As Jewel Walked Slowly Forward, the Guests Near the Entrance Fell Silent . . .

Suddenly a group of people clustered at the other end of the room broke apart. And then there was Skye. For a long moment it seemed that they were alone in the room. As he came closer she saw that his face was filled not only with joy but with a more powerful emotion.

"You came," he whispered.

"Yes," she managed, almost overcome by her feelings.

"You're more beautiful than I'd imagined," he said. . . .

"You must stop . . . courting me, Skye. Tomorrow we'll be off to Scotland."

"Then I must act quickly," he said, his face darkening . . .

Dear Reader,

We, the editors of Tapestry Romances, are committed to bringing you two outstanding original romantic historical novels each and every month.

From Kentucky in the 1850s to the court of Louis XIII, from the deck of a pirate ship within sight of Gibraltar to a mining camp high in the Sierra Nevadas, our heroines experience life and love, romance and adventure.

Our aim is to give you the kind of historical romances that you want to read. We would enjoy hearing your thoughts about this book and all future Tapestry Romances. Please write to us at the address below.

The Editors
Tapestry Romances
POCKET BOOKS
1230 Avenue of the Americas
Box TAP
New York, N.Y. 10020

A TAPESTRY BOOK
PUBLISHED BY POCKET BOOKS NEW YORK

Books by Ann Cockcroft

Pirate's Promise
River Jewel

Published by TAPESTRY BOOKS

This novel is a work of historical fiction. Names, characters, places and incidents relating to non-historical figures are either the product of the author's imagination or are used fictitiously. Any resemblance of such non-historical incidents, places or figures to actual events or locales or persons, living or dead, is entirely coincidental.

An *Original* publication of TAPESTRY BOOKS

A Tapestry Book, published by
POCKET BOOKS, a division of Simon & Schuster, Inc.
1230 Avenue of the Americas, New York, N.Y. 10020

ISBN: 0-671-53019-4

First Tapestry Books printing July, 1985

10 9 8 7 6 5 4 3 2 1

Printed in the U.S.A.

River Jewel

May, 1784

Chapter One

FROM HIGH IN THE GREEN ADIRONDACK MOUNTAINS THE sweet waters of Lake Tear of the Clouds run down and become the beautiful, abundant and clear Hudson River. On an inland hill above its cool banks, a hundred miles south of its source, lie rolling pastures and timberland and several great houses, as well as the small but flourishing town of Hudson.

Less than a mile from the town in a barn next to a large wooden and somewhat decayed house, Jewel Lockridge leaned her thick brown tresses against Tessie, occasionally talking in a low voice as she pulled rhythmically on the cow's full teats. Tessie patiently stood still, swinging her head slowly around to look at Jewel, her ears and flanks twitching to scare off the ever-hovering flies.

Jewel was bemoaning the loss of yet another servant, this time the last farm hand of the once flourishing estate. He had sought employment elsewhere after four months without pay. His abrupt departure meant that someone had to milk the mournfully lowing cow, and Jewel, although she thought such work unsuited for a lady, had decided to do it herself. Fortunately, as a child she had often watched and even tried her hand at milking the cow. She had always been curious and eager to learn, one of those souls who felt she could do almost anything, given the opportunity, by sheer persistence.

"Sam had no faith," Jewel muttered to the cow whose soft brown eyes looked at her. "Couldn't he see it's just a matter of time before the farm will be profitable again?" Jewel sighed. The Lockridges had been the leading family in the area for thirty years and now, just because they had been Tories and loyal to England, people were trying to do them in.

"I'll never be poor, Tessie. Never!" she continued in a whisper to the indifferent cow. "Somehow we're going to get out of this terrible hole and never, never fall back into it again!" The cow lowed complainingly as Jewel's fingers pulled extra hard on a teat in the fervor of her explanation.

"Shush, Tessie, don't fuss." Jewel's dark eyebrows knotted over her large violet-blue eyes, as her soft hand stroked the animal soothingly. Her back ached from the unaccustomed position.

"Sam! That dolt! Just when we needed him," she repeated, irritated anew. "Still, if one has to work, 'tis better outdoors than in, I say. I can't see how Sarah can bear to peel potatoes. Lord! I'd rather pitch hay!"

Jewel straightened and dipped a slender finger in the thick warm cream as she removed the pail from the path of Tessie's hooves, and then hung up the three-legged stool. "Delicious, Tessie!" she said aloud.

Then, as she pitched several forks of hay into the cow's stall, she wondered what her betrothed, Aaron, would think of her out here sweating in the barn. He had such a romantic image of her, that the idea of her pitching hay would probably upset him. Stopping to wipe her brow, she smiled. He treated her like a princess and she loved it, even if it was occasionally boring.

Carrying the heavy pail along the worn path to the kitchen where her mother and sister were preparing breakfast, Jewel thought about the upcoming evening. Aaron would be visiting, and by then she would be dressed in an immaculate dress and smell of perfume, not of hay and cow dung. A breeze played on the budding lilac bushes behind the large brick house and the violets spread beneath them. She stopped before the kitchen door to give the gamboling kittens and their marmalade-colored parents a ladleful of warm milk. Her mother rapped sharply at the kitchen window to forestall a second ladleful in their bowl.

"Jewel!" came the affronted voice. "You shouldn't waste on those beggarly creatures when we need every drop here!"

Jewel toyed with disobedience, but seeing the taut features of her mother, turned the thought aside.

"Oh, Mama, they're so sweet, and . . . we need them to catch mice—they're useful!" Jewel said. She let the muslin sheet fall in the entranceway of the kitchen. It kept the insects out, but let in the balmy spring day and its sunny warmth.

"Never mind, dear," Abigail Lockridge said as she wiped her hands absently on her long, not nearly white apron that was tied in a large bow behind her slender figure. Her thin hands reached for the pail of thick milk and she set it down on a large cross-sawed pine table to skim the top for cream and then pour some in a pitcher for their breakfast.

Jewel raised cold water from the indoor well and poured some in a basin on a stone slab to wash her hands as she watched her mother slowly ladeling the cream.

Her sister, Sarah, with her dusky blond hair tucked in a floppy white muslin cap, sat on a high stool peeling a withered winter apple and slicing it thinly into a pot to be made into applesauce. The hot sauce would top the cornmeal prepared for this morning's meal.

"Not cornmeal again," Jewel said, wrinkling her small nose. She regretted the remark instantly upon seeing Abigail's unhappy expression. She knew her mother was even more affected than herself by the swift decline in the family fortunes, never before having had to run a household without servants. And she and Grandpapa had brought up the two daughters to expect service rather than serving. She remembered all through her childhood her grandfather's stern voice: "A Lockridge is always a lady, and ladies do not do the tasks of servants and farmhands." He hadn't said anything like that in the last few months though.

"Be thankful for what we have," her mother said, her voice quivering. "And please, I'm in no mood for any whining this morning, Jewel."

"I do not whine," Jewel said firmly. "That's exclusively Sarah's province." But when she saw her mother's lips pressed tightly together and her eyes glistening with tears, she added quickly, "I'm sorry, Mother . . . here, let me help!"

"I'll do it," her mother chided, her slim shoulders hunching with disapproval over her children's complaints. "Just take the tea and cereal into the dining room. Your grandfather is waiting."

"Don't worry, Mama, things will get better, they will," Jewel asserted and, planting a kiss on her mother's pale cheek, quickly picked up the tray of tea and cornmeal to take into the dining room.

Her grandfather was waiting, absorbed in staring out of the window, his hands clasped behind his back, his usually erect figure now growing round and slumped at the shoulders. His dark blue waistcoat was worn, but neatly pressed, although his shirt was not as white as it could be, a fact Jewel tried to ignore, knowing that this responsibility, of late, had been hers. If only they still had at least two servants, one for the house and one for the farm, they might manage until autumn. But all of their servants had now fled, as from a plague, the plague being, Jewel thought crossly, the lack of money.

Jewel let out a small groan as she placed the glazed brown crockpot of cornmeal on the sideboard next to the cream and a small pitcher of maple syrup. The blue and white teapot went on the table near her mother's place.

"There are a great many sighs in this house of late," Edmund Lockridge commented, turning his grey head in the direction of his granddaughter.

"I'm given ample reason, Grandpapa," Jewel said, drawing attention to her rumpled robin's-egg-blue dress, a little worse for wear from having been worn while tending the cow and horses. "I'm working like any common field hand. 'Tisn't right. . . ."

"'Tisn't right! 'Tisn't right! Blast it girl, don't you be lecturing me!" her grandfather bellowed, pushing his ample belly out and unclasping his hands as he flung them out to his sides in exasperation. "Your mother's at it day and night. A body needs rest from a woman's tongue. I'll not have it in my own house." He lowered his voice and added, "I've done my best." After walking ponderously to the empty fireplace he stood there looking down at the darkened grate, his feet apart, and brushed his sleeve of imaginary lint.

"Grandpapa, I didn't mean to lecture. It seems all we do is argue. We never used to . . ." Jewel said, aggrieved.

Her grandfather cleared his throat, thrusting his chin out as he did so. "Oh, we used to argue all right," he said firmly. "It just didn't matter before. But now we're tender, all of us, with this . . . " He trailed off.

"It won't be for long," Jewel said encouragingly, thinking he meant the loss of the servants.

Her grandfather said nothing to this, but she noticed a perceptible droop to his usually erect back. Jewel felt a prickly fear race through her, but dismissed it.

"The widower Hibbard came to see me," her grandfather said, not looking directly at her.

"If he's come to court again, the issue is closed. I'm spoken for, as well he knows, and Sarah's hopes are elsewhere." Then she added quickly, "He has a daughter my own age!"

"Spoken for, harrumph," Edmund Lockridge answered, his hand waving airily as he turned to face Jewel.

"I am! That pompous old goat! Thinking he can sow fresh fields with his old oats!" Jewel tossed her dark head, her thick pinned-up hair looking as though it would fall down from the gesture.

"I'll not hear such talk from you! Damn! This new generation is beyond me!" he said while shaking a finger at her.

"Jewel!" her mother reprimanded, coming into the room with a small basket of warm johnnycakes, Sarah behind her with the hot applesauce and butter.

"We were just talking . . ." Jewel said by way of explanation.

"Grandpapa's doing his best," chimed in Sarah. "The least you could do is show respect. You're nothing but a . . . a twit!" With a flounce she took her place at the table.

"It's you, you silly weed, he'd be willing to marry

off to Mr. Hibbard," Jewel launched at her sister. "And he's old enough to be our father and then some!"

"He wouldn't! He knows I love Ashbury Marks! Grandpapa?" Sarah cried, her pretty chin quivering and her eyes on her grandfather.

"He would too, he thinks love is for fools!"

Edmund Lockridge thumped a fist on the table. "By God, we'll have grace now and be done with this bickering, or I'll give Mr. Hibbard both your hands to be rid of your tongues!"

While Sarah sniffed daintily, Jewel sat down with a whirl of her skirts, folding her hands in her lap demurely, and Abigail bowed her head.

Edmund sat at the head of the table and after a good clearing of his throat, called upon the Almighty to bless his house, his food, his estate, and then asked calmly for forgiveness of the disturbance of the peace of the world by the ungrateful women of his household.

Jewel surreptitiously watched her grandfather and mother while the family ate in unusual quiet. Ordinarily her grandfather expounded on some topic of the day or retold yet again stories of his illustrious English ancestors. Jewel had always looked forward to these tales, but today there was an unnatural silence.

"I'll collect the eggs directly after breakfast," Jewel said in hopes of lessening the tension in the room.

Her mother put her teacup down with a clatter, tears again in her blue eyes.

"You will not refer to our . . . present labors . . . at mealtimes," she said.

"But Mama . . . why?" Jewel asked. "We must do these chores until we can find suitable help."

Abigail covered her face with her thin hands.

"Your mother is distraught today," her grandfather chided her. "Desist, my girl."

"But, it's only until you find someone, Grandpapa. I know 'tis awful, but next week . . ."

Edmund threw down his napkin in disgust. "Abigail, we must tell them straight away. I warned you about this," he addressed Abigail quietly. "Your daughters must understand our position." Abigail stared into her teacup, not answering.

"Listen to me, both of you," Jewel's grandfather went on. "What I have to say affects us all. Indeed, I took too long myself accepting the inevitable." He hesitated a moment. "We've lost . . . Riverwatch." He didn't look at anyone but stared rigidly past Jewel.

"We've lost the estate?" Jewel asked after a moment of stunned silence.

"We've had offers," Edmund went on in dull tones, still not looking at Jewel. "And since we're going to lose it anyway because we can't pay the taxes, your mother and I agree we must sell."

"Sell it?" Jewel was incredulous.

Sarah gasped and then wailed to her mother loudly.

"Be still, girl!" her grandfather said. "And stop that caterwauling. It'll do you no good. We have no money. You must marry, both of you, and the sooner the better. Do you understand me? We've lost everything!"

The two young women stared at him in shock while Abigail wept quietly, her pinched, but once beautiful face, wet with tears.

After a few moments of stunned silence, Jewel recovered her presence of mind. "Aaron cannot marry yet, Grandpapa, you know that," she said quickly. "He's just spent his inheritance getting elected to the state legislature. His future is promising, but he is just beginning."

"I thought his prospects better than just promising," her grandfather said soberly. "He'll need something more than just promises in this world. And Sarah's young man doesn't even have promises. I suggest you both look at Mr. Hibbard's bulging pocketbook and not his sagging face."

Sarah wailed again and tipped over her chair as she rushed to kneel next to her mother, throwing her arms around her waist.

"Edmund, please!" Abigail cried, placing her arm around her sobbing younger daughter. "You could have been . . . gentler. Can't you see how you've affected Sarah? There, dear . . ."

"Damn! I'm doing my best! We shouldn't have kept it from them. Now there's the piper to pay and every jackanape in the village besides." He put his hand to his chin and looked at Jewel, who sat disbelieving. "If Aaron Flemming won't have you this summer, then . . . he may never—not when he discovers you've nothing to inherit. So hitch up your skirts, girl, and deliver your message to him in the most persuasive manner possible."

"He may not listen to these idle threats . . ." Jewel whispered.

"This is no idle threat, but fact! Perhaps he doesn't love you. The time to find out is now."

"That's never been a question! He has to spend most of the summer in Albany. When the legislature adjourns in the fall . . ."

"I hope so," Edmund muttered, pushing at his food. "You have little dowry left, my girl."

"What do you mean?" Jewel asked, tossing her head in shock.

"It's been spent. How did you think your mother and I paid for your fine clothes, your tutors and trips to your cousins in New York? We hoped 'twould find you a rich husband!" He shifted uncomfortably, a scowl on his face as he thought about it.

Jewel said nothing, stunned anew.

"I truly hadn't thought Aaron was so dependent on a fortune coming to him," her grandfather admitted. "I even dreamed he might be so smitten with you he'd offer something for your sister's dowry to marry her young apple farmer." He snorted in disgust.

Jewel gasped. "You can't have thought that! How humiliating." Jewel said, her eyes wide.

Sarah began to protest loudly to her mother, who shushed her.

"Hush! We did our best," Abigail whispered imploringly to her daughters.

"We were loyal to England," Edmund went on soberly, "and now we're paying the price for our patriotism. The Americans are gobbling up our Tory estates like hungry pigs." He waved his hand tiredly. "Especially these worthless fur trappers and gunrunners. I haven't the knack in these changing times."

"So, you would have us marry that old goat Hibbard to save the estate! And, pray tell, when the estate is sold, who benefits from its sale?"

Her grandfather reddened in the face but then cast an apologetic eye on his granddaughter.

"I owe most all of it," he said tiredly. "They'll be a pittance left for your mother and I to live out our days." Then he straightened and leaned back in his chair. "Do you think I want to do this?" He shook his large head woefully. "Can you think where we'll go, your mother and I, and be able to hold up our heads? The dishonor to our name? And worst of all, the only half-decent offer for the place is coming from the same mysterious upstarts who've got everyone gossiping. And 'tis my fault!" His shoulders sagged.

"Not the same boorish old man and rakehell son who stole the Norton Estate?" Jewel asked.

"The same. And no one except the lawyers involved even know their names." He shook his head. "'Tis a strange world we have come to when a man has neighbors that are too common to admit who they are."

"But whatever their name . . . they're beneath us! I've heard people tell Mama the son seduced—" She flushed. "At any rate, I've heard he's a scoundrel! And that the old man has the manners of a pig."

"But a rich pig," her grandfather noted gloomily.

"We can't sell to people like them. Why the land is

ours by decree. You yourself built this house," Jewel said, her voice filled with indignation. She got up from the table with a surge of energy, taking quick steps round the room. "We don't have to sell," Jewel said with sudden inspiration. "We can tend the remaining sheep and feed the stock. We can all work to save the farm, and then . . ."

"My dear girl," her grandfather began, turning from the table and pushing his chair back slowly, "spare me your nonsense."

"It's not nonsense, we can—"

"I'll not see my granddaughters turn into milkmaids, and that's final!" Edmund Lockridge fairly shouted at his headstrong granddaughter. Then he went on in a more subdued voice, seeing Jewel's mutinous expression. "I tell you we can't go on. I've been taxed heavily by the new congress. My servants have run off, not content to earn their keep, and I've no money to pay wages. The times have changed and we get no sympathy since we've proven ourselves to have been loyal to the wrong side. It's all I can do to send the linen out for your mother, who's never had to launder so much as her own handkerchief! Now, cease, I'm an old man and can take no more." He coughed to regain his poise.

Jewel subsided and then glanced at the faces of her mother and Sarah who were clearly upset but not about to argue in favor of their sweating in the fields to save their home. Giving her grandfather a long look, she saw there an infirmity she hadn't noticed before. In his sixties, he wasn't capable of the hard work required, nor was her mother, frail and delicate, nor Sarah, who, though a healthy seventeen, was barely able to manage helping her mother with the housework. She suddenly realized her grandfather's admonition to marry was the only possible solution from his point of view, and it galled her.

Jewel's heart plummeted as she took in her defeated family. But marry to save the estate? Her mind whirled. Then with a flounce she lifted her skirts and rushed out of the house, slamming the front door behind her.

Chapter Two

HER CHEEKS HIGHLY FLUSHED, JEWEL RAN THROUGH the garden toward the pasture, her thoughts on the embarrassment of having to ask Aaron to marry her.

"Never! I won't! He won't!" she said aloud. Even if they were promised, it would never do.

"Perdition! I forgot the horses!" Jewel stopped her headlong flight and ran back toward the barn. Fixing leads to the two mares, she walked them both toward the pasture. They followed eagerly, wanting to be free.

Jewel spoke soothingly to the animals, telling them to spare her their fretting, she had enough worries of her own without having to cope with spirited horses.

She opened the gate, unhooked their leads, and let them enter the pasture, watching as they trotted in and settled to graze. Swinging the gate closed behind her she glanced off into the distance. Clouds strolled effortlessly across the vivid blue sky toward the distant Catskill Mountains, and the summer sun glanced off the trees and fences and distant ribbon of river. The fields and woods seemed to beckon her and, gathering her skirt, she flew forward, gliding over the quarter mile of green grasses.

Clumps of dandelions and red clover grew along her path, and the bees hovered over their fragrant heads. A crow cawed loudly overhead. Being young, she forgot her anger quickly, and, struggled to think of a way to save the estate. For, where could they go if it were sold?

It was true that in New York they had aunts and cousins who would welcome a visit, but a visit only. They would abhor taking in destitute relations whose only hope for a solvent future lay in the marriage plans of herself and Sarah. Heavens! Aunt Polly had two daughters of her own to marry off!

She couldn't blame her grandfather entirely, he was within his rights to save his honor and pay his debts from the sale of the land. Still, it rankled! And, remembering that he was a descendant of an old and respected English family, she felt a pang for him.

Her thoughts went to the newcomers, and her brow knit with displeasure. She remembered the one time recently she had dared to hike over to the Norton Estate and had seen the mass of workers renovating the stately old building. She had been rudely told by some flunky that she was trespassing. The gall! She had indignantly demanded to speak to the owner and been told he wasn't "receiving visitors." When she still insisted, the flunky had shrugged and pointed to the roof of the mansion where a half-dozen bare-chested men were sweating away in the sun, repairing the roof. "There be the owners," the man had said, smirking, "and ye be welcome to go visit them." Jewel had fled, wondering how such common men could have earned the money to buy such a grand property. She'd heard they'd made a fortune in furs before the revolution and in arms during it, and had lived among Indians and French trappers. The son had been involved in a scandal with some rich lady in Albany. But, she still wondered, amazed, how, *how* did they do it?

She came to the end of her own land and the beginning of that of her neighbors. Once belonging to the Nortons' estate, it was given upon marriage to a daughter as part of her dowry, and was called Mattoon's Woods. The earthy smells of decaying leaves and sweet blossoms penetrated her senses. She nearly stepped on a small patch of purple trillium, a wild flower blooming beneath a tree. She bent to relish its delicate beauty and was reminded of Aaron.

He would wax poetic about such a discovery, and the thought brought a smile to her lips. Aaron was a dear, so thoughtful and attentive. Last Sunday he had read a poem to them after dinner. She thought back to his words: "Her brow is like the snaw drift, Her throat is like the swan, And for bonnie Annie Laurie, I'd lay me down and dee."

She let a small sigh escape.

A woman needed a man like Aaron in her life. But was she ready to marry him on the morrow? The thought made her frown and plunge deeper into the woods. At nineteen, she should be wed. Most of her friends already were or were preparing their trousseaus for summer weddings, while she was content to wait until someday in the future. Aaron was just establishing himself as a lawyer and could not yet support a wife, not in the style they both expected.

She heard a bird cry out in alarm at her passing, and she paused near a trickling brook running through the woods. Feeling a tingling in her spine, she straightened cautiously.

There, not fifteen feet from her, crouching by a shrub, was a man, as handsome as she had ever seen. He gave her a smile.

She took in her breath, startled, and then noticed that he had just finished gutting a fat rabbit. He bent to wash his knife in the water and, sheathing the weapon in a swift motion, stood up in a powerful, controlled spring. Jewel's heart gave an unexpected flutter, but she stayed, mesmerized by his steady glance as he held the skin aloft.

"How could you, the poor thing!" she blurted and turned away from the sight of the bloody animal.

"It's yours," he said, "with my compliments. The fur will make a warm muff next winter and the meat a fine stew for this evening's supper." He spoke easily in a musical baritone, and his deep-set green eyes sparkled with mischief.

Jewel looked back at him warily, and her dark brows rose.

"I wish you would bag it," she said, pointing to his pouch on the ground, "and if you could stuff yourself in with the rabbit, I'm sure all the woodland creatures would benefit!"

He laughed and bent to comply. "Why so offended?" he asked, squatting. "And you, a country girl." He straightened and shouldered his bag. "When you were approaching, I had the impression from your manner that had you a weapon a pack of wolves would have met their maker. As it is, I think several ants and beetles were trampled to death, no doubt feeling blessed that their end came from such a beautiful foot."

Jewel's cheeks pinked. "It's true, I was angry. I've much on my mind today. Family difficulties. Taxes on the land . . . and such." That was as far into her griefs as she cared to go with the stranger.

"Ahh!" he said softly and leaned casually on one leg, shifting his rifle to his shoulder and looking off.

Jewel had a moment to observe the man, whose muscular length was clad in buff-colored leggings and a soft doeskin shirt that stretched across his wide shoulders like a second skin. His strong features were quite tanned and his thick, dark honey-colored hair was tied in back with a thong. His black eyebrows arched as he caught her perusal. Jewel blushed faintly, but recovered her poise.

"May I ask what you are doing on the Mattoons' land?" Jewel's chin tipped up haughtily.

"Hunting, as you can see," he said lazily, ignoring her tone of superiority.

"You're poaching, and if you don't leave, I'll have to report you," Jewel said authoritatively. "And I'm sure the wolves who have bought the Norton land will be no easier on poachers than are we Lockridges."

"So," he said, narrowing his eyes. "You are a Lockridge? You must be . . . the *jewel* of the family."

Jewel started. "You know my name?" she asked, taking a half step back as the tall stranger began to approach her. "Yes, I am Jewel Lockridge, but—" When he was only a few feet away and she looked up into his green eyes, her breath caught in her throat.

"That's close enough," Jewel barely whispered, giving him what she hoped was a withering glance to stop his advance.

"You're even more beautiful than I'd heard," he said softly.

"I must leave," Jewel said, flushing at his words and turning to go.

"Don't run away," she heard the man say from behind her, "unless you let me accompany you. It's not safe in the woods for a lady. Who knows when you might run into . . . a wolf." He had come up beside her and taken her arm.

Jewel hesitated, uncertain. She was aware of a teasing note, but there was also something in his tone that was quite gentlemanly. And even though he was in hunter's garb, he was clean and very handsome. Moreover, he was in command of himself, and at the moment, that sureness—and perhaps his compliment—was irresistible.

Seeing her hesitate, he turned her to face him. "I am most pleased to meet you, Jewel," he said, smiling down at her.

"Miss Lockridge, sir," Jewel countered, pulling herself free, her eyes sparkling. "You're far too pleased with yourself for any girl's comfort," she chided. "And we haven't even been introduced."

He hesitated briefly and then answered, "My friends call me Skye, and may I ask what brings you out into these woods?"

It was Jewel's turn to hesitate, suddenly frightened at being alone with such a powerful man.

"My family and I were out for a stroll," she lied, hoping to impress him with someone's nearness. "They should be coming to fetch me in a moment." She looked with exaggerated expectation back toward the distant Lockridge house.

Ignoring her look he let his eyes sweep her trim figure and then return to meet her own.

"I will have to find out what flower matches your eyes and have it planted in my garden in abundance," he said as his mouth curved into a smile. "I can't imagine a more beautiful sight to awaken to each morning. I commend your mother, but then I'll be meeting her any moment—if what you say is true." His smile broadened.

Jewel flushed. "They are slow," she compounded her lie uncomfortably.

"I suggest we let them take their time. It would be a crime to hurry anyone on a day like this. I've been up since dawn hunting." He lowered his voice a notch. "I'd be pleased to have you join me. I'm not going far and you'll still be within striking distance of home."

"Hunting?" Jewel whispered, entranced by his offer. Her lips felt dry and she felt an extraordinary glow inside her from his closeness. Why not? she suddenly asked herself, surprised by her own willingness and then sobered again.

"I don't think my family would approve of my going into the woods with a stranger," she answered, but still her feet didn't move to go home.

"Ah, but we've been introduced," he countered easily, "and I suggest that the excitement of the hunt might be a pleasant distraction from the troubles you have already admitted."

"It would not be proper," Jewel said haughtily, almost instantly regretting both her words and her manner.

Skye's face clouded and he shouldered his rifle and shrugged, about to leave. "Then I guess I can't help you. I thought the hunt might give you as much pleasure as it does me." He gave her a polite bow and started off, turning a few feet away to look over his shoulder to see her startled expression. "Oh," he said, "my pleasure to meet you, Miss Lockridge." A smile touched his lips as he turned and slowly walked away.

"Wait!" Jewel called to the retreating figure, hiking up her skirts to hurry to his side. He smiled down at her, a dark brow raised in question, but his eyes shone.

As they strode toward the edge of the woods he slowed his pace to match hers.

"You've decided that rough sorts like myself are not too evil?" he asked her teasingly. "Or at least not as evil as your new neighbors?"

Momentarily flustered, Jewel made a show of picking her way carefully over the rough terrain. "I haven't met them," she said with cool dignity, "and from what I've heard, I have no desire to."

A low rumble coming deep from his chest told her he was laughing at her explanation. "No, I don't think you'll like them much when you meet them," he said, his eyes glittering at her strangely.

"You've met them?" Jewel asked, curious about Skye's strange smile.

"Often," he answered, holding back the branch of a sapling so she could pass along the trail unhindered.

"Do you . . . work for them?" Jewel asked.

"You might say so, yes," he replied, "and they pay me quite well."

"And are they . . . ?" Jewel began, uncertain of exactly what she wanted to ask.

"They are hardworking, brilliant and ambitious, but common, Miss Lockridge," Skye answered, "quite common. All their wealth cannot disguise the fact that they are no better than woodsmen." Skye stopped beside two large boulders and gently reached out a large hand to restrain Jewel from passing him.

"I thought so," said Jewel with satisfaction, wondering why Skye was squinting down the incline, his body in a half crouch. Again she was aware of the enormous animal strength of the man. He turned to her and, taking her arm, pulled her close.

"There's a brace of wild turkey down in that grove of poplar," he whispered, and when he brought his face close to hers she felt a brief wave of heat flood through her. "We're downwind from them but I fear they may have been spooked by our noise. Follow me close and make no sound. Step on nothing, not even ants and beetles." He smiled a warm conspiratorial smile and she could sense his excitement of the hunt and felt herself being drawn into it.

In a slight crouch he began to creep forward, glancing back once to see that she was following. Jewel was aware of every twitter of a bird, croak of a frog or sigh of the wind through the tall pines. She was carefully planting her feet in the indentations made by Skye's large boots. Her eyes were glowing with pleasure when abruptly she felt herself bump into him. A warm shock rushed through her and she pulled away as though stung. He put his strong hand on her arm to steady her, his intense green eyes capturing hers.

"Oh!" she murmured, dazzled by the shock of his touch, her cheeks flushed. Aware of the need for total silence she simply stared up at him, unable to tear her eyes from his gaze. Jewel felt ensnared in a private world of their own making. Her every sense awakened sharply as his broad chest loomed in front of her, and she looked up to see his eyes become a shade of deep emerald. She didn't know why she stayed, except her feet wouldn't go, for she read his intention before it happened and, half-frightened and half-yielding, she felt his arms come around her in a hard vise, as he took her soft lips hungrily in his own.

So sudden was the transition from the excitement of the hunt to the wordless meeting of their mouths that Jewel felt as though she had entered a dreamworld. But as his mouth moved demandingly over hers, forcing it open to allow his tongue entry to the sweetness beyond, Jewel's senses ignited and her whole body seemed to blaze. She returned his kisses with an ardor born of a need she didn't know she had. His hands slid further downward to cup her buttocks and press her against his thighs. She trembled with uncertainty, her eyes flying open.

His mouth left hers and lowered to her throat, the ardor in his kisses overwhelming. Taking a deep breath she put her hands up between them, shaken.

"Don't . . . !" she whispered and twisted to free herself.

Suddenly a great whirring of wings rose up from the floor of the woods and a flock of large grey birds took flight. Skye released her and, whirling, steadied his rifle and fired. The loud noise resounded across the meadow, spooking the Lockridge mares who thundered around the pasture.

Dazed, Jewel staggered and looked up to see a large bird tumble lifelessly from the sky and disappear into some tall grass fifty feet away. In the distance two other birds flew off into the woods.

Skye lowered his rifle and turned back to Jewel. His eyes narrowed in puzzlement as if he too felt he'd been awakened from a dream. When he stepped toward her she felt torn between wanting to go to him and wishing to flee. Instinctively she backed away, her eyes widening.

"No," she whispered again, as if the hunt were still on.

He came to her and again took her in his arms and, when she tried to turn her head away, he took her chin in his huge hand and forced her to look up at him. There was no laughter in his eyes but again the same puzzlement.

"I . . . must go home now," she said, her eyes locked to his. She knew she could no more leave him now without his permission than a fox can escape an iron trap.

"We must first retrieve the bird," he said simply, his eyes falling briefly to her lips.

"All right . . ." she said stupidly, the pressure of his hand on her lower back burning, the light in his eyes penetrating deep within her.

When he began to lower his face to hers she could feel herself growing weak even as her lips parted in anticipation, but then, he abruptly straightened, released her and plunged away to retrieve the prize. Jewel, dazed, followed.

Soon she saw Skye stoop briefly in the grass and then rise, holding a large bird for her inspection.

"A good size," he said, examining it. "Must be twelve pounds." He lowered the wild turkey and bent to the task of wrapping it in a cloth. He was about to stuff it into his pouch with the rabbit when he stood up and with an easy fluid movement came close to her.

"It's yours," he said, gazing down at her, "for your family's supper tonight. You've earned it." He paused. "I wish I could join you."

Jewel's heart thumped unevenly and she fought for control of her poise. "You're very generous." She turned a hand pointlessly in the air. "I'm sure my grandfather would welcome you. He rarely turns away a gift of game." But she knew that as a rule they didn't entertain members of the working class unless there was some special reason, and then not at the evening meal. Never before had she wished that rule broken—until now.

"I doubt your grandfather would welcome me," Skye said, "but what about you?"

"I fear I have enjoyed your presence far too much alrea—" She stopped, flushing. "I mean . . . I'm betrothed!" She flushed again and turned away in embarrassment. "I must go home."

She felt rather than heard his steps behind her, and a shiver raced over her back. She turned her head, but didn't stop. His long strides soon had him beside her, the pouch slung over one arm.

"I think you're a little unfair in your judgment of your new neighbor," he said, glancing at her.

Jewel tossed her head and, happy to focus on some other subject, continued her rapid walk toward the Lockridge land.

"It's obvious you don't know the men well," she replied with dignity.

"I have the feeling I know them much better than you do," he countered with a soft laugh.

Jewel's eyes flared. "It seems you are as pleased with yourself as they are!"

"Most would agree," he responded, his eyes admiring the beautiful flushed face and the shining strands of tumbled dark hair around her shoulders. "Jewel—"

"It's not a good idea, your coming back with me," Jewel threw at him over her shoulder.

"Our dream is ended," he said in a voice so husky and low that she instinctively stopped and turned to him. "So be it," he continued quietly, "but please take my gift of the bird, and one day soon I'll bring you the fur. Is that acceptable?"

She nodded mutely, then added, "I think you've come with me far enough." She indicated a stone wall, the beginning of the closest pasture to her house, which was now visible.

"Jewel, I'm afraid I've a rude shock for you. I didn't mean to carry it so far. I apologize." His voice was serious. "I'm closer than you think to your notorious neighbors. You see . . . I am . . ."

"Don't, I already guessed as much," she said, wondering why he was telling her again how well he knew them. "I'm not sorry for the things I've said about them, but I am sorry we . . . You shouldn't have! It was wrong!" She was as much exasperated with herself as with him for the kiss. "Oh! Perdition! What a day!" She stopped, her cheeks pink with embarrassment. "I was foolish, but I hope you won't misconstrue what . . . happened between us. I'll take the bird and we thank you." She held out her hands and took the bundled bird from him.

"You're more understanding than I thought you'd be," he said, surprised. "I would like to see you again, with your permission."

"Impossible! I already told you why. It would be an embarrassment." She looked at him, hoping for understanding. "You can't be so obtuse! You don't belong!"

He nodded, his lips curling in amusement. "I see. Good enough for the pasture but not the mansion."

Shocked at his allusion, Jewel wheeled around and

left. As she ran toward home she knew he was watching her and hoped he had enough sense not to follow. She glanced back once to make sure he had stayed where he was and saw he was gone. She heaved a sigh of relief. To think she had kissed a gamekeeper! What madness!

Chapter Three

HURRYING HOME, JEWEL TRIED TO BRUSH FROM HER mind her response to the handsome stranger. She had been in need of someone to talk to and he had listened, that was all. She looked down at the bird which she carried cradled in her arms, its feathered body still warm, and trembled as she realized she felt as helplessly the man's victim as the bird. She was frightened by his strength and capability and she wished they had such a man in their employ—their labors would be play to him. But bold, much too bold, and clearly not content to stay in his place. His mocking green eyes rose from her memory to haunt her.

The whinny of a horse tethered in the barnyard startled her. It was barely noontime and they expected no one this early. Then she recognized the cream-colored gelding belonging to Aaron, and her spirits momentarily lifted—only to be cast down again when she realized he would have to be told of the loss of their estate.

Rushing into the kitchen, she dropped the bird unceremoniously on the kitchen table and tiptoed to the back stairs to change. Aaron's soft-spoken tones could be heard coming from the sitting room where he must be sitting with Grandpapa.

"Where have you been all morning?" her mother suddenly asked from behind her, frowning at Jewel's disheveled appearance. "Gracious, you look a fright! My dear child!"

Jewel blushed nervously. "I'm no child, Mother, and I simply needed to get away for awhile. You know the woods have always been my favorite hideaway. I'm sorry if I worried you." Jewel turned to mount the stairs, then stepped back. "How long has Aaron been here?"

"Above an hour, I'd say," her mother answered. "We were about to send him looking for you."

Jewel shivered. "Thank heavens you didn't!" Then realizing how that might sound, added, "I mean, my dress is unsightly. I wouldn't want Aaron to catch me like this." Then she swiftly took the stairs to her room.

Viewing herself in her long dressing mirror, Jewel made a disgusted noise, clicking her tongue. She fingered her too full lips gingerly and, as she recalled why they were so full, twin pink spots appeared on her cheeks. Madness!

Sarah came in and unceremoniously sat on her bed. "You were gone a long time. Mama said you looked like you'd been wrestling with Tessie." She tilted her dusky blond head at her sister speculatively.

"With a wolf, more likely," Jewel mumbled half to

herself as she moved rapidly to shed her dress and quickly don a soft lavender batiste frock with lace ruching. The accidental answer to Sarah struck her, and her heart seemed to skip a beat. A wolf! No, it couldn't be! Skye was a gamekeeper, of course he was, not a land speculator. Any man with pretentions above his station like the new owner of the Norton Estate would be out hunting with hounds and horses, dressed to the teeth. That was how aspiring social climbers would behave—they flaunted their wealth with all the garish trappings they could buy. Nevertheless her heart fluttered with uneasiness.

"Aaron has important news, that's why he came early today," Sarah said, watching her sister's nimble fingers twist her hair in a pretty topknot.

"Well, what is it?" Jewel asked impatiently, a tightness in her stomach she couldn't account for. "And has Grandpapa said anything to him about . . . our marrying?" She dropped her brush and hastily picked it up.

"I wasn't with them all the time, so I don't know," Sarah replied airily, "but Aaron seems pleased, so I doubt too much has been said yet." She shrugged her slender shoulders. "But you know Grandpapa!"

"Oh please, don't let him have begged on my behalf," Jewel whispered, distraught. "It would be so mortifying!"

"If it would be me with Ashbury, I wouldn't care who asked, or even begged, so long as it was done," Sarah said fervently.

Jewel sniffed in disdain, and with a last glance back at her daydreaming younger sister, left.

Aaron was standing with his back to the fireplace and seemed to be listening intently to her grandfather. He cut a handsome figure in his finely made brown waistcoat and fawn-colored breeches. When he heard the rustling skirts from the staircase, he came forward to clasp both of Jewel's hands and bent his silvery blond head to lightly kiss them.

"Jewel," he greeted her, his voice low, "that dress is my favorite and you've never looked lovelier in it." Smiling gently, he let his brown eyes rest on her.

Jewel gave him a tremulous smile and a whispered thank you. Was it her imagination or did she detect a slight flush on his face? He guided her to a chair and took another opposite her, elegantly crossing his legs.

"Your grandfather told me of your family troubles," he began in his soft voice. "I am sorry that you have to sell your estate."

"Yes . . ." Jewel answered, a slight quaver to her voice. "It's very distressing."

"However, as I was just telling Mr. Lockridge, I have brought with me today what I think should be good news," Aaron went on, reaching down to a leather case beside his chair and pulling out a sheaf of papers. "An offer for your property which is much better than I had dared hope."

"At least we shall not be robbed as were the Nortons and the Mattoons," Edmund Lockridge said as he puffed on his pipe with a surprising look of pride on his face.

"I don't understand," said Jewel, looking at her grandfather. "You mean you're happy now to be selling?"

"With this offer we'll have money left over," Edmund explained.

"I don't really understand why these people are buying up property here or why they're being so secret about it," Aaron said, "but as long as you are the beneficiaries . . ."

"They're commoners," Edmund Lockridge said forcefully. "That's why they try to hide their name. If I knew who they were I might not sell to them." He smiled, holding his pipe cupped on his belly.

"In fact," said Aaron casually, "with this offer they had to sign their names. The buyers are one Angus and James McAllister. As far as I can tell—"

"Angus McAllister!" Edmund Lockridge exclaimed, sitting up with a lurch, his pipe falling to the floor. His face, flushed with pleasure a moment earlier, was suddenly pale.

"Why yes," said Aaron, staring, as was Jewel, at the shocked expression of Edmund Lockridge. "Do you know him?"

"The McAllisters want to buy *my* Riverwatch?" he said and, visibly trembling, he came to his feet and stumbled blindly across the drawing room toward a window.

"Grandpapa!" said Jewel, rising and going quickly to his side. "What's the matter? Are you all right?"

Edmund seemed barely aware of Jewel clinging to his arm and looking up at him in distress.

"My God, my God," he muttered. "It cannot be. It cannot have come to this."

Aaron too had risen and walked closer to the old man, who was sightlessly staring out the window at the distant river and mountains. "Please, sir, be seated and tell us why the name McAllister has disturbed you so greatly."

Edmund turned slowly, still not looking at either one of them, shuffled back to his chair and, as though he had aged ten years in as many seconds, sank with a groan back into it.

"We cannot sell the estate to them," he said in a low, hoarse voice. "I'd sell to the devil himself first."

"Sir, you must explain yourself," said Aaron, glancing at Jewel, who was as bewildered as he. "Who are the McAllisters?"

Edmund looked up at Jewel and with a resigned gesture motioned for her to sit. She and Aaron resumed their seats opposite each other.

"They . . . we cannot sell to them," Edmund repeated dully, staring down at the fading blue floral rug.

"Grandpapa," Jewel said gently. "Please let us help you. You will have to tell someone sooner or later. Please . . ."

At last Edmund Lockridge looked up at her, almost imperceptibly nodding his head. He sighed.

"They are the family that murdered my brother and gave me this limp you see me with," he said, raising his eyes to glare into her face.

"Good Lord," muttered Aaron.

"But how? Tell me?" Jewel asked, leaning toward her grandfather, frightened by the look of hatred on his face.

"More than forty years ago it was," he began slowly. "The McAllisters were a good-for-nothing family, former gentry, but hardly worth a shilling then, and suddenly they claimed that their daughter was . . ." he paused to clear his throat and glance briefly at Jewel before continuing, ". . . was with child by my brother Richard." His face took on an expression of sudden anger. "Why Richard was the best young man in the world and the girl no better than a serving wench! I was eighteen at the time and all the boys used to snicker at the mere mention of her name. And Richard was the finest son of the finest family in all of Northumberland. Imagine, they wanted him to marry her! She could have been with child by half the young men of the county! Richard laughed in their faces." He paused with a frown. "Well, the poor lass went and died giving birth to her bastard baby, and Ian McAllister, her father, then came and called Richard a murderer and challenged him to a duel. Now the Lockridges don't deign to duel with riffraff, especially an old man, and Richard rightly refused. And . . . and two days later . . . while Richard and I were out riding, Ian McAllister and his oldest son Michael ambushed us. They killed Richard, murdered him they did, cut me up on my leg, and fled, but not before I got in a shot that left Michael a cripple for life. They lost no time hanging Ian McAllister, and their property was forfeit. The mother and Michael and a young son had to flee to the colonies . . ."

As Jewel and Aaron simply stared at him silently, he cleared his throat a second time and concluded:

"That young son was . . . Angus McAllister . . . come now for his revenge. . . ."

Jewel remembered how in her grandfather's tales of his Lockridge past he had always idolized his brother Richard but had never been willing to talk about why he had died at the age of twenty-three. Now she knew.

Aaron was frowning down at the papers he had taken from his leather case.

"I am very sorry, Mr. Lockridge, that this offer . . . ah . . . is from . . . an undesirable source," he said hesitantly. "Your affairs . . ." He trailed off and flushed. "It's distressing that these past . . . troubles . . . complicate the situation."

Jewel was suddenly very aware that Aaron was embarrassed that without this sale the Lockridge finances were again frightful.

"But can't your father help us?" Jewel appealed to him. "If he could loan us money or even buy our property, we could work hard and buy it back from you in a few years."

Aaron grimaced uneasily.

"You know we would like to help you, Jewel, but this Mr. McAllister is offering for your estate . . . well, frankly more than the property, in these times, is worth. I suppose he wants to humiliate your grandfather and is willing to say 'hang the expense.' "

"We must stop them!" exclaimed Jewel.

"We must certainly try," said Aaron, again looking embarrassed. "But I think you exaggerate the consequences of selling to . . . the McAllisters. I have met the son, James, and he seems a reasonable young man."

"Reasonable!" exploded Edmund Lockridge. "I'll

be hanged before I'll see myself having to surrender this house to any McAllister!"

As a flustered Aaron stuffed his papers back in his bag, Jewel's mother entered from the dining room and, seemingly unaware of the tension, spoke to Jewel:

"Jewel, was it you who brought the turkey home?"

"Yes," Jewel answered, "it's for dinner tonight." Then she added, mustering her most brilliant smile, "You will stay, Aaron, won't you?"

"Why, er, yes, thank you," Aaron responded, getting up and walking to the window while Jewel's eyes followed him.

"Now we shall have to dress it," her mother said, half to herself. "Who gave it to you?"

"A man," Jewel returned quietly, still intent on the cause of Aaron's distant look.

"A man? Just a man?" her mother asked, pausing at the dining room door. "Surely he has a name. We must thank him for the gift."

Jewel let out a sigh and sat on the edge of her chair. "It must have been the McAllister's gamekeeper. There, please, let's end it." Jewel moved restlessly, fussing with her skirt.

Aaron turned and caught her eye. "I wasn't aware they had a gamekeeper."

"They must, I met him in the woods." Jewel stopped abruptly suddenly aware that everyone was staring at her, Aaron with a puzzled frown.

"In my conversations with James McAllister I was led to believe that they either purchase their game or hunt themselves," he explained. "Both he and his father were hunters and trappers before the war." Aaron concluded his speech and, seeing that Jewel had lost all color, came over to her and took her cool hand. "May I get you something?" he asked softly. "Are you feeling well?"

"I . . . ahh . . . Mother, is there some tea?" She turned to her mother, her voice weak, and let Aaron guide her into the dining room behind Abigail.

"Jewel, what is it?" Her mother quickly poured her a cup, sweetened it with honey and brought it to her. "Drink, dear, it'll make you feel better."

Jewel took a few gulps and looked up at Aaron whose brow was knit with concern.

"Aaron," she whispered, "what does he look like?"

"Who?"

"Oh heavens! The son! James, who else?" Jewel put her cup down with a clatter. "I'm sorry, Aaron, it's not your fault. It's silly of me to be so overwrought." She put a hand on his sleeve reassuringly.

Aaron looked down at her, his eyes softening and closed his hand over Jewel's. "James McAllister is something of a giant of a man who looks like he not only used to trap bears but might well have wrestled with a few, too. I—"

"His hair?" Jewel interrupted. "What color hair does he have?"

"His hair? Jewel? What . . . ?"

"Is it dark honey in color?" she croaked in a low tone.

Aaron laughed quietly in a disjointed way. "That's fanciful, 'dark honey.' I'd call his hair a light shade of brown. Men don't have hair colors as women do,

Jewel." He would have continued, but Jewel turned away quickly to hide her flaming cheeks. The man she had met in the woods, the man who had kissed her as had no man before in her life, *was* James McAllister.

"Please, Aaron, I need some fresh air," she whispered. "Will you excuse us, Mother? I'll help you with the bird later."

"Of course, dear," Abigail said, watching her daughter with concern.

Aaron took her by the elbow and steered her toward the formal garden at the side of the house. He bent among the violets and quietly picked a few, handing them to Jewel. She fingered them gently, her head bent.

"I won't pretend to understand all that's going on here," Aaron began in a low voice.

"Nor do I," Jewel said, raising her shimmering violet-blue eyes to his, "and I'm frightened by it!"

Aaron seemed shocked by her emotional statement and recoiled a step. "I can't believe they mean you or your family bodily harm, but I'll do what I can to get another offer for your grandfather, rest assured."

"Oh, Aaron, I fear their vengeance. I'm afraid of the man I met. Oh, not that he'll try to murder me, but that he means our ruin. That he will do anything to avenge his family, just as I will try every means to save mine." Jewel's voice was just above a whisper but every word was punctuated with the intense memory of the powerful man who had held her in his arms.

Aaron walked thoughtfully beside her, his blond head bent and his hands clasped behind his back.

"You don't agree with me?" Jewel looked at him questioningly.

"It happened many years ago and in another place. James is another generation . . ."

Jewel felt an urgency to convince him. She felt threatened—not for her life, but for her future. Feeling a need to expunge the memory of her unexpected response to Skye's kiss, she reached for Aaron's hand. "Come with me over by the mulberry bush, out of Mama's vision." She dragged the wary Aaron with her, lavender skirt flying in the spring breeze.

"Jewel, if anyone ever caught us running like children with snatched sweets, they'd laugh. My dignity would be forfeit." But he laughed at her sudden upturn in spirits.

When they were well hidden, Jewel stopped and with a small whirl stepped close to Aaron and wrapped her arms around his waist. "Kiss me, Aaron, kiss me, and mean it!"

Aaron's face was wiped clear of concern, but had been replaced with a puzzled expression. "But it's broad daylight." He nevertheless put his arms around Jewel, whose face was tilted and waiting.

Jewel pressed her lips to his and felt Aaron respond, holding her tenderly. She felt warm and nice and when he released her, she looked up at him expectantly, wanting more.

"Do it again—with fire!" Jewel commanded and again offered her mouth. When he leaned down to her, she pressed her lips against his and pulled him to her. Aaron responded, and this time when he released her, his face was flushed and his eyes had a darker glaze.

"My dear . . . Jewel . . ." He looked embarrassed by the ferocity of her embrace.

"Aaron," Jewel began, disappointed but not dissuaded from her purpose, "do you remember when we talked of posting the banns for our wedding . . . ?" Her voice was tentative, tiptoeing around Aaron whom she could feel stiffen slightly.

"I do," he said quietly, "it was this time last year. I remember it well."

"And we said in a year's time . . ." Jewel coaxed gently, her eyes wide and clear.

"Jewel," Aaron began softly, "we can't in the middle of this." He dropped his arms from around her waist and looked off searching for words. "I haven't yet the money to buy us a house. You must be patient."

"Patience!" Jewel scoffed, much as her grandfather would. "It's a virtue I've little use for."

"It's the only way to deal with the present situation," Aaron persisted. "In time—six months if my plans work out—I will be quite well-off, and then nothing in the world will give me more pleasure than to wed the most beautiful woman in the world." He reached out his long tapered fingers to lift her chin.

"Then I must wait," concluded Jewel with a rueful smile. "That's what you're saying to me."

"We must wait," Aaron said, taking her by the arm and leading her back to the house. "Time has a way of clearing a path for two people destined for each other. You'll see. . . ."

But as they continued their slow walk back to the house and he began to talk of some important issue he hoped to resolve in the Albany legislature, all Jewel could think of was saving the estate and marrying Aaron. Looming large no matter which way she looked, was the sky-high man who had entered her life, whose touch she had been unable to erase.

Chapter Four

JEWEL AND SARAH SAT ON TWIN STOOLS JUST OUTSIDE OF the kitchen in the warm afternoon sun, dunking the turkey in hot water and plucking the feathers from the bird, their fingers reddened with the work. Sarah uttered little noises of pain and disgust, her stomach turning, and Jewel remonstrated with her to get the work over with.

"Think of the drumstick, crisp and brown," she admonished, "and just do it, for Mama. We'll live, lots of people do."

Aaron returned slowly from the barn after feeding and watering the animals for Jewel. He walked toward them, brushing his neat breeches free of hay, his lean young face screwed tightly in thought. He stopped in front of the two sisters wrapped in smeared aprons and put his hands on his hips.

"Where is Emma?" he asked, referring to their cook, a note of anguish in his voice as he watched their labors.

"She left us two weeks ago and Sam left yesterday,"

Jewel said, her lovely voice full of frustration. She looked up briefly and caught Aaron's tight expression.

"This can't go on," Aaron muttered.

"You won't say anything to Ashbury, will you?" Sarah pleaded. "He mustn't know."

"No, of course not," Aaron returned quickly. "I had no idea it was so bad." He looked off to the distant Catskill Mountains and shifted from one foot to the other, watching Jewel's slender fingers work the feathers. "I must be off after dinner, Jewel, there are things I must attend to in Hudson early in the morning. The town graveyard has been finally settled. There are papers . . ." His voice trailed off as he saw that Jewel was not listening.

"I understand," Jewel said, her eyes downcast, a slight tightening to her lips.

"I can't be drawn into this quarrel, Jewel," he said, disturbed, "but I will do all I can to ease your burden."

"It's not the work," Jewel reminded him. "It's our becoming rootless. Oh, how can I explain it to you. It's the loss of all we've been and done, who we are, and the humiliation of being bested by . . . you know who."

Aaron ran his hand around the back of his neck and reached down to dust off the top of his fobtop boots as if he were searching for an adequate response. Then he straightened.

"We'll find a way," he said, trying to sound confident.

Jewel stuffed feathers into a bag and ignored the statement. He meant well, but had no intentions of marrying in haste or lending money to a sure loss. She understood.

Aaron finally withdrew and later, after a strained family dinner and an equally difficult farewell, Jewel saw him off, his last words, "Depend on me," failing to give confidence.

Jewel saw Dan Buckthorne ride into the yard the next morning. His short body ambled toward the kitchen door where he stood, hat in hand before her. He twisted the brim of his wool hat nervously.

"Mornin', Miss Jewel," he said deferentially, "if I could speak with your grandfather?" His brown eyes questioned her.

Jewel smiled. Dan had worked for them less than a year ago, tending the gardens and helping with the stock, but when her grandfather sold all but a dozen sheep and all the cows except for Tessie, they had let him go. He was a quiet man and Jewel was aware he worshiped her from afar.

"You can tell me whatever it is, Dan. My grandfather is occupied at present."

"It's important, Miss Jewel. Mr. McAllister said to tell it directly to Mr. Lockridge an' not to bother the womenfolk." He looked apologetic.

Jewel felt a coolness invade her as she realized who he now worked for.

"Wait here. I'll ask if he'll see you."

"Appreciate it, Miss Jewel. I surely hate imposin' on you like this."

"It's all right, Dan, it's not your fault." How many more times would she say those words to people? She vowed not to utter one more apology for their circumstances to another soul, but to bear their troubles like a Lockridge.

She found her grandfather in the study, going over his accounts, his grey head bent. He looked up as Jewel approached, a fleeting smile passing over his lips.

"Well, my girl?" he said. "What is it?"

"Dan Buckthorne is here to see you," she said, going over to him and planting a light kiss on his furrowed brow. "He's come from . . . the Norton Estate." Her eyes looked down at the black figuring he had been doing.

"If he's come for his old job . . ." he said, his shoulders sagging.

"I don't think so, Grandpapa. He works—for them now."

"Then he can go the way he came," he said straightening. "I'll not be exchanging secondhand messages with any McAllister. If they've got something to say, they can just come over and say it."

"I tried to find out what he wanted, but he said it was for your ears alone." Jewel said. "I'll tell him you can't see him."

"A minute, my girl, a minute. I'll attend to it." He squared his shoulders. "Send him in and be sure his feet are clean. Sending me his servant is he," he growled, "who was once mine! The audacity," he muttered.

Jewel hurried below to fetch Dan, who was still standing outside looking very discomfited.

When Dan entered the study, he bowed his head

politely to his former employer. "Beggin' your pardon, sir." Jewel lingered near the doorway, too curious to leave.

"Come forward, man," Edmund beckoned, his voice imperious. He waited until Dan stood in front of his desk shifting his feet nervously. "Now, what miserable message did you bring for me?"

"The McAllisters, Angus and James, they'd like to call, sir, a business meeting, they said. This afternoon at five, sir, it being convenient."

"Convenient!" Edmund bellowed, his face getting red. Dan's eyes nearly popped, so wide did they get, and Jewel winced. "There will never be a convenient day, and you can tell them I said so. Be off with you."

Dan's round face reddened and he turned quickly to make his retreat.

When Dan had cleared the study, Edmund said, "Hitch up Lady, Jewel, we're going into Hudson to see Aaron. I'll have this matter of selling the estate settled straightaway. They'll be no doubts about who's allowed to buy my land."

Jewel had never had to hitch up the small open carriage before and had her hands full with Lady, trying to calm her until her grandfather finally emerged from the front door, his gold-tipped walking stick in hand.

She shifted to let her grandfather get up beside her where he settled himself ponderously. Jewel flicked the reins and they lurched forward. Edmund Lockridge sat looking ahead, his face full of thought.

"I've seen you grow from babe to girl, never having to lift a finger to do chores such as you now have to do," he said with a lift of his head as they swayed and bumped along the rutted road to town, "and I'm proud of you, my girl. You're a Lockridge through and through."

Jewel felt her heart quicken with the unexpected compliment and she smiled her thanks.

"We'll come through, Grandpapa," Jewel said. "We have spirit, and that's something no one can take from us."

"True words, those. True words."

As they crossed the bridge that took them onto the main street of the small, but flourishing town of two thousand or so souls, Jewel acknowledged with a smile those she knew. The town now boasted of several fine inns, a malt beverage company, a newly developed tannery and was extensively developing its marine commerce. A fleet of some twenty sloops now plied their trade from the South Bay of Hudson, primarily shipping shad, herring, lumber and barrels to the West Indies. New warehouses and wharves dominated the banks of the river.

Jewel had managed Lady admirably until another horse trotted by and then her horse sidestepped nervously.

"Careful, Jewel, careful," her grandfather needlessly warned as they watched the skittish mare toss her head.

A handsome landau with a matched pair of chestnuts drew along side them, forcing Jewel's attention on the restive Lady, who pulled and snorted her discontent. A tall man with a full head of greying brown hair and dressed in a huge misshapen coat of what looked like bearskin glared at Jewel's grandfather, his bloodshot eyes glittering.

"Remember me, Edmund Lockridge?" he called, showing his strong teeth in a grimace as he reined his horses to a stop. "I be the child you and your family sent to the poorhouse."

As Jewel reined in Lady, she saw her grandfather gape at the wild-eyed stranger confronting them.

"Angus McAllister?" Edmund Lockridge asked incredulously.

"Aye, Angus McAllister," the man replied. "But no more a mere helpless lad."

"And do you plan to shoot me as your father tried to do?" Edmund asked, his face red as he sat stiffly facing his tormentor.

Angus McAllister scowled, his bushy grey eyebrows almost hiding his bloodshot eyes. He spit into the dust of the road between the two carriages.

"No, there be an end of shooting and hanging," he said. "But not an end to revenge." He grinned.

"Let us go, Jewel," Edmund said with dignity to his granddaughter. "We have no business with this man."

As Jewel flicked the reins gently over Lady's back and felt them move away from the nasty old man she heard his reply.

"Oh, ye have business with me, Edmund Lockridge, no matter how far ye ride."

For a moment she thought they were free, but soon the McAllister landau appeared again beside them, the old man's bearcoat blowing open in the breeze to reveal a worn, unbuttoned and dirt-smeared shirt.

They were now trotting down the main street of Hudson.

"I see you've lost your touch, you old geezer," Angus shouted for all to hear. "Have to let a little filly drive you around." With a high wild laugh, Angus lashed his two horses and drove them at a gallop past the Lockridges, leaving Edmund sputtering and red faced.

"Geezer, am I? Lost my touch, have I?" Edmund muttered angrily. "That old crone!" He coughed and dabbed his nose with his handkerchief. "By the heavens, I'll see him blown back to Scotland. Hie me to Aaron's, my girl, I must see him forthwith. Business with a McAllister, huh? We'll see about that. And you, my Jewel, had better not come in. Call on Mrs. Flemming. I have harsh words on my mind and you'll distract young Aaron from my business." Edmund finally subsided pushing his handkerchief back into his breast pocket.

As they stopped in front of Aaron's establishment, a brick townhouse of some substance, Edmund alighted and waved his granddaughter away with his walking stick. "Call for me in an hour or more at the earliest."

Jewel felt shaken when he left, and it took her several minutes to collect her senses. Lady still stamped her feet in agitation and Jewel crooned to her until she finally seemed calm. Then Jewel set her at a leisurely pace toward the river. There was a grassy park near the wharves where she could walk and Lady could peacefully graze, until they both recovered their equilibrium. She had no intentions of calling on Aaron's mother to receive condolences on their present miseries, nor did she want to fend off embarrassing questions about the future.

Several sloops lay tied to the docks and from the strong smell of fish in the air, she realized one must have recently come in from the sea. It still amazed her that in a matter of less than a day those ships could be in New York. Men were still cleaning the decks, and crates of shad were being readied for loading. She watched their activity, letting the tension of the morning leave her shoulders. The river flowed peacefully, its clear depths showing the rocks below. Walking along the green banks, her thoughts, unlike the river, were turbulent.

So that was Angus McAllister! So much rougher and more common than the son. Yet Skye was his son. Skye indeed! Why, who called him that? She had only heard him referred to as James. He had tricked her, deceived her and enjoyed the game. How humiliating! She thought of her grandfather's visit to Aaron and hoped the two of them would find some way to frustrate the McAllisters. But was her grandfather equal to the task? If not, who then?

A gentleman approached the riverbank coming from the docks and seemed to be heading toward her. She watched him for a moment, admiring the superb cut of his clothes, the buff breeches and waistcoat and broad-brimmed black hat, the cuffed black boots. He was muscular and lithe, graceful for one so tall. With a jolt she realized the man in gentleman's clothing was Skye, and he was gaining on her rapidly. Her first instinct was to turn and run, but as before when she came upon him suddenly, she stood rooted, facing him, her feet wingless. She lifted her chin and greeted him in as cool a voice as she could muster.

"Good afternoon, Mr. McAllister!" This said, she whirled, her pastel-striped blue dress fluttering, and started walking away, head held high.

"Skye," he insisted, and caught her by the arm, his strong fingers biting into her tender flesh, not hurting, just staying her firmly.

She turned her dark head with its wide-brimmed straw hat upward, her eyes meeting his to flash a warning.

"There's no need to have an old family quarrel stand in our way," he said firmly, his voice low as he released her arm, the musical baritone floating around her.

"Your father just threatened my grandfather and nearly overturned our carriage," she said with asperity, "and you deceived me in the rudest way possible. I think that's reason enough, without the past."

"Those two have their bitterness dyed in their coats," Skye returned with control, "and their quarrel need not be ours. And as for my deception, I did apologize, if you remember."

"You are not forgiven!" Jewel countered, her violet eyes flaring. "And I assure you, my grandfather's quarrel is mine. I am cut from the same old rag as he and proud of it." Jewel stood her ground as he came closer and took her arm again, his eyes narrowing.

"Old wool from an ancient ram does not a brilliant jewel make," he said, a twist of a smile on his lips.

Jewel ignored his words and focused her eyes on her arm. "Loose me, if you please."

"If you'll stay and talk sensibly."

"No," she said, trying to pull herself free.

"I'm not going to release you until we have this out," he said, tightening his grip. "I mean you no harm and only ask to be heard." Jewel suddenly felt unsettled, and she swayed a minute.

"The Lockridges had become impoverished gentry before we arrived here," Skye said, his eyes fixing her neutrally. "So my father's efforts at revenge are the rather pathetic beating of a dead horse. Thus I feel—"

"The Lockridges are not impoverished," Jewel snapped back imperiously and with a jerk managed to free her arm.

"Fine," said Skye, a quick grin lighting his features. "Then my desire is even stronger. I would like to get to know you better. With your permission, I'd like to court you." He fastened his green eyes on hers, their intensity assaulting her.

"You're mad," she whispered when she recovered from the shock. "Even had the Lockridges not a penny I would never receive you as a beau."

"Even had the Lockridges a million pounds sterling," he countered with a mischievous smile, "I would never stop courting you."

Jewel caught her breath, his eyes mesmerizing. Finally she said, "I'm spoken for, and I don't intend to let my course be altered by any ridiculous dream of yours." She tore her eyes from his and looked across the river at the opposite bank, the cool lush greens reviving.

"My dreams are bold but never ridiculous," he said with assurance. "And I intend to see them fulfilled." He looked down at her with an arrogant smile that irritated her.

"You forget, sir, that I am English, like my grandfather, and royalist," she said haughtily, "and I believe it takes more than money and . . . fancy clothes to hatch a gentleman . . ."

"Quite true," he said with an appreciative grin at her sally. "But I credit myself with having good manners—which I've come to know means more than lifting the correct fork, and has more to do with the intelligent listening to the other fellow's point of view and showing consideration." A single dark eyebrow rose in question.

"Then you've lost there, too! You made sport of me in the woods. Oh, what am I doing even speaking to you! Leave, please, we've nothing to say to one another."

"If I had told you who I was, you'd have left me. If you're honest, you'll remember I did say I was your new neighbor." He pushed the brim of his hat back. "I've no regrets, it couldn't have been otherwise."

Jewel took a step back, unwillingly responding to his words. "Did Dan tell you we were coming to town? Did you follow us?"

"No, I didn't follow you here. I had business to attend to. My father was quite sure your grandfather would refuse us." He pointed briefly to a lovely black ship. "The *Mourning Dove,* the sloop at the dock there, she's mine."

"A stinker—like yourself!"

Skye chuckled, the sound throaty. "Careful, your breeding's showing!" He grinned broadly and Jewel's cheeks flushed.

"You had no excuse for your behavior in the woods!" Jewel said, refusing to let his charm win over her weakened senses.

Skye grinned leisurely as his eyes swept over her.

"And do you have an excuse . . . for yours?" he asked in a low voice, his eyes glowing. Jewel could feel herself flush.

"I'd heard Edmund had two granddaughters," Skye went on. "One of them a remarkable beauty." When she flushed again he added teasingly, "And reportedly vain." Then he turned serious again. "When I saw you put the horses out to pasture, I wished you would come my way. I watched you come across the fields and felt you were flying to be by my side. You touched something inside me with your youthful grace, so proud and yet so fresh. Was I to say then that our families are old enemies, but stay and talk to me? Was I to say forget who I am and let the sweetness of our time together be the thing to remember? Would you have let me kiss you if I had?"

"I don't want to hear it," Jewel whispered, moistening her lips and trying to fight the pull of him.

"Then believe what we felt and trust it," he said in a low voice.

Trembling, Jewel shook her head and put her hands over her ears. "Leave me alone," she said, wanting to flee but feeling as helpless as a trapped animal.

Then, before she saw what he was about, he grasped her by the shoulders and brought his mouth down on hers in a firm, heated kiss, his lips warm and tender and knowing, the brief sensuous invasion of his tongue making her knees feel weak from the rushing, pulsing fire of it. Then, just as her whole being was wanting more, he let her go. She stood disbelieving.

"That's to help you remember why I ask to court you," he said, capturing her eyes with his. "And I mean what I've said. If you change your mind, send word to me. You know where I live." And, with a last smile and a debonair bow, he wheeled and left her, silently gliding like a shadow up the grassy embankment without a backward glance.

Chapter Five

SKYE WAS SWEATING IN THE AFTERNOON SUN, HIS MUScular tanned arms strained as he labored to train one of his new colts. Regal Prince was a magnificent two-year-old Arabian of impeccable breeding. He was worth a king's ransom, and he was willful and determined, but not so hot tempered that he was unmanageable. Skye wanted him honed and obedient, sensing his innate ambition and power, and though this was more his father's province, they shared both the love and some of the responsibility.

He had thrown the fractious colt on his side five times to convince him who was master, finally subduing him. He advised Patrick, a small and gentle black man and his new trainer, to treat him firmly and consistently.

"Never let him get away with any tricks, Patrick," Skye told the trainer. "He's a handful, but worth the time. You'll have to use the whip around the hind legs to remind him." He nodded at Patrick, handing him the whip. "And when he does it right, reward him."

"I see, Boss." Patrick gave Skye a wide grin, his black eyes snapping cheerfully. "You have a way with them colts, Boss. He'll be better now, sure."

Skye was tired but satisfied as he retrieved his shirt and pulled it over his tanned, bare back. His new colt eyed him, his flanks shivering with the exertion of trying to overpower his owner.

"You're a beauty, Regal Prince," he said to the colt. "Like another I know," he added under his breath, thinking of Jewel.

Angus had been watching his son intently. "Aye, Skye! It would've taken months to rid him of his cantankerous habits. That fool Van Heisen knew he had a fine animal, but spoiled him. Will you train him to race?"

"I'll spend some time on him," Skye answered, "but he has a ways to go before I'd race him yet." Skye turned to go back to the house and then called over his shoulder, "I need your opinion on a few matters that want clearing. Have you plans for the evening, or will you be coming in soon?"

"Now where would I be going with a storm brewing?" Angus said, his eyes looking northward where dark clouds were gathering. "We'll have a corker tonight."

Skye, following his father's eyes, agreed with his assessment. "*Mourning Dove* leaves at dawn loaded with timber for the Indies, and she's weighted down," he said, half to himself and half to his father. He rubbed his chin thoughtfully, then added, "Should clear by morning, I'm hoping."

"Aye, and leave a fair wind blowin'," his father

agreed and turned his attention back to Regal Prince and Patrick, who was leading the unruly colt back to his stall.

With long strides Skye abruptly started for the house. The day's work behind him, he needed a drink and wanted to spend the early evening in the study, entering his accounts and business transactions. In the early morning he'd been with his ship's captain going over details of the voyage and then with his foreman about the timber to be cut and planked for the next shipment. He sometimes spent sixteen hours a day working, but never reckoned the time by clocks. He loved his work and building his growing business, but he had another thought on his mind this day—how to handle the other beauty he had become fascinated with—Jewel—and the bitterness between his father and the Lockridges.

When his father had talked of having an old score to settle, Skye had sympathized, knowing how much Angus had suffered from his sister's disgrace and death, his father's hanging and later his mother's and brother's untimely deaths in a harsh Canadian winter. All his life he had listened to the tales with a child's loyalty, and daydreamed of justice for the miseries and hardships the feud had caused his father. And now the tables were turned—it was the McAllisters who had power and money, they who were winning the game of life, and the Lockridges who were weak. As Angus had months earlier outlined his plans, Skye had hoped besting the Lockridges would at last end his father's agonies over the old tragedy.

But Jewel and the present reality made it different.

Skye saw Edmund Lockridge as a pompous old man struggling with failure, his daughter-in-law as a grieving gentle widow, and the two young granddaughters as helpless pawns. He didn't relish a victory over such weakened enemies. Three destitute women and a weakened old man didn't rate a laurel wreath in his book. But the struggle had begun, and because the need for revenge so haunted his father, he didn't yet see the way out of it.

At times like these he wished himself back to the simpler time when he and Angus hunted and trapped up north, the icy streams and cool forests clearing the mind, the testing of his body and instincts a daily habit, all his senses alert, and his troubles were confined to survival in the wilderness. Easier than dealing with civilization. Now he needed diplomacy *and* cunning—all the skills he had learned tracking—the patient wait, the reading of signs, the wariness first, then the quickness to action. He had admired and learned his father's shrewd manuevering and bargaining among Indian traders, French trappers, and English armies. Angus had passed to him the same canny traits, save one—the anguished, obsession to settle this old score. Oh yes, Skye was willing to best the Lockridges, but he lacked the desire to rub the enemy's nose in the dirt, especially when one of the noses belonged to Jewel.

Mrs. Harris could be heard banging pots in her domain, the kitchen, annoyed that supper had been postponed an hour. As he entered the pantry, Skye helped himself to a locally brewed beer from a barrel in the cooling room.

"A body gets no rest hereabouts," Mrs. Harris muttered, her plump figure puttering near the cooler where she knew Skye had just served himself an ale. "And the menfolk will waste to naught, with no victuals in their gullets. An' don't you be tellin' me ale be good fer you. It's good for makin' round bellies and naught else!"

Skye grinned as he stepped into the kitchen.

"Now, Harris, we'd not survive without you," he said. "Why, just yesterday I heard my father say you made the best pudding in the county and he'd not touch another."

"Humph!" Mrs. Harris adjusted her white mobcap on her greying head and straightened her starched apron, then bustled about the black woodstove. But she was clearly mollified and Skye gave her apron strings a playful tug as he left her preparing to serve the supper.

As a rule Skye and Angus ate at the long polished table at one end of the large kitchen. The dining room was beautifully appointed, but was only used on those rare occasions when they had guests. Angus came in and sat tall in his chair, appreciatively eyeing the lamb chops placed before him.

"You're a credit to your Irish race, Harris," he said to her, "and none can compare."

"Supper an hour late! What can you expect but crisper than crisp chops," she complained. "An' there be my best rhubarb pie for dessert. Yer to save room, mind you." She turned and padded to her chair by the kitchen window, leaving the men to their supper. Angus winked at Skye.

"I've been meaning to ask," Skye began cautiously, "about the meeting you had with the Lockridges in Hudson." Skye held his tankard of ale between two hands observing the hardening look on his father's face.

"Wasn't a meeting," Angus said, with a growl. "Was more like a contest, which I won. The old buzzard called me a devil. Stubborn old fool! He's no choice but to sell to me. Grown rounder over the years, and lets a girl drive him about. I hadna' thought him so infirm." His hard speech concluded, he tore a piece of bread and mopped gravy with it before popping it into his mouth.

Skye delayed before speaking, wanting to give his father time to digest his food and lessen his rancor.

"I thought I'd ride over tomorrow and see Edmund Lockridge, introduce myself and get a feel for what lies ahead."

Angus considered his son. "Think you know best now, do you?"

"No," Skye replied carefully. "I simply know we live here. We've vested interests in the goodwill of this community. The Lockridges have few choices, but I want this ended with grace. We'll do our part right, and to the letter of the law. We'll see our enemy to the ground, then let him retire to a cave and lick his wounds."

Angus controlled his temper while Mrs. Harris cleared their plates and served her special spring pie, warmed and cream poured over. Angus managed to give an approving nod to Mrs. Harris who, seeing her food eaten with relish, went away like a well-fed cat.

"Aye, the law," Angus muttered angrily. "The law. . . . Don't ye speak to me about any letter of the law. My father was hanged by the so-called law and I won't forget it. He never ambushed the Lockridges. It was a challenge and a fair fight, but when they lost, the Lockridges paid coin to the magistrate for the hanging, broke my mother's heart, and saw us run out of the country, with nothing but the clothes on our backs! That's your damned law. There won't be justice until a Lockridge pays. No, don't you ask me to forget. I can ne'er forget." Angus set his mouth tight.

"You've always been a fair man," Skye answered, his voice low and serious. "You know I've been your man through smoke and fire, but, there are three women involved," Skye finished, his broad shoulders squared over his elbows on the table.

"Women, is it?" Angus said with asperity. He swore, then attacked his pie, demolishing it before sitting back and staring at his son. He crossed his legs and slowly lit his long clay Indian pipe, drawing on it as his shrewd eyes narrowed. There wasn't much went past him regarding human nature, and Skye, while appreciating the fair sex, had never let his self-interest get tangled with a skirt that he hadn't whipped free of when it clung too close.

"One, in particular," Skye said, his face straight and closed. "The eldest granddaughter, Jewel."

Angus puffed on his pipe, his grey eyes as cool as an early spring mist. Then he withdrew the pipe and looked over his shoulder to see if Mrs. Harris was listening outright or just pretending not to listen. For she didn't let much get past her of the doings in the house and she'd nose around until she found it all out anyway.

"Must be the lass who drove the old buzzard into town then," he said finally, deciding not to care if Mrs. Harris heard.

Skye nodded.

"Bring her here," Angus said abruptly.

Skye laughed. "You're a faker," he said at length. "You've no interest in meeting her at all."

"Now how would you know that?" Angus snorted. "It's time you settled and produced an heir." He eyed his son.

"Did I say I was marrying?" Skye said, amused at his father's turn of mind.

"Nay. But there's a look about you I remember at your age. Aye, we'll look her over for breeding, I'm thinking."

Skye leaned back, watching his father's face for clues. He was up to something, he knew, but he would have to smell it out. He was certain his father was setting a trap and he was feeling oddly like he might be the bait.

"Aye, bring her over, I'll not bite her," Angus repeated. Then he gave a bitter grin. "It'll give the old geezer something to swallow he won't like and that is worth the price."

Skye decided to call his father's bluff, certain that's what it was.

"I'll do it then, if it can be arranged. She's excitable, but exquisite—an uncommon beauty. But not very fond of us roughneck McAllisters."

Angus flushed and took a forceful puff on his pipe and withdrew it, letting a large cloud of smoke encircle his head. "We'll see who's common," he said in a low voice.

"I'll be lucky to get her to speak to me, much less get her to visit."

"Then you've a challenge," Angus said, looking up through narrowed eyes. "Ye like that—it piques you."

"Aye." Skye smiled. "It piques me, the challenge."

"Hmm," was all Angus replied, keeping whatever other thoughts he had about the girl and her parentage to himself.

A gloom had settled over the Lockridge house. The family discussed and lamented, torn this way and that, but Edmund Lockridge finally admitted he was defeated. Aaron had given him papers to sign selling the estate to one Morris Livingston, and they sat on his desk in the study like a small white casket.

Jewel walked through her home, seeing as never before the luxury of it and appreciating the fine craftsmanship in the furniture and woodwork, polished to perfection. There might be cobwebs in certain corners, and repairs and scrubbing needed here and there, but the furniture was never neglected by her mother and Sarah.

She fingered a blue-and-red-flowered chintz curtain at a window, one of three in the salon, and wistfully thought of the many hours she and Sarah had spent dreaming as they watched the comings and goings of fast sloops, and the small boats fishing on the Hudson. She gave a trilling, musical laugh to herself as she dropped her hand from the curtain. "Who knows, you may well become a dress for me before long."

The elegant brick house with its many fireplaces and six bedrooms, its high ceilinged rooms drafty in winter but cool in summer, silently awaited its fate. Jewel mourned its passing even while she yet lived in it.

And never had she seen her grandfather look so downtrodden. He had taken to helping Jewel with the animals, at least the two mares, and he frequently took walks to the upper pasture, walking stick in hand, to see how the sheep were faring, unattended now, except for the sheep dog, Ruffles.

"Like children, they are," he'd said to Jewel, leaning on the pasture fence. "I'll never take them for granted again. What beautiful land we have, my girl. I've loved every inch."

"Don't sign yet, Grandpapa," Jewel had answered, her voice soft as her eyes swept over the rich pasture land, rolling downhill toward the river and covered in sweet clover. "Not yet, I'll think of a way."

Her grandfather hadn't bothered to reply, but had merely turned slowly, leaving her by the fence. Jewel had felt her heart plummet.

Remembering their conversation, Jewel felt saddened, and left the window to go into the garden and begin weeding. Capturing a large black beetle, she played with it, letting it crawl around her pink hand, but keeping her palm around it, not letting it escape. A wicked slant to her clear violet-blue eyes and a tilt to her dark head would have had her mother wishing she could lock her in her bedroom for the day, for it was a look that appeared before Jewel planned an audacious assault on an enemy, and her new enemy was James "Skye" McAllister. He had thought she had stamped on beetles? Well, *he* was now the beetle she would crush.

He dared, how he dared! It would be different when next they met. Oh yes! He would know her presence and not go away unscathed—that big, black-hearted hunter who had entered her life armed to the teeth and marked her with his kiss. So, he liked to play games, wicked games. Well, she could play games, too. No longer would she play affronted lady to his strutting peacock. He was the enemy and she knew her weapons. She would use whatever feminine wiles she could conjure to tease him, arouse him, confuse him. He wanted to court her? Fine. She would make him pay for every glance, every word, every touch. It was fair. He had asked for it.

She lowered the beetle gently back to the earth and then stood up and turned back to the house. She was after bigger game, she thought, laughing softly.

Inside her room Jewel pivoted to her wardrobe, throwing open the doors, and fingered her dresses, assessing them. White, she decided, virginal white. A slim batiste skirt with narrow wisps of lace running around the bottom of the skirt and a low-cut blouse of equally soft, almost see-through Egyptian cotton, its sleeves stopping at the elbows. And her hair, she must get Sarah to help her twist and tie it with rags. A terrible torture, but one she would endure, for her hair must be full and curly to be properly seductive. She smiled, enjoying her game and went to her vanity, opening the drawer. There, nestled in a red velvet box, were her grandmother's pearls, her legacy, to be worn on her wedding day. She fingered their lustrous beauty. Should she wear them? No, too ostentatious, and they didn't suit the untouched look she wanted. She picked them up—they must be worth a fortune.

She stared at herself in the small vanity mirror. A fortune! Of course, they were worth that! Why hadn't she remembered them? Why hadn't her mother remembered? Jewel put aside her plans to be a coquette, took the pearls up with trembling fingers and ran to find her mother and grandfather. Excitement bubbled in her and, after bursting into the drawing room, she let her words tumble out heedlessly.

"I have our way out of this trouble," she said, her voice high and breathless. "My pearls! Why didn't we think of them before? Now we can pay our taxes and not have to sell. We're saved!"

"But that's the last of your dowry!" exclaimed Sarah, who was sitting on the floor sorting clothing. Her mother paused in her knitting, her eyes following her oldest daughter as if she had lost her mind.

"They were your grandmother's," she said, as if Jewel hadn't remembered.

"She wore them on her wedding day," her grandfather said from his chair by the fireplace, his voice carrying the memory, "and they are meant for yours."

"And she would want them to be used to keep the land," Jewel returned, her eyes bright, "I know she would."

Her grandfather stared at her and shifted in his

chair uncomfortably. "My dear girl, had I thought we had any means left, I would have used them. But the pearls—why that's the last of it. You and Sarah will have nothing left, save linens and a few dishes to bring to your husbands. Nothing. I couldn't countenance it."

Jewel knelt by her grandfather's side, looking up at him imploringly. "Grandpapa, if you only knew to what lengths I would go, and this is a simple sacrifice. No sacrifice at all. I feel it's the right thing to do. To save our honor. It's proper, Grandpapa. Please."

Edmund Lockridge felt a surge of love for his granddaughter, and suddenly, seeing her hopefulness he nodded to her. "Aye, my Jewel, I'll try, I'll try."

"Good," said Jewel. "We're not beaten after all," she added, looking up at Edmund encouragingly. "Why I believe the notorious Skye McAllister is somewhat smitten with me. Just yesterday he even asked if he might court me. And he was serious, I'm certain."

Jewel saw Sarah's eyes widen in surprise and her mother look shocked, then confused, her hands groping ineffectually for the shawl she had been knitting. Then Jewel felt Edmund pull away and with a bang of his walking stick push himself to his feet.

"Court you?" he asked sharply, glaring down at her. "When was he so bold?"

"Dear Heavens!" Abigail at last exclaimed, seeming to recover herself. "How could you be so indiscreet?"

Jewel found herself blushing and rose to her feet, trying to collect herself.

"I didn't give permission, Mama," she said quietly, trying to alleviate her mother's fears. "I was just trying to show you that I might have some influence over—"

"Stay away from that man, Jewel," Edmund broke in sharply, his brow deeply furroughed. "He can only mean you harm."

"I certainly have no fear of that roughneck," she said, lifting her chin haughtily, even as she felt a hot tremor unexpectedly quake through her as she thought of him. Her grandfather was squinting at her as if hard at thought.

"Don't you trust his interest, young lady," he said, his hands clasped firmly around his cane which he had planted in front of him. "And don't you let him near you again. It's dangerous. I've . . . I've a terrible feeling about it." His eyes glazed over as he took a flight into the memory of years before, of his brother and a pregnant, abandoned McAllister girl. "'Tis revenge he wants, it's certain, and they will stop at nothing."

"Oh, Grandpapa, he's not going to shoot me," Jewel said, amazed at her grandfather's seemingly unreasonable fears. "Why I was alone with him in the woods for an hour. He could have—"

"We won't speak of what he might have done," Edmund Lockridge exploded and marched with as much dignity as he could muster to the doors leading out to the garden.

Abigail now arose and came over to Jewel, her eyes flitting nervously from her father-in-law to her daughter. She recognized in Jewel a recklessness that frightened her. "Dear heart," she said so quietly that Jewel barely understood the words addressed to her. "You must remember that the ancient feud still separates the families. I'm sure you misunderstood the young man's intentions or words. He could not seriously intend to court you. Why, in addition to the feud, he's not to the manor born."

"Of course, Mother," said Jewel, feeling an unreasonable defensiveness on behalf of Skye. "But though he's not to the manor born, he does own a manor—and much land—while we ourselves . . . oh, I'm sorry, Mama," she interrupted herself, seeing the tears welling in her mother's eyes. "But it's true that in this new country, a man's wealth is becoming as important as his birth."

"You'll stop speaking nonsense," said Edmund from the other side of the room. "He's beneath you and to be avoided."

"I was only suggesting that we might have strengths we're not taking advantage of," Jewel said, turning to her grandfather and becoming suddenly aware of the infirmity and indecision which was overcoming both the old man and her mother. He stood with his back to her, his shoulders slumped forward as if he were leaning on his walking stick.

"We'll be all right, dear," she heard her mother say from beside her. "We'll go live in New York. I'm sure Aunt Polly will be happy to have us visit."

For a week perhaps, Jewel thought, turning with annoyance away from both her mother and grandfather and walking toward the stairwell. No, if they lost the estate, they would be dishonored beyond recovery. They could hope to be no better than servants for the rest of their lives. She doubted if Aaron would ever marry her—his own ambitions were too important to him. She turned at the stairs.

"Please try to sell the pearls, Grandpapa," she announced. "And you may all rest assured that I will do everything to uphold the family honor." With a swirl of her skirts she turned to march up the stairs to her bedroom.

Everything and anything, she said to herself as she pulled her bedroom door closed behind her with a bang. Even if her family seemed ready to surrender, she wasn't. She felt herself equal to the task of rescue, felt that the crisis was making her strong. Yet, as she again sat before her mirror to brush out her hair, a small niggling doubt about her plan to outwit Skye with her charms crept into her heart. Yet, what was there to fear? She supposed he might try to seduce her, but she felt she could handle that, although the sudden thought of his hands on her made her feel a rush of heat. Well, let him try, she concluded. Skye McAllister would find his jewel had facets more dangerous than he had bargained for.

Chapter Six

SKYE DUG HIS HEELS INTO HIS MAGNIFICENT WHITE stallion, Jupiter, and headed toward the Lockridge Estate. If his father was determined to buy it then he damn well better go and have a look at it. Owning the Lockridge manor seemed to be the most important thing in Angus's life for the last year and Skye certainly had no intention of thwarting him. Especially as it seemed to be throwing him into the presence of the most dazzling young woman he'd ever feasted his eyes on.

With the thought of Jewel, Skye spurred Jupiter to an even faster pace and smiled to himself at his instinctive action. Too bad she was a Lockridge. He'd been wanting to marry and sire some sons, but hadn't found a woman who had in the least stirred him. The peasant girls sometimes had a spark of fire, but no wit or drive, and the ladies he'd been meeting since he and his father had become wealthy seemed as insipid as the tea they always seemed to be drinking. Whereas Jewel—by God, there was a woman to match him, either in battle or in bed. He grinned at the thought of bedding her, but, noticing that he was now moving onto the Lockridge acres, he slowed Jupiter to take a look around.

It was rich land, good for farming. As he noted the grade of the hillsides, the color of the soil, the type of growth, he began to relish the ideas flocking to his mind, he thought of stocking it with fine merino ewes, and using the upper pasture closest to his own estate for his studs.

As he neared the manor house, he reined in Jupiter and let his eyes take in the stately building set so perfectly atop the knoll looking down on the distant river. It was a better site than the estate they already owned, he thought, and undoubtedly, a grief to each of the Lockridges to lose it. Well, hell, they'd already lost it before Angus began his scheming. As he glanced toward the barn, he caught a glimpse of a woman working nearby, her long dark hair flowing freely down her back. He knew instinctively it was Jewel and was surprised to feel his heart quicken at the recognition. Although this was only supposed to be a reconnaissance trip, he found he couldn't resist. Spurring Jupiter lightly, he rode slowly down to the barn, his eyes fastened rudely on Jewel, who was watching his slow approach with unaccustomed nervousness. She was dressed in a soiled cotton smock, her hair was blowing wildly around her face, and only as he stopped his horse did she lower the bucket of water she had been carrying. He was unable to take his eyes off her. The soft white dress she wore clung to her firm curves, ripe for the touching, the smoothness of her creamy neck and chest exposed. His eyes leapt from the perfection of her breasts up to her beautiful oval face, tracing for his memory the small nose and the fullness of her red lips. What a temptress, he thought. She's more attractive disheveled than most women are after half a day spent preparing themselves.

To hide his appreciation he dismounted, attaching the reins to a railing in need of a new post and noting the work that needed doing. A frown creased his tanned brow as he realized it was probably Jewel who was now shouldering those burdens.

Jewel was shocked to find Skye there. His clean, close fitting black breeches, shining black boots and tan buttoned vest over a snow-white shirt made her aware of her own none-too-clean dress. She felt as though she must look like a farmhand. And yet the way he had just looked at her was as no man had ever looked at her. She knew that no matter how she must look, his gaze had been filled with admiration and . . . desire.

"The radiant Jewel," Skye said, touching the brim of his hat in salute, his green eyes sweeping over her. He had intended a mocking tone but the words had unexpectedly come out reverently. But Jewel's flashing eyes made him guess that she must have thought he *was* mocking her.

"What are you doing here?" she asked coldly, raising her chin proudly and trying to brush away the dark hair which swirled around her face.

He half smiled and came closer to her. "Trust you to come straight to the point without a greeting," he said, and then on impulse added, "I've come to see your grandfather." When she looked amazed and dismayed, he continued, "Or had you hoped I'd come to see you?" He reached around and gave her a playful swat on the behind, partly for his pleasure and partly to test her reaction.

She let out a gasp, her face flushing, and then slashed her hand across his face so fast he never saw it coming, the sting of the slap stunning him. She whirled out of his reach, glaring at him. It took him a moment to recover himself and he found himself again amazed at her spirit.

"Well, now," he began, managing a smile. "I get to caress your behind and you get to caress my face. Shall we try it again?" When he took a stride toward her, she stepped back and picked up a pitchfork.

"Perhaps not," he said, laughing aloud, and stopping. "I guess it's time to meet your family."

"For what purpose?" she asked with asperity, her heart thudding so strongly from their physical exchanges she thought he might hear it.

"We're neighbors, as I hope you've noticed," he answered. "I thought it time I introduced myself. You were kind enough to hunt me down in my woods, but your grandfather—"

"Hunt you down?" Jewel exclaimed. "You fooled me. I never would have—"

"So you're willing to kiss my gamekeeper but not me, is that it?" he teased, his eyes laughing at her anger.

Jewel simply glared at him. If she had thought he would come money in hand to buy the estate or to ask permission to court her, she was clearly mistaken. He never seemed to do what was expected. Now he came here and swatted her behind and mocked her and wanted, she supposed, to taunt her poor grandfather.

"My grandfather's not well," she answered shortly, regaining command of her senses.

"I'm sorry to hear that," he said. "I fear that means I'll have to spend my time with you."

"You are one of the rudest, most overbearing men I have ever known," she said. "My grandfather will not see you, I'm certain, and I have seen all of you that I want." She then leaned the pitchfork back against the barn and with head held high she marched herself toward the manor house.

"Wait, Jewel," she heard him say as he followed her. "I have been rude, I guess, and I apologize. I'm sorry if my teasing got out of hand. And I would like to meet your family."

Abigail and Sarah must have seen them from the kitchen, for they were at the front door waiting as they approached. Jewel felt almost tongue-tied, so stricken was she over Skye's determined intrusion into their home.

"Good morning, sir," Abigail said, opening the door and offering him entry.

"Mama!" Jewel cried, "This is James McAllister!"

Abigail's mouth opened and her hand went to her throat as if to protect it.

"Madam," Skye said, striding past Jewel as he took off his hat and tossed it nonchalantly on the coatrack in the vestibule. "I'm delighted to make both your acquaintance and that of another of your beautiful daughters." He smiled disarmingly at Sarah and winked.

Abigail flinched at this presumption and clearly did not know what to say. She reached for Sarah's hand as if to protect her.

Skye, however, was equal to the occasion. "I would've called earlier, but I've had . . . pressing business to attend to." Then, as if he assessed her pale face and her question of his intentions, said, "I've come to introduce myself, and to meet Edmund Lockridge and see whether there's a harmonious way to handle this thorny problem of ours." He rubbed his chin thoughtfully a second. "Don't be frightened, little lady, I mean you no harm."

"Merciful Heavens!" Abigail said in a weak voice. Then she let a flitting hand sweep in the direction of the salon. She was clearly in a quandary and didn't know what to do. As he was already in, she said, "Come in . . . ah . . ."

Skye took in his surroundings with an admiring glance, but walked directly where Abigail had vaguely pointed as if he already was in possession.

Sarah followed Skye into the salon, mesmerized until her mother stopped her.

"Sarah, go inform your grandfather that . . . we have a visitor. Right away." She whispered a quick instruction and turned back to Skye, nervously fingering a button on her gown. Jewel hovered near the door watching Skye, anger seething within at his effrontery. He didn't take a seat she noticed, relieved, but walked over to the fireplace and leaned an arm on the mantlepiece, waiting, a damnable calm look on his face, his eyes slightly amused to meet the enemy in their lair and finding them gentle womenfolk and unarmed.

"I'll . . . fetch tea," Abigail said, as if this was what was needed, her eyes flitting from Skye to Jewel, who clung to the threshold as if debating whether to enter or not. "I'll be back shortly," she finished, clearly not wanting to leave the two of them alone.

Jewel entered quietly and perched on the window sill, the light playing over her like a rainbow. She leaned inward with a curved hip, a long, shapely leg stretched out, her tiny waist and the curve of her breast showing to advantage, yet unconscious of the beauty displayed. Her toe tapped in pique with him and herself for being so aware of his presence. She felt trapped by the power of his personality which seemed to fill the silent room. He made no move nor conversation to fill the gap. Her nostrils dilated tensely and she stared out the window seeing nothing, but was filled with an excited tension.

Her mother reentered the room, glancing from one to the other and too brightly announced tea, setting it on the simple, but lovingly polished table in front of her blue satin settee. Never had Abigail felt so awkward socially. What should she do? Her nervousness was evident to them both.

"Don't trouble yourself on my account, Mrs. Lockridge," Skye said. "I don't drink tea, but please have yours as usual."

"Yes, of course," Abigail said distractedly, fluttering over the teapot while she poured a cup. What did one offer such a man? Spirits? She quailed at the thought. How could he have possibly asked to court her Jewel!

Sarah came in, her pretty face paler than usual. "He's coming!" she announced to all, her blue eyes wide, and then she sat down on the edge of the settee next to her mother. Abigail put her teacup down and folded her hands on her lap waiting a small eternity for Edmund to enter. They could all hear his heavy tread and the bang of his walking stick as he descended the stairs, and as Jewel looked around the room she realized that only Skye seemed undisturbed by the coming encounter.

Edmund emerged into the doorway, his face set in a scowl, his body unusually erect, as if he had summoned his entire Lockridge heritage to lift his slumping shoulders. His eyes swept to Skye and fixed on him with a look of dignified coldness.

But Skye seized the initiative.

"Good day to you, sir," he said, pushing himself away from the mantlepiece and taking two paces forward. "I've come to make myself known to you. I'm your new neighbor." When Edmund remained aloof and glaring, Skye went on, "I know there's a tragic past linking our two families and that it must seem luckless for you to lose your land, but I trust we can leave old troubles in Scotland, where they lie dead and buried."

"Not in my heart!" Edmund suddenly said, thumping his chest. "In here they're alive, and if you're Angus McAllister's son then you've some cheek in coming here. Your family killed my brother and we don't want to see any of you in our lives again!" Edmund had spit out the words in harsh anger and his head was trembling as he strove to hold it erect.

"I came here in peace, Mr. Lockridge," Skye responded, flushing slightly at the attack. "I'm a businessman and am interested in the property you have for sale."

"I have no property for sale to you, sir!" Edmund barked back. "No business with you whatsoever!"

Skye's eyes darkened as he looked at Edmund and he compressed his lips. Slowly he moved his gaze away from Edmund to the two cowering women on the settee and then to Jewel who stood proudly next to the window. His eyes softened when they met hers. He turned back to Edmund.

"Then I ask your permission to call on your granddaughter," he said, soberly. "This ancient quarrel isn't—"

"You will not court Jewel!" Edmund almost shouted and took two determined strides toward Skye. "Your father is no better than a pig, and you, sir, no better than a pig in fop's clothing. I do not intend to cast a pearl before a swine."

Jewel's hand leapt to her throat at the harshness of her grandfather's words and all three women looked fearfully at Skye, whose hands abruptly clenched into fists and whose face went pale.

"My father is a stronger and better man than you, Mr. Lockridge," Skye replied in a low fierce voice, "as you are learning to your sorrow. And though you have a pearl, with your failures you will soon yourself be casting it out of this house and into a pigsty. The world does not look kindly on people who can't pay their debts."

The allusion to his responsibility for the plight of the Lockridge womenfolk seemed to stagger Edmund and though his lower lip remained jutted out, as if in anger, his face paled and his eyes began to blink rapidly. He opened his mouth to reply but then looked away from Skye to Abigail as if to appeal for her forgiveness. He looked so pathetic that Jewel hurried to him and took his arm, turning to confront Skye.

"You have said enough, Mr. McAllister," she said angrily, "and I ask you to leave."

"Aye, I've said enough," he said, swinging his head sharply to the right and then back to Jewel. "I came here in peace but find myself attacked by a crazy old man."

"You are hitting a man when he is down," Jewel countered, "and I am asking you to leave."

Skye's eyes were now on Jewel and he flushed at her words.

"Aye, I'll leave," he said, his face showing an unaccustomed hesitancy. "And . . . ah . . . I apologize for the words I spoke in anger. On another occasion—"

"There will be no other occasion!" Edmund said with unexpected fierceness, pulling his arm free from Jewel and regaining his dignified anger. "Get out!"

"I am not a dog to be barked at," Skye replied.

"But good day." He nodded to Abigail and Sarah, glanced briefly at Jewel and quietly took himself out of the room.

Jewel found herself strangely wanting to go after him and comfort him for her grandfather's rudeness, just as she had comforted Edmund for Skye's. She began walking to the door.

"Jewel!" Edmund said loudly from behind her.

She stopped and slowly turned.

"Grandpapa?" she replied softly.

Edmund hesitated, his face red.

"Take the tea to the kitchen," he commanded.

"Yes, Grandpapa," she said, and feeling a deep sadness she went slowly to the tea table to do as ordered.

"And don't ever forget that that man is the devil," Edmund went on in a low hoarse voice. "The devil! Clean the house, women!" he barked. "Open the doors! Bring in fresh herbs! Let not the faintest trace of that man remain!"

As the three women looked at Edmund in shocked surprise, he went to the mantlepiece and began rubbing with his sleeve the place where Skye had leaned.

Jewel picked up the tea tray and walked slowly to the kitchen. But as she moved she knew that no matter how much they cleaned, no matter how hard they scrubbed, there was no way they could erase Skye McAllister. He had left the house but certainly not their lives. He had insulted and been insulted and the war was on. The only question remaining was who would win.

Chapter Seven

JEWEL'S DETERMINATION TO WIN THE BATTLE AGAINST the McAllisters was blunted somewhat by the events of the next several days. Three days after Skye's visit, Edmund Lockridge returned from town and placed her pearls back in Jewel's hands, his face taut with a somber dignity. Jewel's questioning eyes went from the pearls to her grandfather's face.

"Aye, my Jewel, they're returned," the old man said gruffly. "Valuable they are, but not nearly enough for our pack of troubles. Selling them 'twould take from you without ending our plight. There's an end of it." He turned away and slowly went into the salon to sit in his wing chair by the hearth, there to stare into the cheerless black gape. Abigail and Sarah were already seated on the pale blue satin settee against the wall, each of them bent over their mending.

Putting the pearls inside the large pocket of her smock, Jewel followed Edmund and sat down on a pretty creweled footstool in front of him, and soon became lost in thought. Edmund cleared his throat and glanced at the two women on the settee who looked up at him expectantly.

"I've more news from the town," he said, tapping his pipe to clean out the old tobacco. "Carl Spickens tells me everybody's all heated up about a big horse race going to take place at our county fair." He paused, still tapping his pipe, while the three women watched him, waiting. "Seems it's not enough to bring our produce and animals and crafts to the fair to sell, but we have to have a horse race." When he again paused, Jewel spoke up.

"Do you think Aaron will enter and ride his Thunder?"

"Every young blade in the county wants to ride and win," Edmund said grumpily. "It seems the McAllisters have offered to the winner a purse of a hundred guineas."

Jewel gasped. She had never heard of such a large amount of money being offered for any prize.

"And Angus McAllister brags that he's got two horses that can beat any horse running," Edmund went on. "And the betting going on is disgusting. The whole town's gone mad." He snorted and, after one last vicious bang of his pipe, began to fill it with tobacco.

Jewel stood up, her face, subdued since the return of the pearls, again showing its usual spirit.

"A hundred guineas!" she exclaimed. "Why that's almost enough to pay what we owe."

"Sit down, girl, and don't blather nonsense," Edmund said sharply, motioning with his gnarled hands.

"But Lady is a sprinter," Jewel went on, rushing over to him to make her appeal. "Why just last week Lady and I beat Aaron and Thun—"

"Sit down!" Edmund exploded, and both Abigail and Sarah put their mending aside as they listened.

"But I'm sure—" Jewel began again.

"Lady can't run more than a half mile," Edmund interrupted. "Then she tires and is no better than a drayhorse. This race is two miles. No, my girl, if we had a decent horse and I thought we could take that money from the McAllisters, I'd ride in that race myself."

"Then we should bet money on the race," Jewel persisted.

"What money?" Edmund shot back gloomily. "And who do we wager on? The McAllisters?"

"Aaron's Thunder is one of the best horses—"

"Aye, he is, but from what I've heard this Skye and Angus fancy themselves horse breeders, and not all the money they're throwing around came from furs and gunrunning. They say Skye rides a horse like a madman but he wins."

"If I were only a man," Jewel said dreamily, her eyes flashing. "I'd give him a race!"

"Jewel!" Abigail exclaimed, and stood up. "Young ladies do not ride in horse races."

Edmund Lockridge reddened and banged his cane on the floor. "That's enough of your foolishness," he said to Jewel. "This horse race is just another one of the McAllisters' ways of trying to insinuate themselves into the best society, and I, for one, plan to ignore it. And you will, too."

"But surely we must do something," Jewel said, turning to her mother and sister with her appeal.

"We must have nothing to do with the McAllisters," Sarah suddenly piped up primly. "Ashbury says that the senior McAllister is the laughingstock of all the people who count."

"And if we lose Riverwatch we'll be the laughingstock," Jewel reminded Sarah.

"We'll not be going, none of us," Edmund commented firmly. "The race is to be on the McAllister meadow and I'll not set a foot on McAllister land."

"And let the whole town know we cringe before them?" Jewel persisted, her chin tilted stubbornly. "Grandpapa, it's our right to be at any important town event. We can't let them shove us out of society."

Edmund seemed about to bang his cane again, but hesitated, apparently swayed by Jewel's argument. Then he sighed.

"Nay, we're beaten," he said. "We've lost Riverwatch. I'll not go because I won't give Angus the pleasure of seeing me beaten."

Jewel came forward and knelt to put her head on her grandfather's knee.

"I can't let you give up hope," she said, her violet-blue eyes imploring. "We still have three weeks before you say they'll confiscate our property if we don't pay. You certainly won't stop me from talking to Aaron about entering the race, will you?"

When Edmund shook his head silently, she raised her head and turned to her mother with a look of pure mischief on her face. Slowly she stood up.

"And certainly if Aaron invites me to the race you would not have me refuse?" she went on, adopting her most innocent expression.

Abigail squinted at her uncertainly, fearing Jewel's sudden liveliness.

"We will wait and see whether the Livingstons attend," Abigail replied after stealing a glance at the still silent and sullen Edmund.

"Exactly!" said Jewel. "The Livingstons will know what's proper. Now, if you will excuse me I believe I shall go for a walk."

As her family watched her suspiciously, she moved with quiet grace to the door and went out into the garden. She continued to walk in a stately manner until she was sure she was out of sight of the living room. Then she broke into a skip and ran, half dancing toward the barn.

The race! The race would be their salvation! Her idea was splendid! She would wager the pearls! On Aaron! He would be racing not only for himself but also for her family and for her! How romantic! Her beau would ride to victory, saving her dowry and the family estate. Why it was obviously meant to be. It was almost as if the gods had purposely given them these tribulations just so she could prove her resourcefulness and Aaron could prove his love. And Skye McAllister would lose!

As Jewel stopped with bright eyes and gasping for breath before the barn, she pulled out the pearls from her side pocket and kissed them, as if they had come up with the idea.

When Aaron came to dinner the next afternoon, Jewel saw to it she was dressed her very best in a full blue and green lawn dress with ribbons on the skirt and a low-cut bodice. And she smiled and laughed and flirted until she could see the lovelight in Aaron's eyes. When they were leisurely pacing the garden before the meal, she casually asked him if he were going to enter the race and was stunned when he answered that he wasn't.

"But on Thunder you would have a good chance to win," she said, stopping in front of him and looking up at him imploringly.

"Indeed, I believe Thunder to be one of the fastest horses in the state and I one of the best horsemen," Aaron said in reply. "But this race has become a little too . . . rowdy for my tastes. I enjoy a good gentlemanly challenge, but there will be more than twenty horses entered and several of the riders are stableboys. I am a lawyer, not a stableboy."

Jewel searched his eyes to see if this were the real reason but could sense nothing behind the warm glance he was bestowing on her.

"Surely other gentlemen have risen to the challenge and are riding," she said.

"True, there are several," he said, taking her elbow and guiding her to the wooden bench set against the garden wall. Her mother's flower garden wafted perfume to them. "But Hudson is split. Half the families feel it is beneath them to accept the McAllister challenge, while half are happy to accept it. I assumed that you and Edmund would prefer I not race." As he seated her beside himself he looked at her questioningly.

"But there's a prize of a hundred guineas," said Jewel.

"A gentleman can not be bought," Aaron said with a soft smile.

"But I want to wager on you," Jewel said passionately, taking one of his hands in hers. "I want you to beat Skye McAllister. I want you to win the prize."

"Merely wanting won't necessarily make me a winner," Aaron said, gazing at her affectionately.

"It means so much to me, Aaron, I can't begin to tell you how much. I'll give you my pearls to bet against the McAllisters—a private wager—only we need know. I've a feeling that that man will gamble when the stakes are a Lockridge jewel—that will be enough to pique his avarice, I'm sure."

Aaron looked at her meaningfully. "You seem almost more interested in defeating Skye McAllister than in my winning."

"Oh, Aaron, no," Jewel said. "Don't you see, you have a chance to save our family. When you win, some of our debts will be paid and our family less misused by the town gossips. And you and I will be closer to our goals." She smiled at him, catching his eyes and sweeping her lashes low in a flirtatious gesture. She impulsively gave him a quick kiss on the cheek. "You will race, won't you?" she asked, her voice soft with the music of a woman needing a man's help.

"You schemer . . ." Aaron chided gently, his tone relenting and a finger touching her chin briefly.

"Yes," she answered unashamedly, "with every weapon at my command."

"What if I lose?"

"I shall be no worse off than before, and you will still stand as having raced for our honor and given the townspeople and the McAllisters a sign that we still have friends willing to help." Jewel's brilliant blue-violet eyes were steady with purpose.

Aaron sighed. "You leave me no choice, dear lady. I will race." He raised her hand to his lips and brushed them with a gentle kiss. "But one condition—that this will end your scheming."

For answer Jewel gave him a beautiful smile and a sidelong look. "I promise not to involve you in any more schemes."

"Why do I feel that you have made a not altogether satisfactory answer?" he asked with a rueful smile as he escorted her back to the house.

Jewel laughed, the sound lilting. "It's the lawyer in you."

"I want your promise . . ." he began again.

"But I gave it," Jewel whispered, squeezing his arm reassuringly.

Aaron shook his head. "But I don't know to what."

Laughing, Jewel skipped ahead of him back into the house.

Chapter Eight

DURING THE NEXT WEEK, DETERMINATION TO SAVE HER family burned in Jewel like raw lemon in a sore throat. Her continual dwelling on the race drew exasperated sighs from her mother and a look of distant fear in her grandfather's eyes. He believed that Jewel was possessed by the old tragedy and was thus involved in a private duel with the young James. Even Jewel admitted she was spending too much time and thought on her determination to win, but she couldn't seem to stop herself.

Finally, knowing she had to act, she decided to go to the McAllister mansion and see for herself Skye McAllister's famous horses. It was hot, on the last day of June as she pulled on a light cotton dress of palest yellow, fastened a small bonnet under her chin, and quietly slipped out of the house through a side door. She walked rapidly over a field toward the McAllister estate, skirting around the grand brick house with its columned portico. Through the shrubs and trees she noted that the window sashes and trim had been freshly painted white and the grounds newly trimmed. She was in no mood to meet either of its owners and ducked whenever she heard voices until it appeared safe to continue. She made her way steadily toward the stables, which were a distance from the manse.

The McAllisters had had the buildings lengthened and newly refurbished. Three magnificent animals poked their heads out of the top of their stalls to peer at her curiously. Eight other occupants in their stalls watched her approach quietly, munching on their hay. Others she knew were out to pasture or exercising, for she had seen them distantly when she walked. These were no barnyard animals, but bred for their finer temperament and speed. They were showy, and all the evidence pointed to a fine pampering in their sleek brushed coats and healthy bright eyes.

A stableboy stared at her as curiously as the horses, his mouth open and slack.

"Is Dan about?" she asked him, when he stood dumb. The boy nodded and trotted toward the back of the stables to the tack room.

Dan Buckthorne came forward, hitching up the leather apron round his ample waist, his coarse heavy linen shirt stained and his striped ticking trousers looking the worse for wear.

"Miss Jewel?" he asked, his eyes widening with surprise.

"Hello, Dan." Jewel gave him a brilliant smile. "I've come especially to see how you're faring here."

Dan was momentarily taken off guard both by Jewel's radiant beauty and her unusual friendliness.

"The stables . . . as you can see," he swept his

large arm out, "is where I work . . . a fine stable it is . . ." He frowned in irritation as he could think of nothing appropriate to say to a lady who took his breath away. "I . . . ah . . . just finished shoeing Regal Prince."

"Fancy name, that," Jewel said, with just a hint of sarcasm. Her eyes swept the length of the stables. "Your charges are remarkable, and, fleet, I hear."

"Fleet?" Dan scratched behind his overlarge ears, adjusting his pigtail nervously. "Oh, fast—yes, they be very fast."

"And the fastest would be . . . ?" Jewel asked, her face studying the line of overcurious horseflesh.

"Well, Jupiter, over here." Dan walked to a stall where the giant white stallion stood, his coal black eyes watching the two. He stuck his head out to Dan hoping for a treat. "He's pretty fast and the favorite of the master's son."

"The master's son," Jewel repeated with emphasis. "Of course, it suits them to take names befitting the fine house they've . . . purchased," she said meaningfully. She wasn't sure enough of Dan's allegiances to say more. She reached out a graceful hand to Jupiter's sleek white head, his ears forward and seeming to take the attention coming his way for granted.

"A graceful animal," she concluded, not letting on to Dan that she had already seen him. "Dan," she continued, giving him another of her bewitching smiles, "I've been thinking . . . of the race at the fair. You've heard of the big race, of course . . ."

Dan nodded, shifting his eyes away from Jewel guiltily as if he'd been caught seeing too much of her.

"The young master'll win, Miss Jewel," he said with apparently no thought that anyone could challenge him.

Jewel was undaunted, but a small crease of annoyance momentarily darted between her finely arched brows.

"But if he were to lose . . . if he were properly challenged, he could lose, and it wouldn't be much loss to a man of his wealth . . ."

"No, ma'am," Dan said with a grunted reply. "Not as far as money goes."

"Just his pride would be . . . wounded," Jewel added.

"That be it, just his pride," Dan agreed.

"But to some people, to my family for example, why it would mean we might survive."

Dan frowned. "Miss Jewel," he began slowly, sensing that she had more in mind than she was letting on and that it might prove to his advantage, "Lady'd be no match for a McAllister horse, not even the slowest of 'em."

"Oh, I wasn't thinking of our Lady. She's sweet and fast enough for us, of course, but what of Aaron's Thunder? Couldn't he win?"

Dan shrugged, again wondering what she was driving at. "Maybe not against Jupiter . . . Jupiter here's the finest . . ." he trailed off, shaking his head and squinting foxily at Jewel. "I sure would like to give you some hope, Miss Jewel, but I'm bettin' Jupiter's too good a horse and the master too good a rider."

"But if Jupiter couldn't race, wasn't up to the race on the day . . ."

Dan stared at Jewel, shifting his feet nervously, abruptly aware that she was asking for his help in a very ticklish matter, to say the least. When Jewel put her hand on his big arm he started as if a gorgeous bird had suddenly alighted to touch him with its grace. He trembled slightly, frightened at this incredible turn of events.

"Miss Jewel, I . . . ah . . . what was you thinking of?" His eyes darted to her dazzling face, so fine, surrounded by the thick, rich dark brown hair, the violet-blue eyes shining. He licked his dry lips and grinned.

"I don't know, Dan," Jewel said softly, frowning. "I only know that my grandfather is in such straits that we . . . have wagered heavily against Skye—Mr. McAllister. I guess I was hoping that somehow . . . some way . . . you could help . . . me." Jewel leaned toward Dan in her unconscious need to be clear and implore.

Dan Buckthorne's eyes gleamed briefly. "Miss Jewel . . ." his breath seemed to come in a gasp, shocked both by her plan and by her nearness. "A man would give his very soul to help you . . . a man would gladly do anything for a lady as fine as you," he stopped, his eyes fastened on her.

"Oh, Dan," Jewel whispered, brightening. "You will help me, won't you? But what can we do? You say Jupiter is so fast."

"Well," said Dan, squinting in concentration, "if a horse be taken sick I guess he wouldn't be too likely to win a race, would he?" He grinned at his own shrewdness.

"Yes . . . but how?" asked Jewel, feeling a faint stirring of fear at what she was doing.

"I was thinking that someone—someone who liked you a real lot—might just give Jupiter and Outlaw a few green apples the night before the race and the next day they might not be much in the mood for running."

Jewel felt a clear sharp tremor of fear go through her.

"I wouldn't want trouble for you, Dan," Jewel said, then realizing her hand was still on his arm she let it fall away.

"As I said, a man would take on a pack of troubles to help a lady as pretty as you," Dan said, smiling down at her meaningfully.

She was so intent on the plan to thwart Skye and win the race that she failed to sense Dan's rising excitement.

"I'll return the favor someday, Dan, you can be sure of it."

"A favor . . ." Dan said, his voice low and his eyes riveted on Jewel's upturned face. He moved close to her.

"Of course, Dan, you have only to ask." When Dan put his large hands on her arms, Jewel jumped, so surprised was she at his intentions.

"Then I ask one favor now," said Dan. "One kiss . . ."

Jewel uttered a sound of shock before Dan pulled her tightly against him and pressed his wet lips on hers. Jewel pushed at him with her hands, struggling for freedom.

"Dan!" she gasped in a high voice when she was able to twist her mouth free a moment. "Stop! Stop it!"

"A favor, Miss Jewel . . . a favor!" Dan murmured huskily, his forehead beaded with perspiration, and his voice carrying the anguish of his need. He pressed his wet mouth down on her neck and squeezed her roughly to him, his strength overpowering.

"Dan!" Jewel shrieked. "Have you lost your senses!" As Dan's mouth tried once again to take his reward, Jewel fought to twist away from him, her sleeve tearing. She was appalled at what was happening and frightened by the man's strength.

Then miraculously she was free. Thrown off-balance as Dan's body was yanked from her, Jewel fell with a thud on a bale of hay, her lemon-colored skirts flying.

"You bastard!" Skye's voice bellowed through the stables.

Jewel heard a loud crash as Dan's body hit some barrels and crates, knocking them over. A groan rose from the mess where Dan lay sprawled on the stable floor. The horses snorted and whinnied restlessly, their peace disturbed.

"Get up and get back to your job," Skye ordered angrily, standing with his fists clenched over the fallen Buckthorne. "And if I ever see you touch this woman again, I'll hang you by your thumbs!" When he glanced briefly toward her, Jewel was stunned by the ferocity of his look.

Dan grunted and surveyed the livid face of his towering, muscled employer whose eyes glittered angrily. Cowering, he scrambled fearfully to his feet, muttering, and limped away.

Skye turned to Jewel, who was straightening her skirts and checking her pinched arms and the tear in her sleeve. He bent down and, placing his hands on her waist, lifted her up as if she were a feather. Jewel put her hands over his to pry them loose but without effect, a flush on her cheeks.

"You can let me go, too!" she said, her flush deepening and a weakness assailing her knees, which she decided must be the result of her fall and not from the sudden rush of warmth over her body.

"If you had wanted a tour of the estate, you had only to ask me," Skye said, his voice still tinged with anger.

"I . . ." Jewel looked into his hard face and saw a muscle along his jawline jumping, and swallowed the retort that had come to her lips. His green eyes were dark as a stormy sea. "I was curious to see your famous horses," she finished lamely.

He released her and studied her face. "Why?" he asked bluntly. "A purchase, perhaps?" His tone was full of mockery.

Jewel flushed again, this time with anger.

"That was cruel!"

Skye's mouth slanted upwards at one corner and his face relaxed. "There are times when I feel pushed to cruelty in your presence," he said. "I save you from a mauling and all I get for my troubles is more of your anger. But I apologize . . . not for the first time."

Aware that she was indeed grateful for Skye's unexpected intervention, Jewel felt herself soften.

"I do thank you," she said, "for your rescue. I can't imagine what possessed the man . . ." She felt herself blush with embarrassment knowing full well what had possessed Dan.

"Nor can I," said Skye, eyeing her with a trace of suspicion. "But now that you're here, would you like to see the house?" He watched her face for reaction.

"Oh no!" Jewel said. "I mean, I wouldn't think of . . . disturbing your father."

Skye nodded. "I guess you wouldn't, though it might be good for him to meet a Lockridge as lovely as you." When she looked embarrassed, he shrugged. "But as you seem more interested in horses than McAllisters . . ." He swept his hand toward the stalls. "I'm sure they'll enjoy whatever sweets come from your hand, just as I have."

"I would love to see your horses," she announced, her eyes flashing. "They are so beautiful and have such good manners." She adjusted her bonnet and marched ahead of Skye toward Jupiter.

She heard him laugh before he came up beside her and took her arm in a firm grip.

"I'm glad to see you are no longer the ferocious bear you were with Dan," she said.

"You're right, I was angry," he said, in a quiet tone. "The sight of you being pawed by Dan made me go a little crazy, and now that I think about it I want to know why you didn't come to me for what you wanted."

His eyes held the question, but when she didn't reply, he turned to order the groom, who was righting the barrels and crates, to saddle a horse for Jewel.

Then he released her arm and began saddling Jupiter himself.

"As I walked over here, I can certainly walk back," she said, reading his intentions to accompany her home.

"I'd like to show you the foals and one of our new acquisitions," Skye said, nearly finished with his task. "You do ride?" he asked, taking the reins of her horse from the groom, who watched, fascinated by the two of them.

"Yes," Jewel admitted, realizing it would be a pleasure to go for a leisurely ride again. The Lockridges never saddled their horses anymore. "But I haven't in awhile."

"Then why not enjoy it, with me?" he added. "You can't have many opportunities of late if what I saw in your barnyard was how you spend your days."

Jewel reddened, embarrassed. "My grandfather is not well and I'm young and capable!" she retorted defensively.

"Calm yourself, Jewel," he said. "I saw the truth of it, and in case you didn't know I admire people who work hard. And I like your spirit. Come," he said, his voice gentler, "let me help you into the saddle."

Jewel stood indecisively a moment before letting him help her up onto the beast. Gently he tucked her skirt beneath her, the gesture unnervingly intimate. Then he checked the stirrup length and the cinch, his attentive care softening her belligerence.

He mounted his own horse, who was eager to be off. "I don't want harm to come to you, Jewel," he said, smiling fully, and alluding to the care he had taken with her mount. "Even though you think otherwise."

Without replying, Jewel heeled her horse gently and rode ahead of Skye out of the stable area toward the fields, through which a rough road wound upwards away from the river toward the hills and woodlands. Jewel felt a little ashamed of her hypocrisy. The thought occurred to her that if Skye knew about her devious scheming with Dan, he would probably have encouraged Dan to ravage her rather than stopped him. She gave a little shiver of revulsion. Although the incident made it more likely that Dan would be anxious to help her hurt Skye, she knew she must be certain never to be alone with Dan again.

Skye rode abreast of her, back erect, sitting easily astride his mount. He watched as Jewel adjusted her seating to correct an awkward bouncing in the saddle.

"I appreciate this invitation to ride," she said to him, enjoying the outing despite the discomfort. "But I don't know why you trouble yourself on my account. I have given you no encouragement and I never mean to."

"You must have guessed why, by now," he said, grinning across at her. "You give me pleasure, and I think you take your share from me."

She was startled by his statement.

"You're a conceited oaf," she said quickly, "and you take too much for granted!" Jewel flicked the reins and put her horse, a mare named Flying Cloud into a trot, only to find her backside rebelling and she had to slow her mount down again. Skye chuckled.

"Pride will have a fall," he said. "And if you're not

careful, yours could be very hard." His grin was maddening.

"The devil take you!" Jewel's cheeks pinked and she turned her face forward.

Skye ignored her outburst after a brief clucking to let her think she had offended his ears, which she knew to be false. Then he began pointing out the features of his land and what he was doing with it. She saw several foals gamboling with their mothers and he directed her attention to a black stallion named Outlaw in a field adjacent, the fence being quite high to prevent his jumping.

"Will you race him at the fair?" Jewel asked suddenly, her heart skidding with the question. She gave him a sidelong glance and one of her dazzling smiles.

"Ahh," Skye said speculatively, fully appreciating the beauty of her smile, but not led astray by it. "Is that why you were so interested in seeing my horses? I warn you and your grandfather now, you don't have much of a chance." His tone was assured, but without mockery.

"Nothing so foolish, you . . ." Jewel controlled her temper with difficulty, for she was about to call him a braggart. She pressed her lips together. "I was curious, that's all."

"Yes," said Skye, looking forward with a smile. "Most people who wager with precious pearls tend to be curious."

"Oh!" she said. "You know!"

"I believe the whole town knows," Skye continued with his easy smile. "The great Lockridge pearls bet against the upstart McAllisters. Thanks to my father's being rather talkative when he occasionally drinks, there's even rumors about some ancient family feud. All in all, I doubt that the Hudson gossips have had such a good time in quite a long while."

"Do you know who told the story?" Jewel asked, genuinely surprised and dismayed by what Skye was saying. "I'm sure Aaron was discreet."

"My sweet innocent Jewel," Skye said, bringing Jupiter to a halt beside her. "It takes two people to make a bet, so your Aaron had to show the pearls to the man he was wagering with."

"Oh, yes . . . of course."

"I'm sorry to see you being caught up in your grandfather's and my father's bitter quarrel," Skye went on, looking at her seriously. "You and I must respect our families, but we're not obliged to repeat their follies."

"Then why are you trying to buy our estate!" Jewel shot back at him spontaneously.

"My father wants his revenge," Skye said with a sober frown. "And your estate is or will soon be for sale."

"But you could stop him, couldn't you?" Jewel pleaded, suddenly feeling there might be some hope at last.

When he looked at her, Jewel could see his eyes torn with conflicting emotions.

Slowly he shook his head.

"I've tried," he said. "But this is what he wants. It's better than killing someone, and your Riverwatch is lost to the Lockridges in any case."

"No, it's not!" Jewel countered spiritedly. "Aaron will win the race and the wager and even the hundred guineas you so foolishly have offered to the winner."

"I rarely do anything foolish as far as money is concerned," Skye replied with a smile. "That prize is offered as a way of getting men to come and see our horses and possibly buy some. It's good business, especially as I will win the prize myself."

"Oh!" she gasped angrily. "You braggart! Don't you know that most true gentlemen wouldn't even ride in such a race."

Skye laughed. "And I am a man without proper breeding. Whatever would I do without your reminding me?" He watched her a moment and then added devilishly, "I must tell Aaron that you disapprove of his riding."

She was startled to see the hypocrisy of what she had said and unexpectedly found herself laughing.

"I confess I had to talk him into it," she said, turning to him with flashing eyes and tossing a sweep of hair away from her face.

Skye grinned back at her, admiring her swift change. "And the good Lord protect any male you try to talk into anything."

As Jewel laughed with pleasure at this compliment, they rode past the fields to a rise, the road bending toward a copse of trees. A small stream flowed down toward the river. Sheep were grazing in the pasture below them. She could hear the sound of axes in the woods beyond, and Skye explained that his men were cutting timber for another shipment to the Indies.

Skye stopped them under an old spreading oak near the stream and helped her dismount, his hands on her waist. His touch sent such warmth cascading through her, she stepped away from him and walked to the stream. As she bent to dip her hands, she managed to rid herself of the distracting flush. She felt like rubbing her backside, too, certain it was red from the jouncing it had been given, but restrained herself.

Skye seemed to be aware of her predicament and after stretching out beneath the tree, motioned for her to come sit down. "It's mossy and the grasses are soft here," he said.

Jewel sat down gingerly and allowed that it was a cool and shady spot to sit. She removed her bonnet with a sigh of relief, for the day was hot, and while she needed to protect her complexion, the hat held the heat around her head.

"A hot bath tonight will fix your backside right enough," he said casually, putting his hands behind his head and resting back. His eyes seemed to close.

"'Tis none of your concern," Jewel replied, letting her eyes sweep down his length. She was wary of his closeness and felt the pulse of him beside her, hot and powerful. Although she didn't regret coming, she moved carefully a few inches away.

"Do I smell badly, or are you afraid of me?" Skye questioned, his eyes slit a fraction beneath his dark lashes.

"Neither," Jewel returned. "I didn't think before coming with you. My family would be outraged."

"But not you?" Skye turned his head to look at her,

allowing himself to feast on the delicious sight of her. His eyes looked deeply into her own with an emotion that made her stomach muscles contract.

"I . . . am less easily outraged," Jewel said, replying to his question and trying to ignore the desire in his stare. She pulled her gaze away from his and tried to concentrate on the silvery sliding sound of the water over the rocks.

He turned on his side, facing her, an elbow supporting his torso, his eyes still caressing her. Responding to his movement, Jewel made a small jump.

Skye laughed. "Skittish," he said, grinning. Then he lowered his voice to a half whisper. "Did I ever tell you how I tame a willful, skittish colt? One that nips or refuses the saddle, but deserves everything I can give to bring it around?"

"Don't tell me, I don't want to hear your improper tales," Jewel said, tossing her head, a mild panic gripping her.

He chuckled softly. "No tale, only the truth," Skye said, his voice carrying an edge of humor. "I throw him on the ground till he submits." Then he added, still in his husky whisper, "And if he still disobeys, I throw him again, until he knows who's master."

Jewel felt such a rush of emotion at the image his low voice had created that she turned her face completely away from him.

"No doubt you think women are like horses," she returned after a pause. "I would expect such an explanation from you."

"Women?" he said, raising an eyebrow. "I thought

I was talking about horses," he mocked, but gently. "But even they'll eat from your hand when they trust."

"I'm certain you've tested all your skills on many women," Jewel answered tartly.

"None like yourself," he answered her softly and, reaching out a hand, took her small one in his, the shock of his touch stopping her peevish, distancing words.

"Why did you come today?" he asked, his voice lowering, all mocking banter gone, only a serious questioning in his eyes. "I would be flattered beyond limit if you would say it was to see me."

Jewel's lashes fluttered downward and she gave no answer, only parted her lips, a helpless tiny sigh escaping.

"No matter why you came, we are here together now and that's all that matters." Releasing her hand, he pushed himself upright and placed his arms on either side of her, entrapping her. Jewel leaned back against the tree, a small tremor going through her body at the closeness of his face.

"What are you doing?" she asked in a voice so weak it came out as a whisper.

"What I always want to do when I'm with you, when I see you, when I think of you. . . ." His eyes lowered to her lips.

"Your words . . . make no sense," she said, finding herself breathless.

"Words have nothing to do with what happens between you and me," he whispered back to her.

"No . . . that's not true," Jewel whispered, feeling mesmerized by the slow approach of his lips toward hers.

When Skye reached a hand up to touch her cheek with a soft caressing movement, Jewel's lips parted again. He bent his head and brushed her mouth lightly with his. The touch seemed to burn, and she recoiled, bumping her head against the tree trunk in her agitation.

"Please," she said, her voice quavering. "I . . . only came here to . . . to see your horses."

"Aye," he said, "and you've seen them, and now you've let me lead you here. Is it because you want what I want, but don't dare?"

"No . . ." She drew out the word in denial, her eyes avoiding his.

"Yes, Jewel," he said in a hoarse whisper. "Your heart, even now, beats as rapidly as mine." His long fingers came back to lie alongside her jaw and then his lips were upon hers, moving slowly and fanning the fire between them. Her hand crept up to touch his neck and stayed to close tightly on the strong cords.

Whatever plan she might have had to use her charms to sway him, he had disarmed by reversing the roles. Her flesh was weakened by his, her purpose forgotten, lying distantly on a forgotten shore. Here was Skye, able to woo her senses as none had ever done before. And her mind refused to function, lost in the power of his searing touch. His voice was rich with wanting and she hadn't the strength to resist.

"Skye . . . don't," she pleaded, when his lips lifted briefly.

"You won't let me court you," he whispered between soft kisses, his breathing ragged, "yet I'm sure what we feel is right. I want no other but you."

"It wasn't meant to be," Jewel whispered back, but even as the words left her lips, her other hand reached up to touch the hard muscle of his arm.

A light surged in his eyes and he claimed her lips again with his own, aware of the hand on his arm as a surrender, even while she denied him. He slipped an arm around her waist, bringing her closer to him and gently lowered her down to the soft grasses. Restraint gone now, his kiss deepened.

Jewel shivered, her senses swimming with delight as she felt the pressure of him along her pliant curves. His lips left hers to trace a path over her cheek to her ear, his tongue touching it lightly.

His hand came up to enclose the soft swell of her breast. She let out a small shocked gasp, her eyes opening, only to melt, their violet-blue fired by the deep green heat in his. He caressed the nipple through the thin dress and Jewel felt her flesh easing into the earth, his hardened body urgent against hers. He pushed her bodice aside, then fastened his heated lips to the bared swell of her full breast. When a soft groan escaped her, Skye released the taut nipple and smothered her lips again with his.

His hand slid beneath her dress to the smooth creamy skin of her thigh. She protested against his lips, and he lifted his, his breath against hers.

"Aye, my lovely," he whispered, pressing kisses around her mouth. "You belong to me, as you have from the first."

"I am promised to another. You and I can never be," she whispered back weakly.

"Then be with me now, let us taste of each other." His lips hovered over hers while his hand caressed her thigh and hip rhythmically.

Jewel trembled as his hand claimed the moist, soft valley where none had touched her before, his thumb pressing gently against the seat of her excitement and she writhed in an agony of new sensations, gasps escaping from her lips.

"Aye, my Jewel," he whispered hoarsely and then murmured incoherently against her lips, as she shuddered against him, unable to stop the spiraling sensations, her whole body on fire. She clutched his arms as their mouths melded together, devouring each other.

She felt rather than saw Skye adjust his position, his hand sliding away from the place of her hunger. His lips left hers and her eyes opened to register he was lowering his breeches for the final assault. A shock went through her as she realized his intent and she twisted away, pushing against him.

"NO!" she cried out. "Let me go!" As she struggled to free herself, her dress caught beneath him and she tugged on it in vexation. Finally he rolled to the side. Tears of frustration appeared in her eyes.

"You're a beast!" she said, scrambling to her feet. "A black-hearted rogue and I never want to see you again! You are no gentleman!" Her voice shook with distress and she averted her eyes from his, her cheeks aflame with the knowledge of their intimacy and with what she almost allowed him to do.

Skye ran a hand through his mussed hair and

adjusted his own clothing as he watched her clumsily trying to put on her shoes and repair her disheveled appearance. He got to his feet, not bothering to disguise the bulge that was the evidence of his desire.

"There will come a time when you'll want what I can give you, Jewel," he began, his voice low with passion.

"I am marrying another and you . . ." She didn't finish, but wiped a tear from her cheek, then picked up her crushed bonnet.

"Be careful what you say, Jewel, for you and I both know you'll be disappointed in any other lover. We're caught in this together."

Jewel turned away, refusing to look at him and began hurrying toward home a half mile away, forsaking his horse and him. The memory of what he had done to her and her own compliance flamed her cheeks. She had barely escaped with her virtue. She hiccoughed hysterically and her feet flew. It wasn't till she was near her own barn that she remembered the state of her attire and, feeling like a traitor, she hid until she felt she could sneak in unseen by her family.

Chapter Nine

THE WEEK OF THE RACE, JEWEL WAS DISTRACTED, HER thoughts moving to and fro between what she must do for her family and an increasing doubt about it. She regretted having asked Dan Buckthorne to try to weaken the McAllister horses. A war between her good instincts and self-preservation made her wander restlessly in search of things to occupy her mind. In addition to her barnyard chores, she polished and scrubbed the house, weeded the garden, and helped Sarah make jams and tarts from the cherries and strawberries Ashbury brought over.

She was once verging on the point of seeking Skye to beg him to help her family, but hadn't the courage yet to face him, especially after the names she had called him. He would certainly reject her plea, if not from his own feelings then out of respect for his father's wishes, and he might try to take advantage of her appeal to force his attentions upon her. That would be humiliating, she thought, remembering how she reacted in his arms. He might laugh at her, or worse—she might find herself in yet another compromising situation with him. She was torn between her growing doubts about her feelings for him and her loyalty to her family.

Back and forth her restless heart wandered. Did he mean what he said? Oh yes, he desired her, she was sure of that, but what of all those words about courting her? Were those just the words of a clever seducer? When it had happened she wasn't sure, but Skye's whole person had taken on a different aura—no longer that of a hated and feared person but now that of one . . . *desired* was the word that leapt into her mind, but she fiercely rejected it. Whatever it was, Skye must never know, for she was sure he would use it to some advantage. But what had he meant when he said, "I want no other but you"? It was quite different from a clear I love you, and yet, he showed so much feeling. He had said that her heart beat as fast as his, and that meant they both—but she had to interrupt that line of thought as too dangerous.

The arguments back and forth confused her. One moment she would be dizzy with the idea that he was sincere and felt what she felt, that he had meant what he had said, and the next, she would see Angus's face when he nearly overturned them on the road in Hudson and remember her grandfather's warnings about Skye's real intentions. Then her heart would race, full of anxious doubt. Skye was his father's son, and the father was clearly bent on revenge. Her ruination would be the McAllister's final and crowning vengeance, wouldn't it?

No matter how hard she fought it, many a night

went by when her dreams were haunted by a towering honey-haired man, his sensuous lips hovering over hers, till she nearly called out his name in her tossings and turnings. During the day, she shut out his image whenever it jumped into her mind unbidden.

The real man she had seen only once, sitting astride Jupiter on a rise just at the edge of her land, as if he waited for her to come to him. But he did not venture nearer and she took herself swiftly back to her house.

One result of all her thinking was that after three days she knew that she no longer wanted to be a part of a low scheme to endanger Skye's horses. It was not fair. Moreover, the town now knew of the Lockridges' predicament and also of her betting the pearls against Skye. Suspicion might arise that she was behind rendering Jupiter and Outlaw unable to race. Aaron would be faulted and ridiculed for helping her. Such a despicable usage of a good man shamed her. And her feelings for Aaron were now tinged with guilt over her confused feelings about Skye. The fate of Riverwatch must ride with Aaron in a fair race, for to ruin Aaron's reputation when he was trying to save them was underhanded, indeed.

Her decision made to call off the feeding of green apples to the horses, she frantically applied herself to see Dan Buckthorne and tell him. She didn't dare seek him out again in the stables. She no longer trusted him and was afraid of meeting Skye. She reasoned her best chance to see Dan in a place safe enough to avoid an unpleasant confrontation would be at the fair.

An excuse to be at the fair, which was an annual

week-long event providing the farmers with a means to sell their stock, produce and crafts, was supplied by her grandfather. Edmund had made a deal with a drover to take their remaining sheep, their cow Tessie, and True Blue, their six-year-old mare, to the fair for sale. Only Lady was to be kept for a time. He rejected her arguments against the sale, making her sag yet again under the awareness of their financial straits. Her grandfather might hope to win the race, but he no longer had the energy to start anew, nor the means to restock or hire men to help. He now only hoped to sell to someone other than the McAllisters. It seemed he no longer wanted to live at Riverwatch, not with his old enemy next door.

The fair had been in progress for several days before Jewel and Sarah made their way there. Sarah went to be with Ashbury while he sold his cherries and strawberries, while Jewel was determined to find Dan Buckthorne. Her ostensible purpose was to oversee the farmer who had agreed to sell their stock.

The meadow, owned by the McAllisters, was alive with all manner of wagons and carts standing side by side with makeshift tents and stalls. Pens were erected for the livestock, and geese, chickens, sheep, pigs and goats made a deafening cacaphony which could be heard throughout the fairgrounds. The beginnings of the season's produce were hawked, with fruit and greens, herbs for scent, healing and cooking, and the winter's weavings and the spring's shearings all vying for a fair share of the market. Jugglers and Gypsies plied their trade along with knife sharpeners grinding their stones and minstrels singing their songs for pennies or a piece of pie. Itinerant preachers reminded all who would listen that the Good Book held all the truths they needed to know and that salvation lay not in the gathering of treasures on this earth. Almost all stopped to listen, and then passed on, some looking burdened, others looking reassured of their place in heaven. It was at once a colorful spectacle, a muddy melee, and a noisy, necessary market for the farmers.

Neighbors greeted each other after a long busy spring apart; new friends were found and old arguments resumed.

It was a warm and humid day in early July as Jewel walked with Sarah to Ashbury's stall, which contained a dozen bins of fruit. Sarah's face was alight with pride when she set up her own cherry conserve made with the fruit Ashbury had supplied. Jewel thought Sarah had never looked prettier than she did now standing beside her broadly built young swain, his dark hair and eyes contrasting with Sarah's own fairness. Their rightness together was apparent to all who saw them. Jewel's heart contracted to think her sister might lose her beau if they had to leave Hudson. And for where, she wondered, despairing. Aunt Polly, who was Abigail's own sister, had not yet answered her mother's letter tentatively inquiring if they could come for a long visit and outlining their impending difficulties.

At least, Jewel thought, as she made her way to tend her own business with their stock, Sarah was being forgiven by Ashbury's family for the Lockridge fall from prestige, while her own standing with Aaron's mother was waning. That upright woman had been cool to Jewel when she called at her home several days ago, and made a reference about Aaron's racing which made it clear how much she disapproved. Jewel felt the growing coldness toward her as a rejection that she could do little to modify. She had never before dealt with such obvious social disapproval.

Jewel kept an eye on the farmer selling their stock for several hours before she was satisfied that he was playing fair. Her grandfather would not come, embarrassed to be seen hovering near the man as if worried over the loss of a penny. She remembered times in years gone by when he himself haggled and struck bargains with the farmers with relish, and every tinker and tailor as well, but as a buyer usually, not a seller. In those times they had been prosperous. Pride was indeed a troublesome taskmaster. She tossed her head, the unwanted reminder of Skye's words returning, "Pride will have a fall."

One troubling incident marred the day. She had kept a wary eye out for Dan Buckthorne, especially in the area of the horse auction, but didn't see him. She found herself also looking for Skye, her heart beating more rapidly every time she saw a particularly tall man, but none turned out to be he.

It was Angus McAllister she eventually saw. He was looking over the stock with a keen eye and striking mean bargains. Wandering near the pen where her grandfather's animals were kept, he eyed them scathingly and made comments to one of his stockmen, making the man snigger. Jewel kept her own peace, and was shocked a moment later to discover Angus's eyes turned on her, rudely staring, as if assessing a cow or horse for its worth. She quickly averted her gaze from him, but was struck by the similarity of Angus to his son. Angus was tall and rangy, roughly but cleanly clad in a white shirt and brown breeches, his grey head uncovered and his beard trim. She could see Skye in the man's powerful body, but the face was hard and unsmiling, a man who had seen many battles, his will apparent in every line marking his age. The softness and kindness of her grandfather's face contrasted sharply in her mind with Angus's. A dangerous enemy, she thought, as she prayed he wouldn't approach her. The thought of dealing with him made her feel a prick of fear. And just as she realized this fear, the old man was suddenly beside her.

He was grinning at her, but his glittering eyes showed anything but friendliness.

"So ye be Jewel Lockridge, is that right?" he said to her, not offering his hand, but standing five feet from her.

Jewel's first impulse was to turn away from his rudeness, but realized that too would be rude. Instead she looked squarely at him and replied, "Yes, Angus McAllister, I am Jewel. And I have met your son."

"So he told me," Angus said. "So he told me. Said you were a wildcat. Are you a wildcat?" He grinned at her, obviously trying to provoke a response from her.

Jewel stiffened, and decided that her only course was to end the conversation. "I fear our family histories make our acquaintance inappropriate. I'm sure you have much to do at the fair, as do I. Good day." She turned and began marching blindly away, simply to make distance from him, but he moved with surprising quickness to remain beside her.

"Aye, our family histories," Angus said to her, still smiling. "But we McAllisters are hunters, and if you're a wildcat that means you're fair game, no matter what your name."

Jewel simply kept walking, but Angus hurried past her and abruptly stopped in front of her, blocking her path. For the first time his expression was serious.

"I see now why my son is smitten with you," he said in a harsh voice. "You act like a lady but your body moves like a wild animal." He grinned again. "You make even me feel young again."

Jewel flushed and turned to her right and again marched away. This time she was not pursued. For the rest of the day and that night she couldn't erase the image of being stalked and cornered by Angus McAllister. But what disturbed her most was the message that Skye was smitten with her. She spent another night tossing fitfully.

In the next several days a desperate Jewel was still unable to speak to Dan Buckthorne, so that on the eve of the race she realized that, fear it as she did, she must nevertheless seek him out at the McAllisters. She *had* to stop him from acting to help her.

After a light supper she put on a dark blue summer dress and left her house "to take a walk." She hurried through the meadows and woods that separated the two estates, but when she arrived at the stables she found no sign of Dan Buckthorne. Jupiter was in his stall and seemed fine but Outlaw was absent. Frustration churned in her stomach when she caught sight of a stableboy walking from one barn to another and he told her that Dan was in the high meadow.

Her stomach tightening with worry, she ran up the slope. The sun was already low in the sky and she knew she had to be back by dark. At first she saw no one on the hill, only a cluster of horses over on the far side of the meadow. Then a figure emerged from among the horses and she saw it was Dan. Fearfully she lifted her skirts and crossed the pasture toward him.

"Evenin', Miss Jewel," Dan said, removing a weather-beaten hat and mopping his brow of the sweat that was dripping from his face. He looked at her curiously, a half smile on his face. "Come to check up on my work?"

"No, Dan," she replied quickly. "I don't want you to do anything. I've changed my mind. I want Thunder to win without any interference from me or you with Mr. McAllister's horses."

Dan's half smile faded, and a look of bewilderment and then anger came onto his sweaty, unshaven face.

"Ye be a bit late for changing your mind, Miss Jewel," he said after a pause. "I'm an active man, I am, and you asked me to do a job and I'm doing it."

"Oh!" Jewel said, bringing a hand up to her throat as if to ward off a blow. "You couldn't have! Why the race isn't for another eighteen hours!"

"Others besides you been bettin' on this race," Dan interrupted, the anger showing more clearly on his face. "And even if you ain't wantin' to see Skye McAllister lose tomorrow, I do. And your Mr. Aaron don't stand no chance against him 'lessen we do something to slow his horses."

"He most certainly does!" Jewel said, stunned and horrified by what she seemed to have brought about. "What have you done to Jupiter and Outlaw?" she demanded.

"Well, maybe I done somethin' and maybe I ain't," Dan countered coldly, his face sullen.

"I forbid you to do more!" Jewel commanded. "I want you to undo whatever you've done! Do you understand?"

"Oh, I hear you well enough, Miss Jewel," Dan replied, his eyes shifting to the ground between them.

"Well, then, act," Jewel concluded. "If you hurt those horses, I'll see to it that you're fired."

"Aye, aye, I hear you," Dan Buckthorne said, his face taking on the crafty look of a man who thinks he sees a way out of a dilemma. "And be ye offering me another favor for undoing what ye first asked me to do?" His sudden grin was a leer.

Realizing that she had done all she could and had lost control over Dan, Jewel whirled and hurried across the meadow back toward her home. The man's coarse laughter followed her, and made her redden with shame at the memory of both her meetings with him. She had been stupid and now couldn't even be certain she had corrected her error.

The day of the race dawned sunny and bright. Jewel dressed simply but with care, in a dress of white cotton, squared over her breasts, just a suggestion of her cleavage shadowed, the skirt nipped below her bosom and falling in a graceful line to her ankles. Tiny buttons closed the front and dainty lace decorated the elbow-length sleeves, puffed at the shoulders. She piled her heavy dark brown tresses on her head loosely and tied a broad-brimmed straw hat beneath her chin with a wide blue ribbon. Her nerves were pulled taut with uncertainty about what Dan Buckthorne had done and the knowledge that today her grandfather would be at the fair and some kind of meeting might take place between the two families.

Sarah donned a full-skirted dress of pink lawn and chatted excitedly to Jewel while they assisted each other in dressing. For Sarah, the day would be spent with Ashbury and his family, protected and loved. She had steadfastly refused to discuss the coming race or its portent, and Jewel hadn't the heart to awaken her from her dream.

Abigail was impatience itself with the two of them, while their grandfather seemed reluctant to witness any of the day's events. His former enthusiasm for exchanging stories and gossip among his friends was gone.

"Were it not for Jewel's pearls resting on the outcome," he told them soberly, "I would not allow a Lockridge to be present at this spectacle."

Abigail fussed with her bonnet at the last minute, her nervousness obvious.

Jewel, for once, kept her tongue, for she worried that her own anxiety and eagerness would make her grandfather change his mind. If Aaron won, her grandfather would stand proud again and that alone would make all the distress he had been through worth a chance encounter with his old enemy. And they might win with no dishonor attached to them . . . if Dan had listened to her new orders.

The pasture was more crowded than any other day of the fair, on this, the final day. Carriages and carts had drawn up, people on horseback, and townsmen afoot, plus a few notables from afar appearing. Musicians came and were entertaining the crowds gathered round.

Most had come prepared with picnics, but those who did not would not go hungry, for hawkers with cheese and sausages, pies and bread abounded. The brewery was dispatching ale from barrels to all with coin.

Sarah made straight off to be with Ashbury and his family, who had arrived before them. Jewel was happy to see they seemed content to have her with them.

Her mother wore a pinched expression, because two of her friends from the Church Circle of Ladies had been extremely curt and barely polite in their greeting to her. Jewel felt the slight to her mother keenly, for a more tender heart did not exist among them and she knew they wronged her mother undeservedly. But when Jewel told her mother she thought Mrs. Allbridge not worthy to taste even one of her mother's most burnt biscuits, let alone exchange comments on the day's weather, Abigail's lips trembled until she clamped them shut. Jewel was cross with herself for even mentioning that she had noticed the slighting. Fortunately, their minister, Reverend Ebenezer Barrows, and his good wife, Elizabeth, were friendly, and Abigail brightened considerably when invited to share their picnic lunch.

Her grandfather was excusing himself to go to speak with an old friend when Aaron appeared at her side, elegantly suited in brown. He tipped his hat to Edmund.

"I leave you in good hands, my girl," Edmund said jovially. "I see Thomas Brown there wasting his time watching the juggler. No doubt he needs my advice on which of these rascally acts to avoid and which to see." He shook hands gravely with Aaron. "Good luck, my boy. Our prayers go with you."

"Sir," returned Aaron, smiling confidently, "Thunder is groomed and ready."

"You're the best, my boy, you show them."

"We'll show them," Aaron returned, and looked down into Jewel's eyes. Jewel entwined her arm in his reassuringly.

"I know we will," she said, but her own confidence suddenly flagged. Too much rested on the events of this day and the wild excitement she felt earlier this morning seemed to have drained her of energy. She tried to search discreetly for Dan Buckthorne, worry beginning to tighten her features.

"I've packed a lunch for us," she said, struggling for lightness, "a victory repast. Chicken and cherry tarts."

"I've my own contribution," Aaron said, not seeming to notice the edge in her voice or manner. "Dandelion wine, Grandmother Flemming's own."

As they strolled around the grounds, nodding to acquaintances, Jewel tried to cover her searching eyes with chatter, asking after his family and forcing herself to listen, as a gnawing in her middle frayed her concentration.

Jewel returned a wave from a girlhood friend whom she now saw only in church, there being no time in her life for teas and visits.

"Sally looks well," Aaron mentioned in passing, unaware that Jewel had seen his careful survey of her old friend.

"She always was pretty, but now she's quite mode," Jewel said abstractly, becoming conscious of her own dress, still nice, but old and not as stylish as Sally Woodbury's.

Her eyes finally alighted on a group of horses and she saw Dan Buckthorne in attendance with Angus. Neither Skye nor Jupiter were with them. She stumbled slightly and gripped Aaron's arm. He, seeing where her eyes strayed and thinking her upset to see Angus, whispered for her not to concern herself, for she was surrounded by protectors.

Angus was dressed better than at any other time she had seen him, in a broad black felt hat and a black suit. He was showing several horses to prospective buyers, all men of consequence, she noticed.

"Would you mind strolling closer?" Aaron asked her solitiously. "I'd like a look at the animals, to see if they're as fine as is rumored."

Jewel hesitated, then her purpose with Dan remembered, she assented. "Closer, but not too close, please."

"My word on it," Aaron answered, drawing them toward the horses. Jewel stopped him at a safe distance, but told Aaron to go on, she would wait for him. When he left, she quickly moved over to intercept Dan, who was lumbering slowly away from the horses.

"Mr. Buckthorne," she said sharply when he seemed to glance at her and begin to veer away.

"Miss Jewel?" he said, his eyes darting from her to the people strolling past.

Jewel moved up close to him.

"Are the McAllister horses in good health?" she asked, trying to appear casual while actually on tenterhooks to know the answer.

Dan removed his dusty hat and clutched it in his big hands, but stared at her coldly.

"Jupiter's a bit under the weather, Miss Jewel," he replied. "But Outlaw is fine."

Jewel searched his eyes to see whether he was taking responsibility for these developments, but his rough face was strangely expressionless.

"Then the race . . . will be . . . a fair one?" she asked.

Dan Buckthorne's eyes narrowed ever so slightly and a brief nervous grin appeared and disappeared from his face.

"Oh, yes, miss, it be a good one," he replied finally. "And I think Mr. Flemming is the man to bet on, I do."

Again Jewel searched his face, wondering what he meant.

"But Outlaw will run well too, won't he?" she asked next, trying to fathom his cryptic replies.

This time his face broke into a twisted grin.

"Oh, yes, Outlaw'll run well," he answered. "Nothing wrong with Outlaw." He put his hat on his head and grunted. "But I still think you'll be racin' with luck on this day." This said, he grinned again, turned on his heel and trod off heavily.

Jewel felt a weight lifted from her shoulders knowing that Outlaw would race, but then felt it come crashing down upon her again when she realized that Jupiter was ill and that Dan's answers had implied that he felt unaccountably sure that Aaron would win. She wanted her intended to win on his own merits, and again regretted tempting fate by suggesting to Dan such an evil deed. But had he done anything? She simply couldn't tell.

She turned her attention back to Aaron who was speaking to one of Angus's customers, a smile on his face. Jewel thought she recognized the man as someone she had met during a Christmas party at Aaron's home last year, a man from Albany with connections in the state government. The McAllisters would profit indeed if they sold one or two of their horses to this man, for, if she remembered rightly, he had influential friends. So intent was she on her own thoughts, that she failed to take in her surroundings. Aaron at last came to her side, a look of satisfaction on his face, but she was not to find out why until much later, for at the same moment a familiar voice spoke sending rivers of sensations down her spine.

"Mr. Flemming," Skye's deep baritone said.

Jewel turned at the sound of the commanding voice and felt shock waves as she caught sight of his tall handsome figure dressed superbly in a pearl grey suit, his white shirt and stock dazzling. On his arm was a petite, striking young woman with dark red hair, her dress of finest peach silk displaying her curvaceous figure to advantage. She carried a white lace parasol and had eyes only for Skye, her arm on his possessively. Jewel felt her cheeks stain with pink and hoped her big shady hat covered her embarrassment.

Aaron's good manners forbade anything but courtesy and he greeted Skye comfortably, if with reserve.

"May I introduce Miss Melissa Worthington of Albany," Skye said to them both, his eyes looking down on his lovely companion rather than back at them. While Melissa graciously acknowledged first Aaron then Jewel with a courteous, "My pleasure," Skye whipped his eyes to Jewel's face briefly, a bare smile on his lips, his eyes dancing with malicious pleasure—or so Jewel thought.

"The race will begin at two o'clock from the place where you see my father standing now, and will run a course of two miles," Skye informed Aaron, his eyes meeting those of the other man in that direct, intent manner of his. "I've arranged with the mayor and Ebenezer Barrows, your pastor, to have men stationed along the way to act as judges. They're all honest men, you'll find, and none of my choosing." Melissa leaned on Skye's arm while she sent adoring glances up at him. Skye placed his other hand over Melissa's small white hand with a deliberate slowness that seemed to Jewel almost a caress. She felt a wrenching in her heart and looked away. When she looked back, he had removed his hand, but Jewel felt it was not because of her discomfort, for his face was businesslike as he listened to Aaron and ignored her.

"I have every confidence that the race will be run with careful attention to fairness," Aaron was saying, his tone one of his lawyer best. "You have as much at stake in the proper conduct of it as we have."

"Aye," Skye returned quickly, "you see the way of it clearly." Skye touched the brim of his tall hat and nodded to them. He smiled, his white teeth flashing an instant. "I leave you to your pleasures, as I must look to my mount." He turned to leave, Melissa floating with him.

"But where is Jupiter?" Jewel asked, her cheeks flaming suddenly. She hadn't meant to speak, but her tongue was faster than her brain.

Skye stopped, raising an eyebrow in question, his eyes attesting to his amusement with her. He grinned as he cocked his head jauntily. "This concern of yours wouldn't have something to do with a hope for his demise, would it?"

"Of course not," Jewel said, her chin going up. "I merely noted he was not among the horses over there," Jewel said with as cool a voice as she could muster.

"He's neither here nor for sale," Skye returned, his eyes following the direction of her gaze to his father's place with the McAllister's horses. He looked back at her sharply, his green eyes riveting hers. "It seems he found the taste of forbidden fruit too much to resist, and got himself a bellyache, but as you must know, I have another horse quite capable of winning the race."

Jewel felt his eyes watching her reaction and she tried her best to conceal her relief that indeed he felt he had a fair chance to win. Not able to think of anything else to say, she murmured, "I see," and inched closer to Aaron.

"If you've no more questions, Miss Lockridge," Skye said, pronouncing her name with emphasis, "we'll take our leave."

"None, Mr. McAllister," Jewel returned, her violet-blue eyes full of storm. She tugged at Aaron's arm to take them away with dignity before she could say something she regretted.

Aaron escorted her several paces away before he asked why she was so concerned with the whereabouts of Skye's horse.

"If I had known," she began, still smarting at Skye's ignoring of her and of his obvious pleasure at escorting the voluptuous little bird fluttering at his side, but she stopped herself from saying, "I would have fed the apples to Jupiter myself." Instead she covered with, "If I had known what rudeness you would have to deal with at his hands, I might never have asked you to race." But she knew that to be false even while she uttered the words. "Oh, let's not think about the race till it's time. It's too bothersome."

Aaron laughed. "Mother would not have me race, but I pleaded my own cause," Aaron said, unable to dicipher Jewel's other motives. "I'm truly looking forward to the romp. I've even made a few small wagers with my friends for myself."

Jewel made no comment, though she was surprised by this new side of Aaron, who normally did not risk a farthing, nor permit more than a moment to be spent unproductively. Then she felt again her annoyance at Skye's turning up with that redheaded woman.

"Miss Worthington is the daughter of John S. Worthington, the man I was speaking to while looking over the McAllister horses," Aaron said, as if reading the subject of her thoughts. He paused a moment before going on. "Quite a match for the young Mr. McAllister, I should think. Her father sits in the Albany legislature and is quite involved in setting land policies for the state."

Jewel listened with new discomfort to this information. So Skye had himself a catch and would use his connection to his advantage, most certainly. Then what was he doing asking to court her? Trifling! She clenched a small fist and murmured, "Perdition!" Then blushed to realize Aaron had heard her.

"My dear Jewel." Aaron's brown eyes rolled to hers, a curiosity evident. "It's for the best as far as we're concerned. For I'm acquainted with the man and have his ear. Miss Worthington can only have a civilizing effect on her handsome roughneck."

"Civilizing indeed!" Jewel returned. "That man will never rate such a description." Jewel was incensed, no doubt Skye had other fluffy birds fluttering about his gilded cage, too.

"I'm sorry, my dear," Aaron said placatingly. "Of

course, you're correct. I'm sorry to have brought the subject up. It must be trying enough for you today as it is. Shall we take in the entertainment now?"

Jewel walked rapidly toward the tents and carts, wanting to be distracted from her thoughts, and Aaron kept pace beside her. She relaxed somewhat as they listened to a fiddler playing a happy tune. Aaron gave the roughly clad man a coin as they strolled past him.

A small tent, gaily decked with colored scarves, was erected next to a cart where a man sold pots, pans and knives. A large woman with bushy greying black hair and countless creases in her darkly tanned face sat on a stool outside the tent. She wore a voluminous red skirt, a black blouse and beads around her neck. She beckoned with a finger to Jewel. Aaron wanted to walk by, but Jewel stayed him with her hand, drawn to see what the woman wanted.

"Your fortune told, dearie? Any coin will do," the woman said, her voice a husky contralto. "I can see the future in your hand."

Jewel felt compelled to come closer, intrigued.

"Jewel, it's unseemly," Aaron said. "Come away, she can't know anything. It's superstition."

"I see a race . . ." the woman whispered to Jewel, conspiratorially, her black eyes squinting. "There is danger . . ."

"Aaron, please," Jewel turned to him. "Let me. I've never had my palm read." She could feel a restless desire rising in her.

Aaron frowned, but then relented. "I'll pay one

penny, Gypsy, not more for the lady's entertainment." Aaron gave the woman the coin and moved off to look at the knives in the cart next to the tent. "I'll wait here, Jewel," he said, his face controlled, his tone indulgent, though disapproving.

Jewel followed the woman, who smelled of garlic and heavy spices, into her small rough tent made of light worn blankets. Crude crates made seats for the two as the woman slowly lowered her large frame onto one, her hand indicating the other for Jewel. The Gypsy took her time, her dark eyes looking at Jewel carefully, then she leaned closer.

"Your name, dearie?" she asked, putting out her hand and slowly reaching for Jewel's slender one.

"Jewel."

The Gypsy flicked her eyes to Jewel's intent young face.

"A pretty woman always has men sniffin' round her skirts," the woman said, her voice low and her head bent now as she opened Jewel's palm and stretched it, touching the fingertips and tracing the lines with her fat, tan fingers.

"The race this afternoon," Jewel said, looking down at her own hand, "do you see it?"

"It means much to you, this race," the Gypsy said, not a question, but a statement.

Jewel wondered whether the woman was merely going to echo her and decided to remain quiet.

"Yes . . ." the woman hissed. "I see many horses, many men, trouble and danger to someone . . . grave danger, to a man of courage."

Jewel felt an unaccountable stab of fear at the Gypsy's words and, when she became silent, waited breathlessly for her to go on.

"But . . . who will win?" she finally asked.

The old woman's face screwed into an even deeper scowl as she stared into Jewel's palm. "The better man will win," she said slowly.

"Oh, of course," Jewel replied impatiently. "But is the man I want to win the better man?"

The Gypsy ignored her impatience, her eyes fixed on Jewel's palm.

"I can't see who you want to win," she replied huskily. "The lines are all confused. But . . . ahh . . . yes, now I see. Oh, yes, yes." She suddenly raised her head and grinned across at Jewel, revealing large gaps between her teeth. "Your intended will win," she announced crisply, the words striking Jewel like a shot.

Jewel felt herself brighten, giddy with triumph.

"You're sure?" she asked, trilling a small laugh.

"Oh, yes, it's written in your palm," the Gypsy said, "clear as water. Your intended will win and you will lose everything, everything, but in the end you will gain even more. This will be a day to remember."

At these words Jewel felt her giddiness evaporate.

"Wha . . . what do you mean?" she asked. "How can my man win and yet I lose?" She tried to pull her hand away but the Gypsy would not release it, although the woman now grinned into Jewel's face and ignored her palm, the smell of garlic assaulting Jewel's disturbed senses.

"Why it's all love, dearie," the Gypsy said confidently. "You will lose everything to your intended and then he will give back even more to you. Fortune smiles upon you."

Jewel stared at the wrinkled old crone and felt a creeping mixture of fear and excitement. The words made no sense to her and yet they implied that all would be well. Aaron would win and somehow—how could she lose everything to Aaron? She suddenly realized that the Gypsy had released her hand and was struggling to rise from her crate.

"That was worth much more than a penny, no, dearie?" the Gypsy said, grinning at Jewel again and holding out a large hand.

Still feeling both confused and excited by the enigmatic prediction, Jewel stood too. "I haven't a penny," she said, embarrassed by her lack of coin. "But I thank you," she said. Then wondering how to pay the Gypsy, she impulsively took off her hat, stripped it of its wide blue ribbon and gave the ribbon to her.

The Gypsy took the ribbon and nodded her great dark head, smiling, a black gap in her mouth again appearing where several teeth were missing.

"A treasure given is a treasure returned," the Gypsy said enigmatically.

A few moments later Jewel found herself back outside the Gypsy's tent, blinking in the sunlight and so dazed she couldn't remember who she should be looking for. It was almost a full minute before she noticed Aaron standing a dozen yards away with the tradesman, turning a blade over in his hand, but clearly with no intention of buying. Seeing Jewel, he gave it back, and hurried over to her.

"Well, you must tell me my fate," Aaron said to her with a teasing smile. "Who is to win this grand race today? After all, I have sacrificed a full penny to learn the news."

For a moment Jewel felt confused about the answer and then seemed to focus on it better.

"You'll win," she announced with a smile, replacing her shorn straw hat, but even as she spoke the words, doubt flooded her again.

"Brilliant!" said Aaron, still with his teasing smile. "Now I can relax and enjoy the ride."

"Yes," said Jewel, trying to smile back at him, but knowing that the Gypsy's words had left her with even greater uncertainty than before.

Chapter Ten

SKYE HAD MOVED THROUGH THE CROWDS AT THE FAIR with carefree confidence, enjoying banter with new friends, bargaining with prospective buyers and sellers, flirting with Melissa and keeping a sharp eye open for the radiant Jewel. But nagging at him every second was his awareness of the upcoming race and his turbulent feelings about it.

For most of the month since he and his father had conceived of the race and offered the large prize, he had looked forward to the event, to riding Jupiter and winning. And at first the developing struggle with the Lockridges had fueled his desire to win, but the events of the last two weeks had broken the singleness of his purpose. First of all he had come to believe that his attraction to Jewel might be more than simply the healthy physical desire he would normally feel for a beautiful and spirited girl. And when he had learned that she had wagered the last of her dowry against him to back her betrothed, Aaron Flemming, he had felt the sting of jealousy, followed by anger that she had put him in a position to hurt her by winning. Although the prospect of further impoverishing and humiliating the Lockridges had pleased Angus, it had left Skye moody. That the most remarkable young woman he had ever met should be inextricably tangled up with his father's lifelong urge for vengeance seemed a cruel twist of fate. Skye had even begun to find himself considering losing the race, just to help Jewel. But both the thought of betraying his father and the thought of losing to Aaron made him hesitate.

Then this morning, when Jupiter had turned up sick, his first thought was to see it as an omen—*don't win.* Then he grew suspicious of Dan Buckthorne, wondering if he had had anything to do with Jupiter's unusual malaise. He knew he should have fired the man after his crude advances to Jewel. But Outlaw was fine and in good spirits, and though not as dependably fast as Jupiter, he was a fierce competitor who seemed to hate it when other horses ran ahead of him. Skye would ride Outlaw and would still probably win.

But he didn't feel good about it. He had been pleased to see Jewel's face show jealousy at the sight of Melissa on his arm. It was another sign that she had strong feelings for him despite his common upbringing and the bitterness between the two families.

Hot anger surged through him whenever he thought of her willful snobbery. Angus had worked sixteen hours a day all his life from the time of his father's hanging when he was only ten. Working and without parents he had had no time to learn the ways of the gentry, although by birth he was as highborn as the

Lockridges. Instead, Angus had learned first the way of the forest, and then of making money, and then of war, and Skye, who had also been a hardworker since his mother died when he was nine, had learned these ways, too. He dressed better than Angus and his manners were more refined because the last half-dozen years their wealth had thrown them in with the gentry. Angus said he was too old a dog to learn new tricks, but Skye wasn't. Although he found some of the clothing and customs of the gentry ridiculous or hypocritical, he learned their ways the same way he had earlier learned the ways of the trapper and the ways of the soldier. They were necessary tricks of the trade to succeed.

So Jewel's condescension to his father and himself because of their rough-hewn ways angered him. At nineteen, she had seen little of the world and knew nothing of the rough-and-tumble ways necessary for the impoverished gentry to advance in this new country though she might have to learn them soon. But he felt she had the spirit to survive, although her head was still filled with the rigid class-biased attitudes of her grandfather. There were times when her expression of some of these false superiorities had made him want to shake or spank them out of her.

As he swung himself up into the saddle on his big black stallion among the nineteen or twenty other horses and riders who were to race, his doubts were still with him. He found himself searching the faces in the crowd near the starting area for Jewel, but couldn't see her, instead finding his father gazing at him with his hands on his hips.

"Make them eat your dust, Skye!" Angus shouted to him. "Show them what a good horse and a good man can do!"

Skye nodded soberly at his father and turned Outlaw to let him walk toward the starting area. The other riders had had the chance to go over the course that morning and Skye could see that each of them was now beginning to focus solely on his mount and the course, the huge crowd fading into insignificance. Some were dressed as if for the hunt, in their fine coats and breeches, with black hats and shining black boots, while some of the stableboys who were riding were barefoot and shirtless, their sweating chests gleaming in the sunlight. Skye himself was dressed simply in grey breeches, boots and a white linen shirt. When he noticed Aaron Flemming, dressed as if for the hunt, leaning slightly over the head of his buff-colored gelding, patting his neck and talking to him, Skye's ruthless sense of competition was pricked into life. If only Jewel's pearl necklace were not wagered on the race, he would be able to completely enjoy letting Aaron see Outlaw's heels.

There was chaos in the starting area where Reverend Barrows was trying to instruct three or four stableboys to string out the entrants along the hundred-foot-wide start. With at least three hundred people crowded near the start and finish line, this was no easy task. Lance Livingston was to fire the starting gun, but with horses facing every which way it wasn't clear if they'd ever be ready to go. The course was a mile out over a hilly meadow, through an opening in one of Skye's own fences up to and around a large sugar maple that was about a dozen yards from another fence, then back over the same course to the finish line where they had started. There would be confusion and danger when the lead horses turned back against the tide of the trailing horses, but that was part of the challenge. Skye knew that one of Outlaw's strengths was that he wouldn't shy if Skye kept him bearing down on another horse coming directly at him. He planned to get Outlaw out in front and keep him there.

While around him several riders were having trouble controlling their mounts, one reared, bucked and made a sudden rush into the crowd, scattering them amidst screams and laughter, Skye sat erect on Outlaw, holding him steady, his head toward the mile-distant maple tree. He became conscious of Aaron, equally erect, his horse equally calm, directly to his left. Reverend Barrows was shouting at someone to get a horse turned around, and Skye could see that now all but two or three of the horses were facing in the right direction although it seemed that a few were several yards in front of the starting line.

"READY?" Reverend Barrows bellowed in that same deep voice he used to warn sinners about the dangers of damnation.

And then, as Skye felt his body tense slightly in anticipation, there came the loud report of the starter's gun.

Skye's heels dug into Outlaw's sides and he felt the black stallion surge forward in the tumult of charging horses. A chestnut gelding that had been positioned several yards in front of the official starting line was veering to the right in front of Aaron and Skye, who were side by side, and Skye swore as Aaron let Thunder ride right against Outlaw, who stumbled slightly from the bump, lost his stride and fell quickly behind. A hundred feet out, Aaron's Thunder had taken the lead with the gelding second and a cluster of three horses abreast next. Skye and Outlaw were eating their dust in sixth place.

Blocked by the three horses abreast, Skye urged Outlaw to the right to pass them on the downhill side, and when the path was clear he struck the stallion's haunches a sharp blow with his open hand to urge him on. Outlaw responded with a surge of speed and quickly drew abreast of the three horses racing in tandem and passed them. Skye could see Thunder a full four lengths in front, with the chestnut gelding, ridden by one of the bare-chested stableboys, beginning to fall back. They were passing through the twelve-foot-wide open gate separating the meadows and were halfway to the turning point when Skye took Outlaw past the chestnut gelding and closed to within three lengths of Thunder. He was feeling a pleasant excitement and the sight of Aaron's horse ahead of him had him gritting his teeth, crouching lower over Outlaw's neck and urging the beast on. He felt Outlaw still had a large reservoir of speed and decided not to try to pass Thunder before the turn for home. He glanced quickly over his shoulder to see how close the nearest horses were and was relieved to see he led the gelding now by two lengths.

The large maple was looming ahead and he saw Aaron easing Thunder to pass around its right side.

Impulsively, Skye guided Outlaw to the left. He was only forty feet away now, then thirty, now twenty, and suddenly there was Thunder directly in his path wheeling from right to left in his turn for home. Skye kept Outlaw headed right at him, aware of the large crowd lined up behind the fence gasping as the two horses seemed on a collision course. But Thunder, completing his swing around the tree, shied away from the onrushing Outlaw, whinnying, rearing and almost throwing Aaron, who struggled to keep his seat and control his horse.

Skye reined in Outlaw only six feet from the fence, amused at the frightened faces of the spectators scrambling away from his seemingly unstoppable approach. Then he wheeled Outlaw around—and suddenly he was sliding off the left side of his horse.

The sensation was so unexpected, so inexplicable, that it was as if he were suddenly in the middle of a bad dream. He grabbed for Outlaw's thick mane just before he would have been completely unseated, now vaguely aware that his saddle had given way and he was sliding off with it. As the saddle fell to the ground he managed to pull himself back up on his stallion's back, dig in his heels and start back after Aaron.

When Skye saw that the chestnut gelding was now again ahead of him, along with a big grey stallion, he swore bitterly. He couldn't even see Aaron and Thunder. Horses swept by the charging Outlaw in the opposite direction and on either side, and Skye reached back to slap Outlaw's sides.

"Go!" he shouted. "Catch that bastard!"

He was enraged. He was sure that the loss of his

saddle had been no accident and he now wanted more desperately than ever to win this race. He kicked his heels into Outlaw's sides and was glad to see his horse closing the gap between himself and the grey stallion and chestnut gelding. There was a small space between the two and as all three neared the narrow gap at the fence opening he brought Outlaw even with them in between. All three horses surged toward the twelve-foot opening stride for stride until with a screaming oath the rider on the grey stallion slowed his horse to avoid its being crashed into the gatepost. Outlaw and the gelding raced through neck and neck with Thunder now clearly in view five lengths ahead.

With less than a half mile to go, all of Skye's consciousness was focused on overtaking Thunder. He no longer spurred or slapped Outlaw, feeling that his horse could see the other horse ahead and was as filled with fire to win as Skye. With his knees tightening against Outlaw's sides to hold himself on, and one hand clutching his mane, Skye saw ecstatically the gap between the two horses closing. Four lengths, three lengths, two lengths—they sped forward, the crowd now appearing on either side, the unexpected sounds of cheering reaching him. He felt Outlaw surge over the last small rise a hundred yards from the finish line, his head now drawing even with Thunder's pounding hooves a few feet off to the right.

Stride for stride the two horses galloped toward the finish line, Outlaw gaining inch by inch but still behind, now by only half a length, now by a neck, but the finish line seeming to fly toward them. For a sickening moment Skye realized that Outlaw was no longer gaining on Thunder but seemed glued to his position a neck behind and the finish line now only forty yards away, thirty yards, the screams of the crowd ringing in his ears. "Go!" he hissed desperately into Outlaw's ear, his chin tight against his horse's neck, and then the roar of the crowd and the sheer speed of the finish made him lose all awareness of the other horse. He saw the yellow pole of the finish line flash past to his right and slowly let himself come out of his crouch and slow down his courageous mount. As he raised himself he saw Aaron, to his left, still bent over his horse, pulling in front, apparently unaware of the finish.

As Skye reined in Outlaw, he became aware of dozens of people surging in around him, their faces ablaze with excitement, shouting up at him indistinguishable words, laughing, raising big tankards of ale to their mouths. As Outlaw finally came to a halt, trembling, his big black body dripping with sweat, Skye leaned forward to pat his side and neck and whispered his thanks for a gallant race. If his damn saddle had only held he would have won easily, he was sure, and at the thought of his lost saddle he felt again a surge of anger. As he turned on his horse to look in the crowd for Dan Buckthorne he became aware that someone was slapping at his right leg and shouting at him.

When he looked down he saw the ruddy, bright-eyed face of his father looking up smiling and holding up to him a huge tankard of ale.

"Take it, you crazy bastard!" he was shouting. "Come on, take it! Ye may not know how to saddle a horse, but ye sure do know how to ride one!" Giving the tankard to Skye he slapped his thigh and let out a huge belly laugh, turning to poke his elbow into the grinning, ale-swilling man beside him.

Skye looked down at his father with an impatient scowl, unable to share his joy.

"I want a look at that saddle," he said loudly to his father over the din of the crowd. "I think the cinch was cut."

Still grinning, Angus stared up at his son and then shook his head and laughed again, pausing only to down a huge swallow of his friend's ale.

"Who cares?" he shouted happily up to Skye. "Your saddle may come in last, but your horse was first. We won! That's all that counts."

Skye's head swam at these words, so etched in his mind was the vision of Thunder a seemingly eternal neck in the lead.

"Outlaw won?" he asked, leaning down to Angus as if unable to believe his words.

"By a nose," Angus said, slapping his thigh again. "By less than a nose, by a snot hair, ye won. But win we did! Now get yourself off that horse so that the both of ye can drink to your hearts' content."

He had won. As the reality sank in, Skye swung himself off Outlaw and, when one of his stableboys appeared, smiling, he turned the stallion over to him to walk and brush him down.

"Did Robbie saddle Outlaw this morning as I asked?" he asked the boy, who, caught up in the excitement of Skye's victory, was momentarily confused by the question.

"Robbie?" he asked wide-eyed after a long pause. "Aye, Robbie saddled him. And Mr. Buckthorne checked to make sure it was done right."

Skye's face hardened with anger.

"And where's Dan now?" he snapped back at the stableboy, who looked frightened.

"He's here at the finish," the boy answered. "Leastwise he was a few minutes ago."

"Find him," Skye ordered. "And get Robbie to go find my saddle at the maple tree. I want to question him."

"Yessir, Mr. McAllister," the boy said and slipped quickly away through the crowd. And Skye pushed his way through, too, determined to find Dan Buckthorne.

Chapter Eleven

FOR JEWEL, THE RACE HAD BEEN EMOTIONALLY DRAINING. She had stood throughout, about thirty yards from the finish line, overwhelmed by the rush of horses past her at the start and disconcerted by the conflicting emotions which the race still engendered within her. It wasn't until the end that she had become caught up in the excitement of the crowd cheering all around her. When she finally had seen Thunder and Outlaw galloping back toward her, Thunder clearly in the lead, she'd had a brief, piercing sensation of regret. But she'd immediately begun cheering with the rest of the crowd. As the two horses had swept past her, almost even with each other, she had found herself, she realized later, urging Outlaw on, wanting him to gain, wanting him to win.

When the race was over, no one was certain at first which horse had won, but everyone knew that Skye had lost his saddle at the turn. Soon a huge crowd gathered around someone who had retrieved Skye's saddle, and within another minute there was an excited buzz that the cinch of the saddle appeared to have been rasped more than halfway through. Someone had purposely made it likely that Skye would lose his saddle and most likely fall from his speeding horse, thus losing the race and probably being seriously injured.

Dan Buckthorne's ambiguous answers to her questions over the last day made it clear to Jewel that he had done it. His words "There be nothing wrong with Outlaw" now chilled her: he had known that though the horse was fine, the saddle was not.

Feeling angry and ashamed, barely responding to the news that Skye had won the race by a whisker and that she had lost her pearls, Jewel began looking for Dan Buckthorne. He was nowhere to be found in the crowd still lingering near the finish line, and suddenly she was certain that he had fled. Since she herself would not be strong enough to restrain him, she knew it was her duty to warn Skye about what had happened, even if it meant confessing her own involvement.

But when she began to look for Skye he too seemed to have disappeared. One of his stableboys said that he had ridden off toward his manse. Jewel walked rapidly to where she had left Lady tethered earlier in the day and, mounting her, guided her up the hill toward the McAllister main house. Before she was off the fairgrounds, people waved and shouted to her, and one old man commiserated with her on Aaron's losing the race. But it all seemed irrelevant. In the copse of woods that separated the meadows of the fair from the main grounds and manse, she was finally alone and she heeled Lady into a gallop. She had come to within a hundred yards of the house, which was barely visible through the last of the large trees, when a horse and rider came plunging at her at full gallop around a bend in the path. As Jewel reined in Lady the other rider did the same, but the man's horse swerved, stumbled and fell, throwing the rider forward over his neck to plunge face first into the earth. Lady reared up on her hind legs, but Jewel was able to stay on and steady her, finally turning her to see how badly hurt were horse and rider.

When the man got shakily to his feet and turned around to face her, she saw with shock that it was Dan Buckthorne. Beside him the horse was whinnying in pain and struggling unsuccessfully to rise back on his feet. His right foreleg seemed unable to support his weight.

Dan was staring glumly down at his mount, which Jewel recognized as one of the McAllister's horses.

"Are you all right?" Jewel found herself asking, forgetting for the moment her anger at the man.

Dan limped slightly as he moved to his fallen horse and, staring down, cursed its helplessness. He reached down to unbuckle from the horse's side a large saddlebag filled to overflowing. He then turned back to Jewel, who sat erect on Lady, gently calming her.

"Aye, I be all right," Dan answered, squinting up at her. "But ye've damn near killed my horse."

Jewel felt a return of her anger.

"And you almost killed Skye McAllister!" she shot back at him.

Dan scowled.

"I'll have none of yer tongue," he said to her. "Now get yerself down from that horse. I need her."

"Need her to run away," Jewel countered, responding to his threat by backing Lady a few paces away from the glowering Buckthorne. "When Mr. McAllister—"

With surprising agility and quickness in a man who had just been limping, Dan Buckthorne leapt forward and grabbed Lady's bridle. Under Jewel's urging, the horse tried to back away, but Dan's grip held, and with his other hand he reached up and grasped a fistful of Jewel's skirt and pulled down hard. She screamed and kicked, fighting to hold her seat, then heard and felt the skirt of her dress tear. When Dan sensed he had lost his grip on Jewel and had been left with a handful of cloth, he cursed hoarsely and, still holding the bridle with one hand, clawed at her again with the other.

Lady tried to rear, but could not. Jewel felt herself being pulled sideways off her saddle and, to avoid falling, finally threw herself onto Dan Buckthorne. Caught by surprise by the sudden weight of Jewel, Dan lost his grip on Lady and staggered backward and then down, Jewel falling on top of him. With a panicked whinny, Lady galloped away toward the manse.

For a moment both Jewel and Dan were too stunned to move, but then Jewel rolled off him and tried to get up. Again she felt a tug on her dress and, as she strained desperately to break free, felt the whole skirt tear away, the sudden release sending her a second time into an undignified sprawl. As she started to rise, she felt Dan's boot suddenly smash into her back and press her to the ground. When she began to struggle he pressed harder, the pain in her back and in her breasts pressed against the earth making her groan and gasp out a scream.

"Stay down, damn it!" Dan bit out hoarsely, looking angrily first up the path where Lady had disappeared and then at the helpless mount that had just thrown him. "Damn, ye'll be the death of me yet."

"Let me up!" Jewel gasped out, furious at her helplessness.

"I'll not let you up until—"

Dan's speech was cut short, by what Jewel couldn't tell, and she squirmed beneath his boot to look up at him when she felt—and then heard—hoofbeats pounding down the path toward them. Dan's boot disappeared and as she sat up she saw him running away off the path and into the woods and, as she turned, Skye thundering down the path on Lady. Although she pointed into the woods where Dan had gone, Skye reined in Lady and threw himself off to kneel beside her.

"Are you hurt?" he asked, his eyes showing concern as he reached under her arms to lift her up.

She swayed against him and shook her head, almost too stunned to speak.

"Dan—" she finally managed.

Skye's face went from caring to rage so rapidly that

Jewel gasped. He held her a moment more, and, when he saw her fear, softened again.

"Go to the manse," he said, "and wait for me. I'll take care of that bastard Buckthorne."

When he released her and turned to go after Dan, Jewel uttered a spontaneous "Take care, Skye!" before he disappeared into the woods.

Still a little disoriented and forgetting the loss of her dress, which had left her in only a thin chemise and her bodice, she finally moved over to Lady, who this time was standing patiently, and took her reins. She began to lead her back toward Skye's manse, but feeling a sudden rush of fear for Skye, she pulled herself back up onto her mare and plunged into the woods. She hadn't gone more than thirty yards when she saw the two of them at the edge of the woods where the lawns rising up to the main house began. As she reined in Lady in the clearing she saw that both men were crouched facing each other, and that Dan Buckthorne had a knife.

"It's Miss Jewel made me do it," Buckthorne gasped out as Skye, weaponless, slowly circled him. "She's the one."

Skye didn't answer but kept moving slowly closer to Dan, who was backing nervously, holding the short-bladed knife pointed out at his antagonist.

"No, Skye!" Jewel said, but even as she shouted Skye lunged forward, grabbing for Dan's knife hand.

For a moment it seemed to the frightened Jewel that the two men were caught up in some fearful dance, locked together in a tense embrace, two hands fighting for the knife, the other two grappling for leverage, as they staggered around in a slow circle. Then she saw Skye swing an arm and slam a fist into Dan's stomach, heard Dan curse and then stagger away, his knife abruptly flying into some brush.

Skye was after him in an instant and slammed another fist into his chest and then another into his face, sending Dan staggering backward against a tree trunk.

"No—" said Dan, holding up a limp arm half in appeal and half to ward off the next blow, which came crashing through against his face, blood shooting out from his nose and mouth. As he began to slump toward the earth, Skye hit him one more time in the ribs and then stood over him, gasping for breath and glaring down at the man he had beaten. Dan lay unconscious at his feet.

After glancing seemingly blindly up at Jewel, he then pulled off his belt, turned over the limp body of Buckthorne and began to tie his hands behind his back. Then he removed Buckthorne's belt and doubled the binding on his prisoner. Finally he unfastened Lady's reins from her bridle and tied one end of the lead to Dan's helpless hands and the other to a high branch of the tree under which Dan lay. Then, suddenly and inexplicably, he leaned against a tree, bracing himself with one hand.

"What is it?" said Jewel, sliding off Lady and moving quickly to his side.

"Nothing at all, m'lady," he said, catching his breath, a twist to his lips. "I'm ready for a ball, aren't you?"

"You needn't be so—oh!" Jewel stared at his left side, slashed by Dan's knife and bleeding. She gasped, paling, her eyes flying to his tight face.

"It's a nick, no more," he rasped, "but if you feel you're going to faint, put your head down until you recover."

Jewel snapped to with that reprimand and announced, "I'm not going to faint."

"Good. Fainting is for the weak."

"Nor am I weak," she countered.

"Better," he clipped, having recovered his equilibrium somewhat.

He heaved himself upright and slowly weaved a path toward his house some forty yards away. Jewel became conscious of her torn dress and muddy and unpresentable chemise, but felt her embarrassment evaporate in her concern for Skye as she hurried after him.

"Let me help you," she said, hurt by his cold and angry attitude, yet stricken that he'd been injured.

"Your interest in my well-being is rather late," he answered, his voice low and strained, never stopping his tread. His face looked drained, the hard lines forbidding.

"I . . . never thought anything like this would happen," Jewel said, an agony of guilt in her hushed whisper.

Skye didn't answer, but kept to his unswerving path until he came to the back door of the manse. His hand pushed open the door and he called out.

"Jeremiah! Peter! Mrs. Harris!" There was no

response in the silent house and he swept a hand through his hair. When he stepped inside, Jewel followed, her heart racing with her own fears of being in his house.

"They're still at the fair," Skye said flatly, remembering he had given them the day off. "No matter," he added, half to himself. He went into the hallway, past the kitchen and dining room, Jewel trailing him.

"Shall I fetch someone?" she asked.

"It's not necessary," he said, not looking at her. "Bring water from the kitchen," he commanded gruffly, "and find linen—in the dining room cupboard."

Jewel looked around to do his bidding, then saw that he was still moving further into the house. "Where are you going?" she asked.

"To lie down," he said, steadily progressing toward his study.

Jewel flew to find a pitcher, her hands trembling, wishing there was someone to help her. She opened one cupboard after another, leaving them ajar, till she found a surplus of damask napkins. Grabbing a small pile in one hand and the pitcher in the other, she rushed to follow him, sloshing water as she went.

At the end of the hall she swung into the study and found him sprawled on a large divan, his head on a pillow, one leg on the divan and the other stretched out on the floor, his boots discarded. She quickly put the water and linens down on a small table next to the divan.

Pushing himself up, Skye stripped off his shirt and

blotted the slash on his side with the blood-stained shirt.

Jewel hovered near, her eyes avoiding the wound, her fingers dipping a cloth into the cool water and wringing it.

"Will you let me . . . clean it?" she queried, her voice full of doubt over her own capacity as nurse, but intending to do with courage whatever was necessary.

"Have you done this before?" he asked, dropping the shirt on the floor and putting out his hand for the wet cloth she held in hers.

"No," she murmured.

"Then I'll do it," he said. "Wet another cloth."

Jewel did as he asked, her fingers trembling as she took the blood-stained napkin and replaced it, watching him apply pressure and wipe himself clean. Her eyes were wide and face pale, but as she refused to turn away, she saw the wound was not deep, and let a sigh escape.

"Sit down," Skye ordered, giving her a quick glance.

Jewel sat beside him, letting her shoulders sag with fatigue. "I haven't been much help."

"At least you're no longer trying to kill me," he answered as he applied a clean cloth over the wound and held it there. He raised his head to look at her, a swift appraisal in his eyes that made her flinch with the memory of the things she had done against him. "One more favor," he added, his voice lower and less brusque. "I'll need a salve from the kitchen."

He gave her quick instructions and she retrieved it

in moments. When Jewel held it out to him, he gave her a quick smile.

"Will you apply it for me?" he unexpectedly asked.

Jewel hesitated a moment, then bent down while he removed the cloth. She was relieved to see that the bleeding had stopped, and, dipped her fingers into the salve. The scent of sweat, leather and horses filled her senses as she delicately touched her fingertips to the four-inch gash. She tried to keep her mind on what she was doing but waves of warmth shot through her at the feel of his firm heated flesh.

"There!" she pronounced when she finished, and stood away. "Better?"

His answer was a low chuckle, as if he knew she was trying to pretend he was a hurt child and not a man.

"Shall I bring you tea?" she asked to cover her nervousness.

"Tea?" he repeated. "No, woman . . . spirits—rum—over there, in the corner cupboard. Pour one for yourself, too, you need it as much as I do."

Jewel hesitated, but complied, pouring two small glasses and bringing one to him, careful not to let her fingers touch his.

Skye expelled a quick breath through his nostrils, his lips curling upwards as he watched her retreat a few steps. After studying her a moment, he lifted the glass and, tossing back his head, drank it in several swallows.

Jewel took several small swallows from her own glass, then put it down, her eyes watering and throat burning, unaccustomed to the strong drink. Skye said nothing as he continued to watch her, as if searching for a clue, a puzzled, then suspicious look in his storm-darkened green eyes.

"You are barely pricked, but you've lost some blood, and rum will only make you dizzy," she admonished him, wanting to keep his mind on the business at hand.

"I'm swooning already that you cared enough to come running to my side," he said, with a touch of sarcasm.

Jewel felt irritated by his cool tone and responded in kind. "A fool is born every minute," she answered. "I'm no different, it seems. For I find you quite alive!"

"Do you? And does that bother you? Had you hoped I might not live past the race?"

Jewel was momentarily stunned and stood rooted to her spot several feet in front of him. "I never held such a thought in my mind," she said, her lovely voice filled with conviction. "Would I have followed you or tried to stop Dan if that were true?"

"As much as I would like to, shall I believe you when everything points to your conspiring against me?" His eyes glinted dangerously and Jewel felt her temper rise.

"I notice your Melissa hasn't come running to your side!" Jewel tossed at him. "Perhaps now you'd like to play wounded hero to her weeping willow? Shall I find her for you?" Jewel blushed as she realized what she had said, her tongue leaping before her head had considered the thought.

Skye looked startled a moment, then his lips twitched with amusement. "Little claws sharpened already, are they?" he said, his voice more relaxed. Then he added, "No, I don't want Melissa here, nor would I like weeping either. I prefer your scratches, even though they leave me bloodied."

"Oh," Jewel murmured, chastened suddenly, remembering her own guilt and the reason for her lingering with him. "I . . . did want to . . . apologize. I hadn't intended any real harm . . ."

Skye sank back on the divan and closed his eyes a moment, his face taut.

"Did you hear Buckthorne accuse you?" he asked quietly.

Jewel murmured yes, swallowing hard and feeling her knees weaken. She wanted to convince him of at least her partial innocence but it was so complicated. All of her reasons for stopping Dan were not clear to her and she was riddled with guilt for inciting him in the first place. She needed to sit down and started for a chair.

"Sit here," Skye said, his eyes opened and following her. He spread his hand on the divan.

Jewel hesitated, sensing his dangerous mood. Yet she was both fascinated and afraid. She sat gingerly on the edge of the divan near Skye's waist and tilted her chin upwards. "You're not afraid of wildcats?" she abruptly asked.

Skye raised an eyebrow in question, his eyes narrowing. He knew she was delaying explaining her actions but decided to wait patiently.

"You called me a wildcat, so your father said," she persisted, smoothing her chemise over her legs self-consciously, resolutely refusing to be disturbed by her state of undress.

"The description suits you," he answered, a smile tugging at the corners of his sensuous mouth. "Though there are others that leap to my mind—bedeviling beauty, heart-stomping vixen, fascinating wench . . ."

"I am not a wench," Jewel countered.

Skye laughed.

"Does that mean you admit to being a heart-stomping vixen?" he asked, putting an arm behind his head, his intense green eyes watching her.

Feeling her cheeks color and her pulse racing at his sudden closeness, she averted her eyes. A long breath escaped her lips, and she felt lightheaded.

"And bedeviling beauty . . ." he added in a low husky voice that seemed to vibrate through her.

She kept her gaze averted, trying to focus her thoughts when, in a voice suddenly sharp and cold, she heard him ask, "Why did you do it?"

Jewel was instantly alert.

"I didn't!" she answered, turning to look at him. "That is, I did ask Dan to help me . . . make you lose, and he suggested we give your horses . . . green apples." She stumbled over her words. "I meant to correct my mistake. Last night I came over here and ordered him not to do anything that would damage your chances."

Skye snorted, his strong features hardening. "Jupiter's bellyache," he interjected, interpreting for her the result of that gambit.

Jewel nodded again, tense. "But I told him I didn't want any part of it. I wanted Aaron to win fairly." She took in a deep breath and looked at him, saw his searching look turn to disbelief. "I swear it's the truth. I had nothing to do with the saddle." Her voice was edged with a plea for understanding. "I didn't know about it or I would have stopped him or warned you." In her desire to clear herself of the damaging implication, she leaned toward him, unmindful of their nearness.

"You would have come to me? Told the hated beast that his stable manager was plotting against him?" Skye raised himself slightly on the couch, his eyes fastening on hers. "Somehow I doubt you would have had the courage to face me with that tale."

"I'm here," she said, as if that took daring and he should know it.

"I could have been trampled by the onrushing horses behind me," he said and in one swift motion gripped both her arms and drew her nearer to him. "If you'd warned me, I could have checked my saddle and discovered the damage."

"I . . . know," Jewel whispered, feeling guilty, almost welcoming the pain of his fingers digging into her bare arms. "I can only say, I'm sorry it happened. I didn't want my grandfather to lose Riverwatch, but I never should have tried to do what I did. But I tried to stop it all. I did. I . . . was frightened for you."

"Someone might rightly say you inflicted this

wound on me by proxy," he said, his low, harsh voice penetrating her.

"Do you believe that?" she asked, her eyes begging.

"Why don't you pay me what you owe me, Jewel?" he asked, his voice suddenly soft and his eyes alive with a sparkle that could have been either anger or desire.

When Jewel registered what he was saying, a stain appeared on her cheeks. "No!" she whispered hard.

"Then I'll *take* my payment," he rasped in reply, pulling her down onto his chest, a hand snaking around her head to force her lips to meet his. Jewel resisted one brief moment, then the heat of his mouth on hers sent a sweet wave crashing over her and she molded her fired body to his, desire pulsing swiftly between them.

When he released her lips, she was lying beside him on the divan, and he hushed the protest she started to make by planting light kisses on her lips, on her face, lightly playing with her hair, and tenderly touching her ear and jawline with a long finger.

"I don't care which is the right or wrong way of it," he whispered to her. "The only thing I care about is having you in my arms." He brushed his lips over hers deliciously, teasing, taunting, till they begged for his, pursing sensuously, her small pink tongue emerging to lick his.

His eyes leapt with delight as he caught the tiny, unconscious overture, the lick only the beginning of what he could coax from the pliant, luscious woman in his arms. Jewel moaned as Skye sank back on the divan drawing her with him, capturing her with a powerful thigh.

"My love, my beautiful precious Jewel," he whispered huskily, his breath warm on her face.

Jewel, hearing his words dimly, tried to pull away, aware of her own failing resistance to his potency.

"Don't . . . say that. You don't mean it," she said, her voice shaky.

His arms tightened around her and his eyes took on a brilliant grey green depth.

"I do mean it, Jewel," he said huskily, and brought his mouth down on hers in a ravishing, burning kiss.

Jewel struggled momentarily against the fury of his devouring passion, frightened by its intensity. Although he finally released her lips, his hands relentlessly pursued her, unbuttoning and pulling at the bodice of her dress until it parted and bared her creamy breasts to his eyes.

"Please . . ." she gasped, trying to cover herself, but he was beyond hearing her pleas to stop. He lifted her with one hand and slid her bodice from her and tossed it on the floor, his hands then flying to remove her chemise, Jewel weakly pushing at him.

"Skye . . . Skye!" she cried, his name torn from her, half in protest, half in passion, as she watched him helplessly, unable to summon the strength to resist, her thoughts incoherent.

Kneeling beside her as she lay stretched out on the divan, Skye drank in her exposed beauty as a thirsty man in a desert, his eyes tracing her rosy-hued curves in such a bold caress that it seemed as if his hands were touching her. "I've wanted nothing else since I first saw you," he said, the words rushed and then his mouth crushed down, his tongue parting her lips and invading her with its sweetness. She felt his chest against her soft breasts, hot and rousing. His body writhed against her, touching her everywhere, his hands sliding over her soft curves. His tongue, meeting hers, roused her own emotion to a pitch, and soon her fears faded, leaving a woman joining with her lover in their mutual hunger for each other.

When he released her lips yet again, their eyes met, and an unnamed feeling raced through them both, claiming each one for the other, their hearts racing as one, and for a brief instant Jewel felt their souls reaching toward one another.

"Aye," Skye whispered, barely intelligibly. "Aye," he repeated, his voice hoarse. He rose and removed his breeches, his eyes still fastened on hers. She moistened her lips, not knowing what was to come, but knowing, whatever he wanted, she wanted with him. Her body was molten, flowing toward him, no words coming, only feeling. He slowly lowered his body to hers, his head bending to lick the peaked perfection of her rosy breasts. Jewel closed her eyes and clasped his head to her, feeling his hot mouth suck gently at her nipples, sending a piercing current of pleasure through the length of her body and making her breath come in little gasps. As his mouth moved in excruciating sweetness over her breasts, his hands were sliding down her firm flesh, caressing her hotly. Then she felt a hand sweep lower, to the joining between her soft thighs, stroking her gently, his fingers sliding in and out, while his thumb nestled pressing against the peaked point of her desire, until her thighs parted.

Jewel moaned and writhed beneath his touch, the pleasure so intense her face was locked in ecstatic concentration, her hips lifting to meet his hand. When he raised his head from her breasts and his hand ceased its tantalizing gentle probing, she at first simply lay still, her eyes closed, her breath now coming in deep sighs. Then she felt him kneeling between her legs, gently pushing her thighs apart and she opened her eyes to see his erect, throbbing manhood poised to enter her. Slowly he was lowering himself, the head of his member suddenly hot against her womanhood, pressing. She gasped in fear and pleasure, and he paused, lifting his eyes to meet hers, his aching desire striking her like some ultimate caress, and her eyes answered his. With a joyful cry, Skye pressed forward and fell upon her, and Jewel felt a sharp pain followed by a warm dizzying wave as she felt him plunge deeply inside her. For a moment Skye didn't stir, gasping to keep his own raging fire under control, and lifting himself slightly to look down on her.

Jewel knew a moment of shock, a slight burning sensation, then a fiery excitement flooded her entire being. She opened her eyes and lifted her arms to his neck and urgently pulled his lips down to hers, the heat of their mouths sending a second wave of ecstasy through her. And when Skye felt her legs press instinctively around him he had to tear his lips from hers as a piercing pleasure tore through him. Then he lowered his lips again to Jewel's and began a slow thrusting, feeling her arching and thrusting with him, abandoned sounds wrenched from them in an agony of love and need. A wild soaring took them both together, a blooming, opening ecstasy bursting through them. Jewel softly moaned against his shoulder, her nails digging into him, until she felt she was no longer there, only her heart beating in a wild tandem with his.

They lay spent, clasped in each others arms. Skye was planting tender kisses on her shoulder, her neck and her flushed cheeks, their bodies glued together with moisture and heat. After a while he raised his head to look at her and stroked her dark, tumbled mass of hair with a gentle hand. Her head was back and eyes closed, her long black lashes like small fans on her cheek.

"Jewel," he whispered, not wanting to wake her from her dream, but wanting to see her beautiful eyes shining into his. "My love," his whisper was husky with tenderness. "You met me," he said, whispering the words with awe.

Jewel's eyes fluttered open, her face suffused with pleasure, and for a moment she gave him a loving smile, her violet-blue eyes shining like twin stars. Then, as he watched, the smile left, and she seemed to see him in another light, from a darker, murkier place. And the stars faded, falling. Before his eyes, he saw tears gathering and knew she felt regret—wanted to take back what she had given him.

His brows knit together as he watched her heart retreat. When she put her hands up to push at his shoulders and turned her face away from his, his spine stiffened and he felt himself leaving her. He raised a hand to stroke her face to try to bring her back to him.

"Don't!" she said, cringing from his touch, then bit her lip to still its quivering.

Skye removed his hand and eased himself off her, sitting up on the divan. He ran a hand unevenly through his tousled dark honey hair.

Jewel reached blindly down to the floor for her chemise to cover herself, but was not able to reach it. Skye, seeing what she was about, retrieved it for her, his green eyes studying her tormented face.

"Are you blaming me?" he asked, a note of anguish in his voice. He hadn't meant to force her, he had never forced a woman to his bed. It had been love, not lust, desire, not hate. But in her innocence would she know which it was?

"Now you have won all!" Jewel's voice trembled as she struggled to make sense of her chemise and shield her nakedness from his eyes. She wanted to sob for her forfeit dignity, her womanhood given.

"Leave it," he instructed her, his voice ragged. "I'll find a dress for you."

"I'll not wear a maid's garment," she said wretchedly, to cover her distress.

Skye's eyes went cold. "I think this time you'd better squash your pride and use your common sense. I hear my servants returning now from the fair. Would you have them see you half undressed in that rag?"

"'Tis my rag," she cried absurdly.

"I said leave it," he ordered and got up to pull on his breeches.

Jewel saw the angry red slash on his side, marring

the lithe muscular chest. She also saw her own nail marks on his broad shoulders. She turned her flaming face away.

"There's a dressing room off through there," Skye said, pointing. "Go and wash while I find something for you." He put his large tanned hand down to help her up and she refused, scrambling to the side of the divan and clutching her chemise to her.

He looked down on her, his eyes darkening. "My God!" he spit out, pained by her actions. "That you could turn so beautiful a moment to one of grief. It was so rare a thing!"

"Shame! Not grief!" Her full, red lips quivered as she answered him. "My grief will come later, when we must move from here for . . . I don't know for where, but far, far from you and your revenge."

"Revenge?" he said, incredulous. "This was no revenge, Jewel. Never revenge. Revenge is planned!"

Jewel ignored his impassioned words and made for the door, left open she now saw, and stopped, horrified, when she heard the voices of servants coming down the hall. Going pale, she closed the door and went instead as Skye had ordered to find the dressing room and put herself in order.

While she poured water into a bowl from a pitcher on an oak stand and toweled herself, tears spilled down her cheeks. She rubbed at them frantically as if their removal would remove their cause. Finally, having put back on her torn chemise and bodice and smoothed down her hair, she gathered herself to leave. She tightened her features against any further signs of her distress. Her mind raced to thoughts of getting home undiscovered, shutting out any images of her tryst with Skye with a feverishness that made her face flush. "Be angry. Be angry." she admonished herself, forcing thoughts of Skye from her mind. "Forget him! You must forget him!"

She opened the door of the dressing room that led to the hall, but hearing voices, panicked, fleeing again to the study and closing the door behind her. Guiltily she cowered there afraid she would be accosted momentarily by a servant, or worse, Skye's father. Her cheeks blazed with shame.

Skye returned, startling her into a near shriek. He had put on a clean shirt and brought her an oversized striped smock. He handed it to her and she threw it unceremoniously on the divan.

"I've sent two of my servants to take your friend Dan Buckthorne to the constable in Hudson," he said, his face set and expressionless. "I'll take you home."

"No!" she whispered, afraid to meet his eyes. "Who . . . who's here now?" she asked as again she heard voices.

"Mrs. Harris, my cook. And probably a few others."

"Perdition!" Jewel wailed softly. "I'll be caught here."

Skye's eyes blazed a moment, then went cold. "Aye, you're caught out, but Mrs. Harris is in her kitchen preparing our supper and won't see you leave. I'll see to it." His words were short and, had she the presence of mind to note it, hurt.

Feeling stricken, unconsciously catching his tone,

but not able to identify it, Jewel fiddled with her hair, afraid to leave and afraid to stay.

"Look at me!" Skye commanded.

Jewel marched for the door, refusing, but Skye was near it and blocked her path.

"Don't touch me!" she said.

Skye flinched as if struck, and Jewel's face crumpled, its fierce defenses gone, her eyes flying to his, tears swimming again in their lovely depths.

Skye trapped her eyes with his for a moment. He had taken her in love, and deep beneath her fears, Jewel knew it, but was not ready to accept it.

"Aye, my Jewel, I'm a rough lover, but my body spoke true . . . and I would speak more of—"

Jewel wrenched her eyes from his, shutting them out and putting her hands over her ears to stop the words.

"Let me go home," she murmured beneath her breath. "Let me go home," her soft musical voice intoned, pleading like a desperate child.

Skye abruptly ceased what he was saying, his eyes snapping angrily.

"Then go, little girl," he said, his voice edged with irony. "Run away, run back to your old love, run back to your grandfather, sit upon his knee."

When Skye opened the study door for her, Jewel felt such a sense of loss that she barely had the strength to move, but the anger in his face finally propelled her out. In the hallway she stood confused for a moment and then, hearing voices, she gathered herself, lifted her head high and marched down the hall toward the front door. As she neared it, two male servants appeared from the living room and stared at her open-mouthed. When she slowed before the front door one of them abruptly ran to open it for her. As the door opened and her tear-filled eyes blinked at the sunlight, she dimly heard Skye's voice from far behind her—a single sharp anguished "Jewel!" and then she began to run for home.

Chapter Twelve

THE NEXT EVENING, BEFORE SUPPER, SKYE AND ANGUS had the confrontation over the Lockridges that had been building for weeks.

Skye, with a wicked hangover from a bout with a bottle of rum after Jewel's infuriating departure, had spent most of the day training Robbie to take over Dan Buckthorne's job of managing the stables. Several horses had been sold at auction and two new ones bought. Stalls and stableboys had to be assigned for each horse. Although Skye threw himself into the work, his mind frequently leapt back to the previous afternoon—to the ecstasy, the pain and the frustration of his affair with Jewel.

He was still enraged that she had let the feud between her grandfather and Angus make her mistrust him and blind her to their deep feelings for each other. The Lockridges' foolish wagering against Skye on the race only meant that now the Lockridge Estate was hopelessly lost. At noon his business manager had ridden in to tell him that the Lockridge creditors, frightened at the folly of Edmund and Jewel, had instituted proceedings to have the estate sold at auction. The Lockridges would be soon forced to move, back to England if the pattern of previous Tories was repeated, or at least to Canada.

In a violent mood, wanting to ride over and see Jewel but fearing that he would find only more of her guilt and distrust, Skye came in from the stables late in the afternoon. He washed his hands, face and bare chest under the outside pump, and sat down on the long front porch. Fifteen minutes later his father returned from a trip into town, turned his horse over to a stableboy and strode across the lawn to join him on the porch. Without being asked, Mrs. Harris brought out two tankards filled to the brims with Angus's favorite home-brewed ale.

"It's to be Wednesday," Angus announced without preamble, swinging a saddlebag with his business papers into a corner of the porch and pulling up a rocking chair to sit near Skye. After taking his tankard of ale from Mrs. Harris, he slapped her playfully on her rump, receiving in return a clout on the head that made him laugh as Mrs. Harris returned to the kitchen.

"What's to be Wednesday?" Skye asked.

"The auctioning off of Riverwatch," Angus replied. "The creditors refused to let Edmund sell to the Livingstons without an auction, so within three days I'll be the laird of Riverwatch." He tilted back his head and took three big swallows of ale, licked his lips and with a loud sigh, smiled across at Skye, who lowered his head to stare into the brown liquid in his cup.

"Most of my life," Angus went on when Skye remained scowling down into his drink, "I've been waiting to let a Lockridge taste the kind of dregs Michael and I had to settle for for fifteen years, and now it's coming to pass. It's not justice—there be no way that family could ever pay for what they did to Margaret, my brother, my father—and to me, too, by God—but I'll rest easier knowin' I didn't forget, that I've finally begun to repay them in kind."

Skye knew that nothing he could say would make his father feel that such a revenge was unnecessary or wrong so he said nothing, sipping gloomily at his ale.

"And you've done your part, son, and I'm beholden' to ye," Angus went on, downing the last of his ale and contentedly handing the quietly appearing Mrs. Harris his cup to be refilled.

"What do you mean?" Skye asked, looking up sharply. "What did *I* do?"

"Oh, the servants told me," said Angus with a sly grin.

"Told you what?"

"I saw Peter and Hopkins sniggering together, so I asked what they were so chirpy about. After a little prodding they told me." Angus smiled at Skye conspiratorially. "Seems everyone here is jabbering that your Miss Jewel came stomping and crying out of the library yesterday afternoon with her dress torn and her petticoat bloody. From that I gather, she lost more than one treasure yesterday." Angus whooped and slapped his thigh, sending his rocking chair into brief rapid motion.

Skye threw himself up out of his chair, filled with a sickening awareness of the mess he had made of things. He could neither deny nor confirm his father's conclusion, in either case it made no difference. If their servants were talking, then soon the whole town would be gossiping. Jewel was ruined. Uttering a fierce curse he strode to the white wooden porch railing and gripped it with such force that his knuckles went white.

"And if ye planted your seed good and deep," Angus went on from behind him, "then the Lockridges can taste the shame that we tasted forty years ago. The filly will swell up nice and round and let the whole world know that a Lockridge lass has a pussy like the rest of her kind."

Skye whirled on his father, his face red with rage.

"Shutup!" he shouted.

Angus's mouth fell open in shock.

"What the hell . . . ?" he said, frowning and straightening slightly in his chair. "What's the mat—"

"I won't hear you demean Jewel Lockridge!" Skye snapped back. "I'm not proud of what happened yesterday afternoon. I didn't intend it. You should be ashamed of me, not proud."

Angus squinted up at his son as if trying to decipher a new language.

"She's a Lockridge," Angus said in a fierce low growl. "Whatever you did to—"

"You wouldn't have anyone speak of my mother, your wife, that way and I won't have you speak that way of Jewel."

Angus stared at his son for a long moment and then let out a long sigh.

"Ahh . . ." he said. "So that be the way of it."

Skye felt his anger beginning to ebb and paced away from his father back to the railing to stare out across the lawns to the distant river.

"Ye . . . ye be truly . . . smitten?" he heard Angus ask harshly from behind him.

Skye hesitated a moment but his heart made the answer too clear to ignore.

"Aye," he said in a low voice. "I love her."

"And . . . would ye want to take her as your wife?" Angus asked next with quiet seriousness.

After another pause Skye turned to face his father and silently nodded.

Angus swirled the last of his ale in his tankard and peered down into it.

"Well then, the Lockridges aren't bankrupt yet if they got a line around you," he said, musing. He looked up suddenly. "But Peter says the girl was angry. Said you went chasin' after her, but that she marched on home with her nose in the air."

"That's right," Skye barked back. "Because of this damnable feud she doesn't trust me and doesn't want me."

"Doesn't want you?" Angus said, sitting up straight and banging his empty tankard against the arm of his chair. "You're the best man within a hundred miles—

and rich—and the McAllisters go back as far as the Lockridges. She should crawl on her hands and knees and beg for your favor."

"She wouldn't crawl anyplace for anyone," Skye corrected, a bitter smile creasing his face. "And I like her for it. But if you buy Riverwatch on Wednesday I fear she will never trust me."

"Well, I'll not back down," Angus replied, his face darkening. "That ye may count on."

"I'm asking you again. Don't!" Skye countered, coming closer to Angus. "Let Edmund Lockridge fall of his own weight. Don't push his face in the mud."

Angus raised his head slowly to meet Skye's gaze, and Skye saw the etched furroughs on his brow and the ice-cold eyes and knew his appeal had fallen on deaf ears.

"We ate mud for fifteen years," Angus answered stonily. "Let Edmund chew on it a while."

"We don't need Riverwatch," Skye pleaded. "I've got my hands full already with this estate. Let the Livingstons buy it. We—"

"No!" Angus threw himself forward and came to his feet, his rocking chair almost toppling over backward. "It wasn't your sister that was disgraced and died, nor your brother maimed and father hanged. It was mine! And that fop of an Edmund Lockridge still thinks his family pure as lilies. Well, I know! My brother, your uncle," he emphasized, "begged me to avenge our father on his deathbed, and I gave him my oath!" Angus was trembling, and his eyes were sharp and angry. He expelled a breath and continued with less stridency. "You were five and still hangin' on your mother's skirts, but he thought the world of you. Gave you your first knife. He was never strong after we left Scotland. There were nights when we went to bed wrapped in skins in our lean-to without a morsel, the wolves howling, an' the black Canadian night so cold trees snapped like twigs, an' I was prepared to die, didn't see any other way out. But he didn't give up, kept me goin' so I could recoup for us all. An' you, my boy, are what's left of us McAllisters. You're the last of the line." He paused, his eyes lost in a distant line of hills. "I gave him my promise an' I'm keeping it."

"The women don't deserve to suffer with him," Skye said wearily, after a long silence in which they both were lost in their own memories. "They're innocent of the evil you want to avenge."

"They're Lockridges," Angus shot back. "If they stick with that old man then they fall with him."

"Jewel *has* to stick with him," Skye persisted. "He's her family."

"Aye, she'll stick and fall just as I had to fall with my family when the Lockridges pushed us down." Angus shook his head and came forward and put his hand on his son's shoulder. "No, Skye, you'll not dissuade me. In three days I'll buy Riverwatch. If you haven't got the stomach for it, ye'd best not be here then. Better make that trip to Albany to see Worthington."

As Skye looked into his father's eyes, he could feel a rising sense of hopelessness. He couldn't fight his father any further on this no matter how strongly he felt about Jewel. Edmund Lockridge probably deserved no sympathy and it was Jewel's fate, as Angus had pointed out, to have to fall with him. Skye knew that he himself would continue to fight for Jewel but nothing could now stop Angus's revenge.

"Aye," he said, nodding. "I'll go to Albany while you play your hand."

"To the last card!"

"But when I return I plan to win Jewel Lockridge."

"What for? You're asking for trouble! There's nothing left to win."

Skye brushed aside his father's hand and strode away.

"For me there's everything left to win," he said and disappeared into the house.

The change in Jewel after the day of the race was as great as the change in their home. She kept to her room as much as possible, shunning the auditors, lawyers and auctioneers. She was unable to smile at the sympathetic townspeople, even those she knew well, especially not while they were looking over the Lockridge furnishings in order to bid for them at the auction.

The day of the auction was even worse—all their beloved furniture, sold and gone, and the house, her home for all her life, sold, sold to the highest bidder. Sold to Angus McAllister.

She let her mother and Sarah think her silence the result of their losses, unable to tell them that the loss of all of Riverwatch couldn't match the pain she felt from her conflicting feelings about Skye. How could she tell them she was utterly unable to resist their worst enemy and had just given him what she had expected to bring to her husband? They would have been shocked, their worries tripled. That they would feel pity and shame for her, her pride could not bear. No, better they were left in ignorance. All this would pass like a terrible storm, whatever the wreckage to her. But there were moments when she remembered those ecstatic moments in Skye's arms, and then the humiliation of having been used by him would wash over her, and she would be sure that her body could not bear another ragged sob, that her breath would not catch again and that her heart would not go on beating. She hated him and loved him, and from one moment to the next didn't know which she feared more, succumbing again to his evil seduction or that she had lost him forever.

Her mother was patient, but had too many other things to worry about to spend time consoling her daughter. Abigail decided she would take in sewing and the girls would become tutors or lady's maids, though it was barely possible for her to reconcile herself to these things in her own mind.

Jewel's grandfather seemed to bear it all with fierce dignity, summoning all his strength to wrest the best possible deals, accepting with bitter forbearance his losses and winning the respect of his neighbors and old friends. He seemed determined that the Lockridges should leave the valley with grace and good wishes, perhaps to show one last time their superiority to the McAllisters.

Jewel was proud of him and kept her secret shame and longing to herself, seeking solace in the overgrown garden when she couldn't bear to be in the house, and always feeling unutterably alone. Sarah had Ashbury, who took time from his farm—time which he could ill afford in this season—to bring vegetables from his family's garden and cheerfully help Sarah with the heavier tasks. After he had bustled loudly and helpfully around the usually gloomy Lockridge home, he would leave Sarah bright with hope and energy. His constancy only pointed out to Jewel the tragedy in her own choice of lovers. The one, Aaron, was so intent on his ambitions to become a wealthy leading citizen and so concerned with what others thought of the Lockridge downfall, that he kept himself apart from the auction and Jewel as if he himself might become tainted with their misfortune.

And then there was Skye, outrageous in his flaunting of everything she had been taught was proper, dastardly in his use of her, ready to see her family ruined, and aiding his father's revenge at every turn. He hadn't even sent a message to her, either to apologize or to gloat, or put in an appearance to witness the results of his father's cruelties. And from his memory she ran and hid, whether in her room, the garden or the woods above their home.

She also lived daily with the dread of gossip reaching her mother or grandfather. She knew that while the McAllister servants didn't know the whole truth of her fall, they had seen her retreat from Skye in a state not fit to be seen by anyone, and they would draw their own conclusions—and not in her favor, she was sure.

Deep in her heart, she wanted to believe Skye

would want to protect her reputation, but would he? Or did he care whether she could hold her head high in public again? Was her shame simply part of the planned McAllister revenge?

Her nights were a tumbled journey into a world where she waited for dawn, dark circles under her eyes attesting to her maddening inability to forget Skye's touch, his words, her own response to him. In her dreams she would sometimes relive those moments in his arms, almost feel him between her thighs, awakening her desire, the ecstasy returning, and then his warm image would turn into a pair of cold, mocking green eyes and his arms would swoop down to gather her fiercely, sweep her through the air like a giant hawk carrying its helpless prey and then, the fearful joy of sailing through the sky in his arms turned to pure terror—he released her and she fell . . . fell . . . fell helplessly down. The dream would vanish and she would awaken, startled, frightened, half fearing, half hoping he was outside her bedroom window calling to her, waiting to sweep her away. Tossing restlessly, she would fight to regain her lost tranquility, wondering how that one day could change her whole future, and one man could so devastate her life.

Jewel would lie on her bed, clutching her pillow as if it too would disappear into the holds of the wagons that had taken their most prized possessions away, her face swollen from a fresh bout of tears. She heard a wagon depart and felt the silence in the house as a threat. She had survived another day with no word from Skye, or even from Aaron, whom she now suspected had heard some unsavory gossip. And she felt that if he had heard she had been alone at the manse with Skye and been seen leaving in such a state of undress that he would consider her unworthy to be his wife.

Jewel heard a light tapping at her door and dabbed frantically at her face, hoping to erase the evidence of her tears. Her mother opened the door and came in.

"Jewel," Abigail began, twisting her hands worriedly as she approached her daughter. "Dear heart, please come downstairs. I've tea waiting."

"No thank you, Mama," Jewel said, not looking at her mother, who sat on the bed and gently stroked her silken dark tresses.

"Shall I bring it up to you?" Abigail asked gently. "It's your favorite—peppermint."

Jewel lay still, feeling too wretched to reply.

"I can't bear to see you waste away like this," her mother begged sweetly. "You've always been my oak in troubled times. Your grandfather and Sarah need your strength."

Jewel slanted her mother a look. "Oh, Mama," she said, "why did this have to happen to you—you who are so good and kind to everyone!"

"Shh, dear! We'll manage. Haven't we always?" Abigail gave her a wan smile, her blue eyes tender, her pale hand resting on her daughter's shoulder.

Jewel sat up and put her arms around her mother. She swallowed hard. "Has . . . have you heard when he . . . they're coming?" she asked, not able to say the name Skye or Angus.

"You mean Angus McAllister?" her mother said.

"No, dear, not yet. His lawyer said he would be here some time soon." She sighed. "It's nearly over. The papers signed by both lawyers. There's little left to do but pack our personal belongings and leave. When Angus McAllister—" She broke off, unable to continue. She hadn't yet told her daughters that she had received a letter from her sister telling her they could not come to stay. Where they would go, Abigail simply didn't know.

"And . . . his son?" Jewel barely whispered, sitting back, her head resting on the headboard. Her eyes were like large pools of deep blue sea.

"I was told he's in Albany, gone on business to the Worthington's. You won't have him to contend with either."

Jewel felt a cold hand on her heart. Skye had gone to seek his pleasures elsewhere, with Melissa Worthington. A terrible darkness invaded the room as she realized he had achieved his purpose with her and now she was superfluous. What she had feared was now confirmed.

"Why didn't you tell me about—what men can do?" she suddenly cried out to her mother, her voice strained. "I wasn't warned!" She slumped backward, her eyes brimming with tears. "I didn't know!"

Abigail was unable to follow her daughter's distraught questioning.

"You mean Aaron?" she asked. "You must realize he's doing his best for us. If he hasn't come to call, why, he lost the race and men are . . . vain when it comes to losing. I'm sure he'll come, give him time. I've no doubt he loves you."

"Love!" Jewel nearly laughed hysterically. "'Tis a dirty word . . . bandied about like leaves in fall, and just as dead! Men do not love. They use us like they would rum. We're a sop to their appetites!"

Abigail sucked in her breath. "Jewel! How crude! You know all men are not that way. Why your fa—"

"They are! Skye McAllister is a deceiver!"

"Mr. McAllister?" Abigail said, standing in shock and now looking at Jewel in bewilderment. "What has he—"

"And Aaron Flemming," Jewel continued, unaware of how unexpected her mother found her words. "All men treat us no better than brood mares."

"Jewel!" her mother shouted. "Enough! I will not listen to these thoughtless remarks. This petulance must end. Come now, dry your tears and let your grandfather see the old Jewel. He has enough to contend with without our falling apart now when he needs us most." Abigail put out her hand to her daughter and Jewel clasped it, at last sitting up.

"I'm sorry, Mama," she said, suddenly realizing how close she had come to betraying her real problem. "Whatever happens, Mama, you can depend on me." Jewel straightened and swung her feet down from the bed, her beautiful features working as she tried to summon her courage and control the desire to cry.

Abigail smiled, relief flooding through her. "We do, dearest, more than you know."

"Let me just freshen up," Jewel said haltingly, "and then I'll come down for tea."

When her mother left, Jewel washed her face and applied powder to hide the blotchy patches on her face. Had she been another, she might have known her tears made her look appealingly vulnerable and she might have used them as a weapon. But she regarded tears as a weakness and wanted no one to see them.

She heard voices below and knew someone had arrived and hoped it wasn't another townsman come to collect his purchase. The voices were loud and she felt her heart hammer with anxiety. She rushed to finish her toilet and made for the stairs, straightening her simple blue frock as she went. She could hear her grandfather's voice filled with anger.

"You dare come here?" she heard him say. She rushed into the hallway and saw her family assembled and her grandfather, red-faced and trembling, facing the tall, darkly clad figure of Angus McAllister. He seemed to be hovering on the porch, one arm leaning on a supporting post.

"I dare, Edmund Lockridge," Angus replied in a low voice, his face set with hard determination, "because I now own Riverwatch and you can't deny me entry."

"Aye, you own it," Edmund said with a grimace of bitterness. "But is there no Christian charity left in you? Would you see three women cowed by your hatred?" her grandfather's voice intoned righteously.

"Christian, say you?" Angus said, his eyes narrowing, his stance now erect and unbending. "I remember the Lockridge charity well enough—me father hung by a Lockridge judge, me brother maimed by the cold iron of the Lockridge sword, me sister, no more than a child, bleedin' to death with the breeched Lockridge bastard in her belly. Nay, don't preach to me from your pulpit," he raged on, pointing a finger at Edmund, his eyes glinting fiercely, "until you confess the black doin's of your own family. Charity?" he scoffed. "Mine is the charity of the hunter—a swift death."

Edmund paled, shaken. Finally he expelled a held breath and gathered his forces to speak.

"Then say what you have to say and be gone, for I'll not forgive your persecution of my family. My Maker will hear any confession I have to make and not the devil's own son!"

"So be it!" Angus uttered, his wrath now cold and forbidding. He moved closer to the open door, then suddenly stopped as he became aware of the three women standing mutely in the hall behind Edmund. He stared at Abigail's white face, Sarah's large and frightened eyes and then saw Jewel's sorrowing face, translucent with a cool beauty. He stood mesmerized a moment, and a transformation took hold of his angry face, one he hadn't been prepared to let them see. A nerve jumped near his jaw as he tried to reconcile his warring impulses.

"Ladies," he growled from deep in his throat, giving them a curt nod. "I mayn't appear just to you, but you've been told a pack of lies. I know ye be innocent of this man's crimes, but justice must be done, and this crusty old fool and I will bear our grudges to our grave like the mean buzzards we are.

I'm askin' you to understand. Evil was done to me and my family years ago that now must be repaid. I'm sorry. By the look of ye, you've never known what suffering is like."

"You're wrong, Mr. McAllister." Jewel's soft voice floated to him, calm in the face of his obstreperousness, and she came forward to stand in front of him. "We've known sorrow and loss, but it has not left us bitter. And I know of no evil my grandfather has done that he should suffer for an ancient wrong. Generosity is born in a loving heart and I'm sorry you have so little of it in yours."

Angus blinked, dumbfounded.

"Pretty words, those," he said, rubbing his chin thoughtfully a moment. Then he stepped back a pace. "I see what my son—never mind," he corrected, recalling himself and wrenching back to his purpose. "You can stay for now," he went on at length, getting the words past his clenched teeth. "I'll give you two weeks to clear out. Until then you can earn your keep and work this place." He waved his hand to the overgrown grounds behind him. "Ye've let it go to seed. It needs attending to."

"I'd sooner sleep in the fields than lift a finger in toil for you," Edmund retorted, his face still distorted with his suppressed fury.

"That's my charity to you, Edmund Lockridge, or you can lie abed and let the women do it for you. Aye, that's your style right enough. If ye don't want to lift a finger here, let the lasses come over and clean our stables." Angus released a cruel laugh.

"Get your carcass out of my sight, you bellicose buffoon!" Edmund roared, striding forward, his face red.

Angus sniggered, amused to have enraged Edmund. He touched a finger to his wide-brimmed hat to the ladies.

"Two weeks," he repeated, then turned on his heel, mounted his horse, and abruptly left.

Turning from the door, Edmund Lockridge walked in a peculiar lurching gait to his worn chair in the almost-bare sitting room and sank into it. Abigail followed, hovering near him, offering tea.

"Brandy," he gasped.

Jewel and Sarah stared at their grandfather's ashen face, while Abigail fluttered uncertainly. Then Jewel rushed to the wall cabinet and poured him a drop from the almost-empty bottle.

Edmund reached for it, grasping the glass shakily, then slumped forward and fell to the floor, the glass shattering near him. As Abigail let out a scream, Jewel reached out to her grandfather.

"Grandpapa," she whispered. "Please speak to me."

Edmund blinked, but couldn't utter a word, his face grey with agony.

"Sarah!" Jewel turned to her sister, who was holding Abigail, desperation on her face. "Fetch someone, anyone, to help us. Hurry!"

It was another hour before Edmund was finally put to bed and Jewel and her mother had made him comfortable. Jewel thanked the two McAllister employees that Sarah had fetched, but it wasn't until late in the afternoon that Doctor Norton arrived and announced gravely that Edmund was suffering from a mild stroke. He added that given time and good care he would undoubtedly recover since he could now speak, though haltingly, and seemed to have the use of his limbs.

As the doctor rode off, Jewel was surprised to see Aaron come riding up on Thunder. She felt a surge of hope at realizing that he had cared enough to come.

As he tied his horse to the porch railing and turned to her, she thought she saw a fleeting expression of anger and suspicion in his normally bland brown eyes, but the moment passed. She greeted him with a restraint to match his own, feeling again a hurt that he hadn't seen fit to call before this. Their years of friendship should certainly have yielded that much concern, she thought.

He took off his black tricorn as he followed her into the house, but once inside he froze. The customary oak coatstand was missing and only a simple old wooden chair remained on which to place his hat. The mirror, the claw-footed long table, the elegant side chairs and the rugs were all gone.

He looked at Jewel, and all anger vanished, his eyes spoke silently of understanding.

"You knew about the auction," Jewel said airily, not wanting to dwell on it.

"Of course," he answered crisply. "I simply didn't grasp its extent." He waited a moment before going on. "I came to inquire after your grandfather's health. Doctor Norton told me of his illness." He stood stiffly as he waited for Jewel's response.

"We all thank you," Jewel said coolly. "He's improved, though weak. I regret it wouldn't be a good idea to visit with him just yet. It's too tiring." Jewel moved slowly into the sitting room and motioned with a hand to a straight-backed chair, one of several old chairs remaining, the blue satin settee and side chairs having been sold. Aaron chose to remain standing, his hands behind his back.

Jewel felt awkward, wanting to say something that would dispel Aaron's stiff-backed discomfort, but also wanting to forestall any pitying words for their plight.

"Poverty is no disgrace," she said testily, in the brief silence, wanting to bite her tongue the instant the words were out. She did not want to discuss it.

"No," Aaron agreed quietly, turning his brown eyes on her, his face tense. "There are worse disgraces."

"I beg your pardon," Jewel said, disconcerted both by his words and the return of anger to his face.

Aaron turned away and walked to the window, looking out toward the river, his hands clasped tightly behind his elegantly clad back. He cleared his throat.

"I know you're not to blame," he said, pausing, his voice gravelly. "Angus McAllister was in town yesterday, drinking, heavily, I might add, at the White Horse Tavern, and bragging about his purchase of your estate and of his son's . . . capture of Dan

Buckthorne." He stopped again, still keeping his back to her and Jewel could feel the tension in him rising.

"I wouldn't expect any less of him," Jewel said passionately. "The man is rabid. His visit here caused my grandfather's collapse."

"It's all hearsay, of course," Aaron went on in a low voice, not responding to her words. "He also claimed that you were . . . at the McAllister's after the race—with his son—alone."

Jewel sucked in her breath, her cheeks flaming, and indignation rising in her breast.

"So I am damned as well," she said, her voice low, her body still.

Aaron turned to look at her, his eyes beseeching. "Just tell me you weren't with him and I will believe you. His father was drunk, raving, and my servant only repeated what he heard."

"What did he say?" Jewel persisted, cold creeping through her veins.

"That you had lain with his son!" Aaron's anguished voice said as he stared at her.

Jewel paled and whirled away from him, pacing the room in agitation.

"Just tell me it was a lie!" Aaron implored again.

"I was there," Jewel returned, not able to deny or agree. "Mr. McAllister was wounded by Dan and it was my fault!"

"The man has taken everything you own! His father has done everything possible to break your grandfather's will, he's ruined your reputation, and you make excuses for him?"

Aaron strode with rapid steps to take her by the shoulders and force her to look at him, his fingers biting into her arms.

"I make no excuses for . . . Skye," Jewel said, her heart fluttering unreasonably when she spoke his name. "And . . . I can't undo what is done!" She could no longer meet Aaron's gaze.

Aaron's grip slackened. "Then you don't deny it," he said, his voice forced.

"Does it make a difference to you?" Jewel asked, her eyes darkening, knowing it would.

Aaron's face registered shock and he dropped his arms.

"I don't know you," he said, staring at her.

"You do! But I'm not the angel you thought me, I never was. The pedestal is toppled, but I'm still a living, breathing woman and, I care for your good opinion of me. I need your friendship, now more than ever."

Aaron stood rigidly for a moment, his nostrils flaring with anger.

"You're no better than a whore!"

Jewel gasped and let her hand fly to his face, stinging his cheek and her own hand as well.

Sarah chose that moment to enter the room, hearing their voices from the kitchen and feeling she had given them enough time alone.

"Aaron!" she said cheerfully, unaware of the tense atmosphere, and coming forward to greet him. "It's so good to see you," and then she seemed to understand that all was not well. "I, ah . . ." She stopped and looked from one to the other and then started to retreat. "Shall I tell Mother you're here?" she asked tentatively.

"No," Jewel said, recovering her poise. "Aaron is not staying long. He merely wanted to see how Grandpapa was doing." She ushered her sister to the door, and said, "I'll be in to help with the soup soon." Then she closed the sitting room door and retraced her steps to Aaron who had walked once more to the window. This time his hands were nervously twitching behind his back.

As she looked at him Jewel felt a brief sad throbbing of her heart and then a numbness.

He turned and the coldness in his eyes was unmistakable.

"I'm sorry, Jewel," he apologized in a clipped tone. "For the sake of our old friendship, I . . . just please accept my apologies. I can only assume you went with him willingly. But," he hesitated, "you must realize that our betrothal must be rescinded."

Jewel would have laughed at his choice of words had she been herself.

"The barrister wins his case," she said, making light of it, though that was not what she was feeling. "And his tainted lady is banished forever."

"You've changed," he said. "You've grown bitter."

"Aaron—" her shoulders slumped with fatigue—"I've been under terrific strain. I . . . my whole world has turned upside down and I beg you to understand. I release you. You're under no obligation to me. I only ask you not to tell my family what you've heard. I fear my grandfather cannot handle more."

"Of course, that's understood," Aaron said, a relief in his voice that would have given Jewel pain had she been less stunned by everything that had happened in the last few days.

They stood solemnly for a moment.

"I must be going," Aaron said finally. "Please extend my wishes to your grandfather for a speedy recovery and my sympathy to your mother for her losses," he finished formally.

Jewel gave him a sidelong look. Was this the man she would have spent her life with? This cool, contained man? But could she truly blame him for his coldness? Hadn't she betrayed her chances with him in Skye's arms? She shivered involuntarily and made for the door. Aaron followed her, lost in thought, his face grave.

He put on his tricorn and faced her at the entryway, the door open, a light drizzling rain beginning outdoors.

"Thank you for coming," Jewel said softly, "and for all you've done for us."

Aaron compressed his lips tightly.

"I did mean to marry you," he said levelly.

"I know," Jewel said.

"I'll be in town if you . . . if I can be of any further assistance."

Jewel nodded, a smile forming on her lips that had no reason to be there.

Aaron looked perplexed.

"Is there a joke on me?" he asked.

Jewel finally let her lips smile, a tiny tinkling laugh escaping.

"Not on you. On me! I've lost so much, Aaron, that it's like the final curtain on a drama, a purge and, well, a freedom, too."

Aaron looked at her strangely.

"I'd see Doctor Norton, if I were you. You could be suffering from melancholia."

"Now that would be the *coup de grace,* wouldn't it?" Her eyes snapped with energy.

"Jewel, stop it. I'm serious."

"Aaron," she said sincerely, suppressing her ill-timed gaiety. "Don't be concerned. I'll be too busy to waste my efforts on staging an Ophelia, and I'm not so fragile. I'm a Lockridge. Something my grandfather taught me well. We survive!"

Aaron was stopped by that thought, a surprised look on his face and an admiration for her pluck.

"You always did the unexpected. I wonder that I never saw it rightly before."

He turned and stepped off the porch and touched his tricorn in salute, an odd look of regret on his face. He mounted his horse, Jewel watching him from the porch. He was struck as never before by her uncommon beauty.

"Jewel, I . . ." He seemed at a loss for words, yet clearly wanted to retrieve something from their estrangement.

"Don't say anything, Aaron. Truly—not now," Jewel said firmly.

He looked at her for one long minute and then kicked Thunder into motion.

Jewel went back into the house, lighter in step and she couldn't understand why. But something inside her had been set free. Perhaps it was the last thread with the past breaking, she thought. Sarah thought her as mad as a hatter when she joined her in the kitchen.

Chapter Thirteen

JEWEL'S EMOTIONS SEESAWED OVER THE NEXT SEVERAL days between her terrifying sense of loss and her peculiar nothing-more-to-lose gaiety. She knew she had to tell her family about her broken engagement to Aaron, but hesitated, not wanting to hurt them with the knowledge of the rumors about herself and Skye. The opportunity came when all three women were in the kitchen. After Sarah made mention of Ashbury, Jewel announced that she and Aaron had decided not to marry, adding that it was fair of Aaron to release her since so much had changed in their lives.

"I thought better of Aaron than that," Abigail said disappointedly.

"Mama, please don't blame him. There are other reasons, too." Jewel took a deep breath and decided it was time to say something of her involvement with Skye, though loath to do it.

"He also heard some evil gossip in town," Jewel began, her voice tremulous. She went on in a rush to describe her confrontation with Buckthorne, the fight,

Dan's capture and Skye's wound. She omitted the detail of her losing her dress. Finally she concluded: "I dressed Mr. McAllister's wound at the manse and was seen there by his servants. The end result was some unsavory gossip. . . . Aaron heard all this and you know how concerned he is that his and my own reputation should be spotless." Jewel let out a long sigh, silently praying the worst of the gossip would not reach her mother's ears.

"My word!" Abigail said, sinking down on a kitchen chair. "Will you never give me peace of mind, Daughter? How you managed to keep all this to yourself is beyond me."

"Mama, please don't fret. It's over, and the decent thing has been done. Aaron is released and I, well, what matter now, as we'll be leaving."

Abigail was silent a moment.

"I'm afraid," she said at length, "that I have more bad news. My sister Polly can't have us. There. It's out." She sighed resignedly. "She's a dear, but times have been hard for her own family in New York, and Alfred, your uncle, can't see his way clear to have us there." She fluttered her hands helplessly. "So you see, we've no place to go."

Jewel felt her mother's distress painfully.

"We'll be better off on our own," she finally said, as cheerfully as she could manage. "I never did care for being a charity case."

"Well, I don't want to leave Hudson anyway," Sarah suddenly said from her perch where she was peeling potatoes and listening silently. "And Ashbury doesn't want me to leave."

"Of course he doesn't, dear," Abigail said. "He's been a brick."

"And I plan to marry him," Sarah said firmly, her young face held high.

"Has he asked you?" Abigail asked, turning to her with a hopeful look.

"We've made plans," Sarah said quietly.

Abigail was silent a moment, frowning. "I do hope they include marriage."

Sarah wiggled on her perch and said, "They do."

"And when, may I ask?"

"Soon, Mama, you're not to worry."

"My, but you're full of secrets, too. I fear my daughters have grown up when I wasn't looking."

Jewel gave her mother a quick kiss on the forehead. "There, our paths are not so full of rocks after all," she said with a confidence she was far from feeling and walked to the window to look out.

"Angus McAllister said two weeks," Abigail reminded them.

Out in their pasture, Jewel was stunned to see a flock of McAllister sheep grazing and felt a rush of anger. Angus McAllister couldn't even wait until they'd left. And there were men working around the barns! She hoped her grandfather didn't see what was going on from his bedroom window.

She excused herself and strode angrily out of the house to speak to the men. As the door banged behind her she saw Skye on his great white stallion, Jupiter. He was hatless, his honey-blond hair ruffled in the wind, his white shirt-sleeves rolled up exposing his tanned forearms and his tan breeches stretched over his powerful legs. Seeing him for the first time since—that day—Jewel's cheeks flushed and her heart raced. Then she was annoyed by her response. This was the man that had ruined her and her family! As he rode up to her and dismounted, she tilted her chin defiantly and her eyes sparkled with unsuppressed ire. So the black prince was back!

"Beautiful," he said, his low baritone caressing her, "aren't they?" he finished, his hand gesturing toward the sheep with a teasing smile.

"Yours, I presume," she answered coldly, resisting his lightness.

"Aye," he said.

"And the men?" she asked, keeping her voice steady.

"Mine." He paused, turning to face her. "I thought you'd like to see the land being used."

"My grandfather lies ill and knows nothing of this, nor was he asked, not so much as a 'by your leave,'" she responded, relieved that he'd touched a topic that helped her recall her anger with him.

Skye rested his arm on the fence.

"Haven't lost your spit and fire, have you?" he said, a smile creasing the corners of his mouth. "But I'm sorry about your grandfather. I didn't want to disturb him. At the same time, a shipment of ewes arrived and I thought the pasture a good place for them. I mean you to share our good fortune, Jewel," he finished meaningfully.

"By eating our grass before we've even left? That takes incredible gall, Sir Scot!" Jewel tossed her gleaming dark hair and stubbornly refused to look at the disturbing man beside her—afraid of the quivering muscles in her middle, afraid she would reveal how much his closeness unnerved her.

"Aye, I have gall, Jewel, and patience, otherwise I couldn't take your constant insults without upending your sweet backside and paddling it soundly."

Jewel took in a breath. "I'd bite and kick," she said.

"The thought almost makes my palm itch," Skye said, amused.

Jewel raised her stormy eyes to his, ready with a stinging retort, but the sharp stabbing desire in his gaze made her avert her face. A sudden intimacy wrapped itself around them and she lost the thread of her thoughts. Strongly aware of his magnetism she stepped away, turning irresolutely toward her house.

"I must care for my grandfather," she said.

"Of course," he replied easily, taking hold of Jupiter's reins and walking beside Jewel. "And I'd like to offer my services to him and your mother. We know some Indian remedies which may help."

Jewel could feel his eyes on her, a prickly feeling like gooseflesh running over her.

"That's not necessary," Jewel said, her anger melted by his concern. "Please leave."

"I'll follow your lead, Jewel," he said, making one of those statements of his that seemed to be saying more. "But I warn you now, if I ever see a crack in that armor of yours, I'll leap to fill it."

Jewel's eyes flew to his face, and she was nonplussed by the watchful openness of his gaze on her.

"What are you talking about?" she asked, dreading the answer, even while her heart drew her to know everything he meant.

"I'm talking about you and me," he said stirringly. "About us. But don't worry your lovely head about it now."

"We," Jewel said unsteadily, "don't exist. *We,*" she emphasized the word, "have only to work out the problem of when you will force my family to leave."

"I have no desire to force either you or your family to leave," Skye responded, "although I confess my father still insists that you vacate . . . his premises in two weeks."

"Oh!" said Jewel.

"But sooner or later you'll admit that we have much more to talk about than that."

Skye hitched Jupiter to the iron post outside their house and followed Jewel, who ignored his final thrust, inside, his sharp eyes taking in the alterations without comment.

Jewel led him into the dining room, where Skye took a chair without waiting to be asked, his eyes following her. Jewel walked restlessly to the window.

"We can't possibly be ready to leave here in ten days' time. My grandfather needs time to recover. He's very ill." She stopped at the window, the sun's rays playing over her like a rainbow.

Skye put his arm on the table, his large tanned hand relaxed.

"I'll try to get my father to give you as long as you need," Skye said quietly.

"I can only assume that he handled the auction and

eviction notice to your satisfaction," Jewel said heatedly, not trusting his acquiescence.

"As I wasn't here, he handled it his own way and without approval or consultation with me," Skye said with tight control.

"Oh, yes, I remember now, you couldn't bother with such mundane business. You were courting Miss Worthington!"

"Ahh . . . Miss Worthington," Skye said, smiling maddeningly. "So you thought that I rushed off to be in her arms? Doing some kind of penance for having made love to you? Your admiration of my prowess does me credit, but I don't think I like the character sketch." He was more relaxed, a faint ironic smile playing over his sensuous mouth, but there was still palpable tension in the room.

"Does she know you dally with other women when the opportunity arises?" Jewel asked scathingly, her cheeks flushed.

Skye's eyes leapt to hers, but she pulled hers free. Her stubborn refusal of him was fraying his control. "You're like a cornered little fox, yipping and snapping at me," he said angrily. "But maybe a little jealousy won't hurt," he said, half to himself. "Yes, I told her about you, and she was disappointed, but what could the poor girl do? She had to accept my capitulation to the valley's most beautiful woman."

Jewel looked at him disbelieving, not willing to trust the blatant, cocky flattery, and reminded again of being the victim of the McAllister revenge.

"You disgust me!" Jewel said, rushing to the window with her back to him, tears threatening. She was so wrapped up in her fight to prevent them from spilling, she didn't hear Skye approach until he was behind her, his arms suddenly pulling her against his hard chest. Jewel caught her breath, a fierce shock running through her. She pulled herself away as if stung, turning on him.

"Don't touch me!" she whispered desperately.

The look of tender indulgence disappeared and his eyes glinted with temper.

"I seem to recall those words said to me before."

"I mean them," Jewel said. What demon made her deny the feelings that roared through her body? She could barely hold herself from him, hoping the strength of her resistance masked the strength of her desire. Honor, she reminded herself. Family honor and self-respect. If she didn't fight him at every turn, she could become his mistress. Oh, how easily she could slip into that role.

"Then I won't touch you again until you ask. And you will, Jewel," he said fiercely. "You will."

Jewel whirled to the other side of the room away from him, clutching her arms to herself, as if they would betray her, or her wildly beating heart would be exposed for him to see.

"I think we've said all there is to say," she said from her safe distance, knowing her dismissal of him pricked his pride.

"I'd like a word with your mother first," he said.

As if by command, they heard Abigail's step on the stairs.

"Jewel?" Abigail said quietly. "I heard voices and . . ." She stopped in the doorway, almost dropping the tray she was carrying when she saw Skye standing in the room. He stepped forward to take the tray from her, placing it on the table.

"Mrs. Lockridge." Skye inclined his head respectfully. "You'll excuse my intrusion without warning. I came to express my concern for Mr. Lockridge's illness, and to assure you I will do everything in my power to permit you to stay as long as necessary. I've asked the twelve-year-old son of one of my men to help you with the heavier chores. Tommy will be here on the morrow."

"Why, I . . . hardly know what to say," Abigail said, her voice full of surprise.

"Mrs. Lockridge, my father is a bitter man. Maybe now that he feels he's avenged a past injustice he can forgive—even himself for his own helplessness all those years ago. Aye, that's one of the things that's rankled him—he was helpless and powerless."

"Your father helpless?" Jewel said with asperity. "Like a snake!"

"Jewel!" Abigail chastised.

"She's got a point, Ma'am," Skye said, smiling disarmingly. "He's hardly helpless now. But I don't take all her barbs to heart, otherwise I'd have bled to death a month ago."

Abigail noticed both the warm, playful look Skye cast at Jewel and her daughter's proud anger and she felt bewildered.

"Before you make any decisions to leave," Skye went on to Abigail, "I want your promise that you'll come to me with your plans. I may be able to help."

"We will not!" Jewel interjected, listening avidly to

all Skye said. "We're quite capable of helping ourselves."

"Jewel, dear," Abigail said. "I believe that the younger Mr. McAllister is less frightening than his father. It would please me to have you mind your manners."

Skye quirked a smile at Jewel. "Then she is not such an expert on manners after all."

"Good heavens!" Abigail said. "Whatever gave you the idea she was? Jewel is precious to us, but hardly tactful when crossed."

"Mama," Jewel said haughtily, "I'd rather you didn't get into a discussion of me with this . . . rapscallion!"

Skye laughed. "Rapscallion? Now why do I think she means that's a cross between a reptile and a mouth-hot scallion?"

Skye was beginning to charm her mother and this set Jewel's teeth on edge. She made an impatient sound.

"Let's get back to our discussion," she said. "We won't need any further help from you than a little time for my grandfather to recover, and . . . we'll repay you every cent it costs," she added recklessly.

"I mentioned no costs," Skye said, his face losing its pleasant ambience. "However, I confess my father certainly will. And how had you planned to pay this self-imposed debt?" Skye asked, his eyes whipping across hers.

Jewel was momentarily taken aback. "Why . . . I can work." Once the words were out, she regretted them, but her pride wouldn't let her take them back. She lifted her chin in a challenge. Let him be charitable.

Abigail wanted to redress her daughter's rash decision, but Skye held up his hand to forestall her. "She's an over-weaning pride, Ma'am," he said to Abigail, "but I'm curious." He trained his eyes on Jewel. "What had you in mind, Jewel?"

"Your father mentioned cleaning the stables!" Jewel said sarcastically, sure that Skye wouldn't allow her near his precious horses, owing to the fact that she once allowed Dan Buckthorne to give Jupiter green apples.

"Did he now?" Skye said, a smile forming on his lips. He seemed to weigh the matter. "Done," he said, finally, his eyes bright with amusement. "Unless you've decided to accept my *charity,* I accept you on as a groom. But please let me know if you think of something more pleasant, more . . . womanly, I may be open to it." He raised an eyebrow in inquiry.

"How dare you suggest . . ." Jewel stopped, blushing furiously.

"Did I suggest anything?" Skye said, his eyes dancing with pleasure.

"What on earth are you two talking about?" Abigail said, deciding to step between them. "Skye, my daughter has been hasty. I'm sure you realize that." She turned to Jewel. "A lady doesn't groom horses, Jewel."

"Mama, this man wouldn't know what a lady does. He has only one use for them, and it's unmentionable!"

"Jewel!" Abigail said, her cheeks pinked with color at her daughter's audacity.

Jewel thrust her chin forward mutinously. "It clearly pleases the black-hearted rogue to let me soil my hands. Let him worry whether his costly horses will fare safely in my care."

Abigail sighed with exasperation and turned appealing eyes on Skye.

"Ma'am, I promise you no harm will come to your daughter at my stables, but as she's determined, I think we should let her try. She'll soon tire of being mulish."

"You don't know my daughter well," Abigail said, and gave him a kind smile.

Jewel saw her mother's smile and felt betrayed.

Skye gallantly took one of Abigail's slender hands in his and lightly kissed it. "My pleasure to meet you again, Mrs. Lockridge," he said, and giving a nod to Jewel turned to leave.

"Oh, Jewel," he said, offhandedly, at the doorway, "I'll tell Robbie to expect you tomorrow morning at, ahh, about six." He grinned broadly and left.

Chapter Fourteen

ROBBIE WAS, JEWEL DISCOVERED THE NEXT MORNING, A capable young man her own age who took his new responsibilities very seriously. He made at least that part of her self-imposed duty bearable.

She realized belatedly that Angus McAllister had a great deal to do with the stables. His coldly rigid stance as he eyed her washing down one of the mares told her he found her presence there distasteful, even though the suggestion had originally been his. She eyed him just as coolly but said not one word to him. He didn't seem to expect acknowledgment from her and gave his instructions only to Robbie and Patrick in the harsh, clipped tone she associated with him. Rather than gloating over her menial labor, he seemed to wish she was not there, was safely tucked away on the moon.

Dirtier, hotter work didn't exist, Jewel thought, as she wearily brushed down the magnificent animals. She hadn't thought that working in the stables could be dangerous until a frisky mare accidentally stepped on her toe. She yelped in pain, sure it was broken.

Robbie made her dunk her foot immediately in a pail of cold water, then rubbed it with a liniment until she felt she could hobble back to work. Never was she more grateful to her mother's admonitions to wear proper clothing than she was this morning when she had been scolded into wearing her riding boots.

Skye was away until noontime when he came to the stables carrying a pail of food. She had prepared herself to greet him coolly, but as always his appearance caused her undue excitement and she dropped her brush. Stooping to retrieve it, she cursed. He made a low whistle.

"I think your hands and mouth could both use soap," he said grinning. He held up the pail. "To sweeten your disposition—lunch."

"You needn't have," she said.

"Did you remember to pack something?" he asked, surveying her soiled smock and heated face, surrounded by the tumbled mass of hair.

Jewel shrugged, rather than admit she'd forgotten or that she was hungry.

"I thought not," he answered and directed her to come to the tack room to eat.

"You're staying?" she asked suddenly.

"Do you want me to?" he asked, smiling.

For an answer, Jewel walked off to wash her hands, not wanting to give in to him in the slightest.

His laugh echoed in her ears as she washed her hands, and then she saw him leave the stable, striding back to the manse, and leaving her feeling disappointed. Tomorrow, she vowed, she would remember to bring something to eat.

When she arrived home late in the afternoon, hot and cross, she noted the swept and polished floors with wonder and was informed that Tommy, the twelve-year-old boy Skye had sent, had indeed been an enormous help around the house. Her mother and Sarah were more relaxed than they had been in weeks. Jewel, on the other hand, was so tired from having thrown herself into the grooming tasks, she didn't have the energy to talk about her day. Tommy, she was told, had brought a basket of food for them as well, freshly baked bread and game, all plucked and ready for the pan.

Jewel dragged herself to bed early that evening, barely able to look in on her grandfather and read to him, as she had been doing before she took this cursed job. They had decided not to tell him what she was doing during the day, knowing it would upset him. He was sitting up and it was hoped he would soon feel well enough to go downstairs and perhaps sit in the sun awhile. For the moment, they were content to see him eating well and regaining his strength. His spirits, however, were another matter. He was subdued, pensive, and said nothing about their leaving or the McAllisters. It worried them.

In her room, she suppressed the tears that threatened. Where would it all end? She stared at the white cotton canopy of her four-poster bed and unexpectedly remembered the Gypsy fortune teller's words at the fair: "You will lose all your treasures, but in the end, regain them." There was something more, she reflected, something about a gift being given, a gift of love, but she couldn't recall the exact words. In any event, the Gypsy had been wrong about her intended winning the race. Aaron hadn't won. So much for Gypsy fortune tellers!

Her eyes flew open wide and her heart pounded furiously. The Gypsy couldn't have meant Skye, could she? It was Aaron to whom she had been betrothed. Skye had never mentioned marriage to her. Her racing heart decelerated and she felt an almost crushing defeat. Where would it all end, indeed. She was too tired for coherent thoughts, and images of horses and her recurrent dreams of Skye rushed in until she fell asleep.

The next day followed much the same pattern, with Skye appearing at lunchtime. When she proudly said she had her own lunch, he simply informed her he would eat what he'd brought for her and joined her, sitting on the table in the tack room, eating the fresh bread with thick slices of ham and drinking cold tea. Jewel sat on the long bench and doggedly tried to ignore him, answering his questions about her work and her grandfather's health very briefly.

"I'd like to speak to him on a personal matter when he's able," Skye said.

Jewel looked up sharply. "What personal matter?"

"About a woman and her future," he answered.

"Not mine!"

"Why not yours?" he asked.

"I won't allow it."

Skye laughed, swinging his body off the table and standing up.

"Maybe it has to do with your present occupation. Maybe I have something less strenuous in mind. Is that allowed?" he asked quietly.

"Then speak to me," Jewel commanded. "Any words with a McAllister would anger him. Surely you know that."

Skye paced the room a moment, then leaned one arm on the wall above her head, the effect making her feel surrounded by him. Her eyes ran up his body to his face, where they met his and she blushed.

"Won't you believe that I want to help your family?" he asked impatiently.

"No. You've gotten what you've wanted, and I wish you would just leave us in peace."

Skye's face clouded.

"You can end this war, Jewel. You have the power to do it. Just tell me what you'd have me do. There isn't anything I won't try."

"Oh?" Jewel said sarcastically. "Then why don't you donate our estate back to a poor widow and her two daughters?" She felt her eyes suddenly fill with tears and tried to suppress them. She could feel Skye's body tense, but she went on. "You have everything, and as you're a successful businessman, surely you can be generous." Jewel knew the futility of her request.

"I thought the Lockridges accepted no charity," he answered after a moment's strained silence. "An astute man of business always wants a return, Jewel. Some kind of—exchange."

"What would you have?" she asked, beyond using her common sense.

"You."

Jewel flushed deeply, spilling her tea on her dress. She dabbed at it nervously. "You'd have me become your mistress?" she asked, when she recovered from the shock.

"Aye, why not?" He shrugged, a nerve jumping at the corner of his mouth. "I'll take you on those terms."

The air in the small room was suddenly stifling and Jewel felt a dizziness begin to overtake her.

"I'm sure. An object of your passion!" Jewel made a dismissing gesture with her hand, reddened from contact with the herbal powders used to keep the insects off the horses hides.

"Then why goad me?" Skye said, his eyes trained on her. "As for the charity you had in mind, I don't own your estate. My father does."

"Haven't you anything better to do? You hide behind your father's evil, benefit from it, but never manage to stop it!" she countered, sliding along the bench away from him and getting up slowly.

Skye's face reddened in anger. "And you are blinded by your grandfather's spite, unable to see us!" he returned angrily. "You're spoiled rotten, and your pride rides a mighty high horse."

As the two glared at each other, he suddenly withdrew a white envelope from his breast pocket and let it fall on the table.

"An invitation," he said. "I wouldn't expect you to lower yourself so much as to come."

Then he quickly left, leaving Jewel to stare at the white envelope.

At first she wanted to throw it in the trash bin, but curiosity overcame her and she opened it.

It was an invitation to Skye's birthday celebration, a barn dance on August fourteenth. A bold, black script had penned in her name and his own initials at the end.

She pocketed it. She and Sarah would at least have a laugh at it.

When she arrived home that afternoon, hot and miserable, Sarah informed her that several boxes had been delivered and awaited her in her room.

"Boxes?" Jewel said, not able to focus clearly on the fact.

"Yes!" Sarah returned excitedly. "Let's do open them. They're large and have a gold-embossed label from a dress shop in Albany."

Jewel couldn't take it in. "I need a bath. I'll open them later."

Sarah was disappointed in her lack of enthusiasm and followed her to the tub room off the kitchen. "Do you think Aaron sent them?" she persisted. "The man who delivered them wouldn't say."

Jewel began filling the little copper tub with water, adding rose petals and lavender while she thought about Sarah's suggestion.

"That would be sweet, wouldn't it? Aaron is capable of acts of contrition. But not, I think extravagance." She began to peel off her soiled clothes and then remembered the invitation. She extracted it from her pocket and handed it to Sarah. "Read that. It'll tickle your fancy. Now leave me to soak this grime away."

Jewel lowered herself into the tub of tepid water and let her tension melt away. A gift from Aaron, she mused. Interesting. It would redeem something. Not that she wanted her engagement reinstated, but at least it would show he'd forgiven her. Perhaps it was a hat? She'd lost hers at the fair during her anxious flight. It would certainly signal a change of heart.

She toweled herself dry and smoothed on an oil scented with rose geranium, taking special care with her blistered hands. Then she pulled on a billowy cotton robe and went upstairs.

Sarah was waiting for her on the bed and beside her were the anonymous boxes. She stared at them longingly. Christmas and birthdays had always been great occasions in the past but she couldn't remember when she had last received a costly present. The gold embossing leapt out at her: Madame Archambeau's of Albany. When she touched the largest box, a tantalizing excitement seized her.

"Open it!" Sarah squealed.

Jewel took off the top and slowly folded back the tissue paper and her eyes widened. Nestled in the tissue was an exquisite lace gown of violet-blue. Its bodice was low-cut with off-the-shoulder sleeves, and a narrow blue silk sash that defined the waist. The style was the latest. She held it up and heard Sarah gasp.

She opened the other boxes joyously and lavender silk mules fell from one, a silk chemise of palest blue fell from another. Delicate undergarments and silk stockings followed a white lace fan onto the bed. Finally the smallest box yielded a silk handmade nosegay of forget-me-nots and violets. A white card fell to the floor from this one and she picked it up eagerly. A bold black scrawl proclaimed her benefactor: "A replacement, J.S.M."

Jewel was stunned. She let the card fall back on the floor and sat down on her bed amid the finery. Sarah picked up the card and read it, her blue eyes rushing to Jewel's face.

"Skye," Sarah gasped. For a long moment she was silent and then she began extolling the virtues of the French lace and the choice of colors as if it didn't matter where they came from.

"Sarah!" Jewel stopped her. "They must be returned. It's all part of a devious scheme of his to . . . to lure me into his bed!" Jewel caught her breath. "If I were seen in these, gossip would be rife."

Sarah did see that and then told her she had also received an invitation to the barn dance. Moreover, Skye had invited the entire family and Ashbury as well.

"Even if you don't accept the gifts, we must go," Sarah said. "If you don't go, people will think that you're ashamed of something. Going will put an end to the gossip."

"Attending Skye's birthday party?" Jewel said incredulously. "That would be playing into his hands. I wouldn't trust him an inch with my reputation."

"Then think of mine," Sarah said plaintively. "I plan to live here with Ashbury. The taint is mine, too, and Mama's. Those old biddies at the Church Circle are still snubbing her."

Jewel hadn't thought of that.

"Can we hide our going from Grandpapa?" Jewel asked Sarah, capitulating for the moment.

"We can see to that," Sarah said, helping Jewel to repack the beautiful gifts.

Jewel was doubtful, and tremulous. She had a fear of being in a social situation with Skye where she would be at his mercy. But she noticed that her exhaustion melted as ice in fire at the prospect of going.

The next morning at the stables, Robbie told her she was wanted at the manse.

"What for?" Jewel asked.

"Master Skye said you was to report there before work, that's all," Robbie said. But he knew more, Jewel thought from his refusal to look her in the eye.

Jewel hesitated, but went, deciding it was at least an opportunity to tell Skye to send someone for his gifts.

She went to the front door, noting the skipping beats of her heart, and took a few deep breaths to control her remaining senses. A plump, grey-haired woman answered her knock, looking her over with obvious interest and forming an opinion of her that Jewel decided was not entirely favorable.

"Mr. McAllister sent for me. I'm Jewel Lockridge," she said in her best social voice.

"That'd be James," she said. "I'm Mrs. Harris. He said you were coming." She gestured with a plump hand inward, as if Jewel were a backward child. "He's in his study, but his foreman is there and you'll have to wait your turn."

Jewel followed, knowing the way, but deciding she wouldn't acknowledge that fact to his housekeeper.

"You're the one what spotted the dining room table the day of the fair. I'm telling you now, young woman, fine furniture doesn't take to water spilling on it in puddles and, then for pity's sake to be using the damask for bandaging!"

Jewel thought the woman had cheek, and bristled at the reminder of that infamous day.

"I'm well acquainted with the running of a proper home," Jewel said, irritated, "and I needed bandages!"

Mrs. Harris looked her in the eyes a moment. "What you need is a strong hand taken to you and a whopping good talking to, in me own opinion. Wildness in a lass, no matter how pretty, is for beer halls and bawdy houses."

"You've a bold tongue, Mrs. Harris. I'd discharge you if this were my house."

"Well, that's not likely, is it?" Mrs. Harris sniffed indignantly.

Jewel was on the point of storming out of the house when Skye's study door opened and his foreman left, giving her a nod of greeting.

"Miss Lockridge," Skye said formally, "please come in."

Jewel marched in, her eyes bright with frustrated rage.

"Your fur is nearly crackling," Skye said, his lips not smiling, but his eyes full of amusement. "Mrs. Harris scratched you the wrong way, I take it."

"She's rude!"

"Aye, she can be," he agreed. "And kind-hearted, a great cook and loyal to the core." Skye grinned, looking down at her.

"Why did you want to see me?" she asked, still bristling.

"You're through as a groom," he answered quickly.

Jewel felt oddly crestfallen for a moment before she recovered.

"Why?" she wanted to know.

Skye picked up her hands, turning them palm up, his touch sending a warmth rushing down to her toes. She jerked her hands free.

"I saw your abused hands yesterday and meant to end it then, but you so riled me, I forgot," he said, hooking a thumb in his wide belt. "I also wanted to be sure you read the invitation. Did you?"

Jewel nodded.

"Will you come?"

"I will attend in order to dispel the nasty gossip about us, for the sake of my family."

"Reason enough," Skye said, his keen eyes watching her.

"You may send someone for your gifts," she added, wanting to shake his ease of manner with her.

Skye was slow to answer, but there was no trace of a smile on his face and his eyes were a cool green.

"Keep them," he said, finally. "Mrs. Harris has a more-ample figure and no daughters."

Jewel headed for the door, dismissing herself.

"Be careful what you throw away, Jewel," Skye

said to her retreating back. "You may wish you had it back—too late."

"I wish all manner of things back and it's all foolishness. I mean never to retrace my steps. And since I do not accept charity, I will continue to work as a groom." Jewel opened the door and left, feeling she had gotten in the last word. But once outside, her face fell and she felt hurt inside. Her ruthless words had given her no comfort.

At home that evening, Jewel piled the boxes in her armoire, throwing an old sheet over them, but late that night, by candlelight, she pulled them out, and opened them. She tried the gown on and discovered it fit perfectly, marveling at the delicate lace and the transformation of herself in the mirror. She had never before had a gown so beautiful. She fingered the nosegay, so real she could almost smell springtime on their petals.

After repacking the gown, she blew out the candle and lay awake for a long while. How was it possible that one man could so dominate her thoughts? If he but knew how close she was to accepting whatever he was willing to give—the power she would place in his hands. His last words came back to her.

"Be careful what you throw away, you may wish you had it back—too late."

"Oh, Skye, there is no place for us, none that I can see, except back doors and barns and the woods."

Chapter Fifteen

THE VERY NEXT DAY, EDMUND LOCKRIDGE CALLED HIS family together in his bedroom directly after his evening meal. Ensconsed in a comfortable chair, he was neatly dressed in his burgundy robe, cleanly shaven and looked more like his old self than he had since his collapse. Once they were all gathered, he launched into his announcement.

"We'll be leaving Riverwatch for New York on Sunday," he said, his hand clutching his walking stick firmly. "Reverend Barrows has an old friend who has found us an inn there that will be adequate for our needs until we sail for home, for Scotland."

Jewel felt shocked to have the decision she'd known was imminent spelled out so concretely.

"For Scotland . . . ?" she repeated in a whisper.

"Yes, for Scotland," Edmund replied sullenly. "In three weeks. There's no home for us here in this country."

Seeing Sarah sitting rigidly, Jewel's eyes fixed on

the floor in front of her, she knew her sister shared some of her own feelings. The wrench from their childhood home, the coming uncertainty and the separation from a loved one, all in one quick sentence, was like a death knell. No sooner had her grandfather made his announcement then Jewel knew with no doubts she didn't want to leave Skye. It was unreasonable madness, but it was also the undeniable truth of her heart.

"Are you well enough to travel?" Jewel asked, grasping at anything that might delay their leaving.

"I will not spend more than one day here beyond my ability to leave," Edmund replied, jutting his chin out belligerently. "The air is fouled, as are my lands, by yon cutthroat and his son." He paused for emphasis, then went on. "You will all consequently prepare yourselves. Bid your adieus, pack your trunks and be in readiness. The good Reverend is making our arrangements. We'll travel by boat to New York, it's two days' journey, no more. A carriage will meet us at dockside." He stopped and looked at Jewel.

"And you, my Jewel," he added with more force, "have destroyed my confidence in you by your labors at the McAllisters. You will immediately cease such work."

Jewel's head snapped up. She hadn't thought he knew and she glanced at her mother wondering if Abigail had told him.

"No, it wasn't your mother gave your secret away. 'Twas young Tommy this morning made the slip." He banged his walking stick on the floor impatiently.

"That you allowed yourself to be drawn by those . . . !" He trailed off angrily, unable to find a word suitably degrading.

"I meant only to pay our debts," Jewel defended herself, having to squelch all the other feelings that went round that decision.

"I'm cognizant your loyalties were with us, my girl, when your tongue tripped itself into that foolish bargain. That they would allow you to perform such work speaks for itself of their true character. I'm only glad I've found you out before any real damage was done. That bastard son of his has the look of an unprincipled scoundrel." He coughed to clear his throat and switched his attention to a morose Sarah.

"Sarah," he said, with more restraint as he looked at the distraught girl. "I've a pity for you and your young man, but as Ashbury has neither home nor land in his own right, but must labor with his parents, I cannot with clear conscience consent to a marriage. You'll bide your time. When he's established himself, he may present himself and I will gladly give my permission."

Jewel thought Sarah would burst into tears at this pronouncement, but Sarah amazed her by remaining stoically quiet, her head bowed.

"You've naught to say for yourself?" Edmund asked Sarah, his brow furrowed.

Sarah shook her head negatively and Abigail sighed.

"'Tis too much, Edmund," she said to him.

Edmund said nothing, tapping his stick impatiently.

Finally he lifted a hand of dismissal to his granddaughters. "I'm sure you have much to do and I'm weary now. Abigail, I'd like a glass of port before retiring."

Jewel and Sarah rose, both giving their grandfather a kiss on the cheek as usual. Jewel was tempted to tell her grandfather that the port he called for was provided by Skye, but seeing his fatigue, decided against such a rash move. He was nobody's fool, and no doubt he already knew and would not like to be reminded of the unwanted generosity foisted on him by Skye. She left the room feeling that her life was over.

Saturday, four days later, they had completed their preparations for their journey. Jewel had done her packing in gloomy silence, and noticed that Edmund and Abigail seemed to do so as well. It brought tears to her eyes to see the pitiful collection of belongings they were able to bring with them, and tears, too, to see the trivial but treasured things they were forced to leave behind. Her mother had gently ordered her to choose from among her childhood dolls and toys, and in the end she decided to leave them all. Leaving meant the end of her childhood, the end, she thought when she remembered Skye, of her life.

Only Sarah seemed to be able to put a strangely happy energy into her preparations, startling Jewel with sudden bursts of laughter.

"Sarah?" Jewel called as she trailed after her into the downstair's dressing room. Sarah had carefully hidden their gowns for Skye's barn dance earlier in the day in the room's cupboard. Sarah ignored Jewel, so intent was she now that supper was over on preparing for the dance, and she began undressing.

"Why are you so excited?" Jewel finally had to ask. "We're about to leave everything we've ever known and loved, and you're merrier than St. Nick."

Sarah looked up quickly with a hint of guilt on her innocent face. "I . . . I'm going to the barn dance," she whispered to Jewel finally as she began to wiggle into her pretty white sprigged lawn dress, having outgrown her one ballgown.

"I wonder if I should, too," said Jewel. "With our leaving tomorrow, I haven't the heart for it." Jewel knit her brows a moment as she looked at Sarah's intent expression. "You look like you have a secret. Are you keeping something from me?"

Sarah stopped and her face was flushed with tenseness and joy. Slowly she pulled one of the straps of her gown over her bare shoulder.

"Ashbury and I . . . we're eloping tonight, right after the dance," she said, her eyes gleaming in the light of the oil lamp.

Jewel was stunned.

"Oh, Sarah!" she exclaimed. "That's wonderful!" She rushed forward and hugged her sister jubilantly. "Sarah, oh, but I'm happy for you!"

"Then you think I'm right?" Sarah questioned shyly as the two sisters held each other with beaming faces.

"Very right. You belong together."

Sarah's eyes shone with happiness. "You are the best sister ever!" She released Jewel to swirl around the room, her skirts flying.

"As I'm your only one, I must be the best," Jewel

teased, with her heart lighter at the sight of her sister's happiness.

"Then get yourself dressed," Sarah abruptly urged, stopping her dancing. "I want you to come with me and wear Skye's dress. Show them, Jewel, all of them. We'll make a grand entrance and a grand exit." Sarah opened the cupboard and pulled out the carefully wrapped lace gown for Jewel.

"I can't wear that!" Jewel said, catching Sarah's feverish excitement. "It's not the townspeople I fear in Skye's dress, Sarah, but what he will think."

"It's a way to thank Skye for the food and for sending us Tommy, and you'll look glorious in it," Sarah said, watching her sister thoughtfully. Finally she set the gown down on the dressing table and came up to Jewel. "You care for him, don't you?" she said, her young face showing unaccustomed seriousness. "I've known it for some time, despite your denials."

Jewel looked at the gown in its wrappings, her thoughts in a whirl. She wanted to go, to have one last night with Skye.

"Yes," Jewel admitted with a sigh. "It's hopeless, but I do."

"You have a more difficult decision before you than my own then," Sarah said quietly. Jewel didn't answer.

"Does Mama know of your elopement?" Jewel asked, wanting to change the subject.

"No, though I've hinted," Sarah said. "I left a letter explaining all. I know she'll be happy for me once it's done."

Jewel agreed with her. "What will I do without

you—you've been my best friend," Jewel said as she brushed her hair, sweeping it up high, but still for some reason unable to begin getting into the gown.

"Ashbury and his family will welcome you, Jewel," Sarah said as she bent to straighten her hem. "And I shall always want to see you."

"But I'll be in Scotland!" Jewel said, her eyes misting at the thought of all she was losing.

"Skye does have exquisite taste," Sarah said, pulling out the gown and holding it up to Jewel to distract her. "I wonder where he acquired it."

"That's one question I wouldn't dare ask," Jewel said ruefully, but looking at herself in the mirror, "unless I'd like to add a list of French brothels and such to my New York itinerary!"

Sarah tutted disapprovingly. "I doubt he's ever had need of them," she said, and then her color heightened—with her own wedding hour close at hand, the subject of sexual relations was very much on her mind.

Jewel wrinkled her small nose in distaste. No doubt Sarah was right on that score. There were probably as many Melissas in his past as there would undoubtedly be more Jewels in his future. She quickly dismissed the painful thought from her mind.

She then decided to go to the dance, but in her old blue ballgown, and she quickly donned it, flushing with pleasure. Sarah helped her put on the finishing touches, smoothing out the folds of silk.

"Sarah?" Abigail knocked at the door of the dressing room. "I want to talk to you, dear."

Sarah and Jewel exchanged looks, Sarah hoping her

mother had not overheard their conversation, and Jewel feeling caught in the act of going where she knew she shouldn't.

Abigail opened the door and gasped at seeing her daughters dressed for a ball. She quickly closed it.

"What are you girls doing?" she asked, looking shocked.

When Sarah sheepishly explained about Skye's barn dance, Abigail slowly shook her head. "I suppose there's no harm in your going, Sarah dear," Abigail said in her most imperative tone, "but you, Jewel," she continued, turning to look at her eldest daughter sternly. "You can't! I forbid it! Your grandfather would die if he knew you were going there to see that man."

Jewel's shoulders sagged. "I'm sorry, Mama," she said quietly. "But I wanted to be with Sarah and Ashbury tonight." It was not the entire truth, but at least that part of it was true.

"I haven't the heart to refuse Sarah this final outing with Ashbury," Abigail said. "But you must see that it's all wrong for you to go. He'll barely forgive me for letting Sarah go."

Her mother was right, of course. Her grandfather would be enraged if he knew. As it was, Sarah's elopement tonight was going to be a shock.

"I understand, Mama," Jewel said softly, "I just . . . it's our last night here . . ."

"You mustn't go," Abigail said sharply. "Your grandfather . . . he's so concerned that before we get away from here something even more terrible will happen. And he's especially worried about you."

"I can take care of myself, Mother," Jewel replied. "It wouldn't . . ."

"Jewel! Don't even consider it," Abigail interrupted, looking frightened at Jewel's mild resistance. "You must stay here tonight. I hope you'll call in to see your grandfather before going to bed. He does so love you and hates to see his grandchildren leave their home. It's been a burden to him. I believe even he does not want to leave."

"Yes, of course," Jewel said desultorily. Then she turned to Sarah.

"I'll see you off, Sarah," she said. "And then I'll be back, Mama," she added to her mother.

Sarah gave her mother a hug, tears in her eyes. "I love you, Mama."

Abigail patted her gently on the back. "Yes, dear, and I, you. Have a wonderful evening. You do look lovely."

Jewel accompanied Sarah out the door, the two skirting around the back of the house to avoid being seen by their grandfather. They hurried down the lane to where Ashbury waited with his horse and cart. A full moon was rising in the east and its glow heightened the dark green grasses and shrubs, shading them with a golden splendor. The moon looked so close, Jewel felt she could almost touch it. The night was full of promise, but it was for Sarah and Ashbury, Jewel thought, refusing to be sad until she'd seen Sarah off. She could hear the distant sounds of fiddlers drifting on the soft night wind.

Ashbury reached out his hands to Sarah as they

approached him, a broad smile on his dark face. Sarah curtsied, laughing giddily.

"You look wonderful!" Ashbury said, and then seeing Jewel as he clasped Sarah to his side, "And so do you, Jewel. I'll be the envy of every man at the celebration tonight with two such beautiful sisters by my side."

Sarah laughed, forgetting for the moment Jewel wasn't going with them. "Just be sure you remember which one of us you're marrying."

Ashbury was startled a moment and threw a glance at Jewel, his dark eyes worried.

"You know?" he asked, referring to their plans to elope.

Jewel nodded. "Sarah told me this evening and said you were a passing fancy, but one she couldn't resist," Jewel teased.

Ashbury looked askance at Sarah and both sisters laughed, enjoying the joke. It relieved their tension somewhat.

He leaned toward Sarah, smiling. "This deserves some thought."

"No thinking allowed, only dancing," Sarah said lovingly.

Jewel heaved a great sigh, content to have this last happy moment with them. She gave Sarah a kiss on the cheek and hugged them both, fighting back a strong desire to cry.

"I'm so happy for both of you," she said, her voice tremulous. "I'll think of you every day and wish . . . I know one day we'll be together again."

Ashbury was taken aback by all this. "You're not coming with us?" he asked.

"Mama forbade it," Sarah supplied, all her gaiety gone for the moment as she clasped her sister's hand.

"Then . . ." Ashbury hesitated. "Then we'll see you again at our farm," he concluded on a happier note.

"You will indeed," Jewel said over-brightly. "Now, be off, before I shed tears. I want you both to dance for me, too, dance till your feet beg for deliverance!"

Jewel and Sarah embraced once more, both silent with their own grief-filled thoughts. "I'll write often," Jewel said, brushing back a tear and smiling crookedly. Sarah nodded her own agreement to do the same, and she and Ashbury climbed into the cart and left. Jewel watched them go with a heavy heart.

When she reentered the darkened house, realizing that her mother had gone to her own room, she was reluctant to bid her grandfather good-night as instructed. She was afraid her sadness would only aggravate his own depressed feelings. But taking a deep breath, she decided to follow her mother's wishes after all. Perhaps they could comfort one another.

She threw on a large shawl and apron to hide her gown and then went to his room. After knocking, she entered to find him sitting up in bed with a book. When he looked up he seemed pleased to see her. He had been writing in the family Bible, she saw, recording dates and events. Sighing, he put it aside.

Jewel gave him a kiss on his furrowed brow. "I

came to bid you good-night, Grandpapa," she said hoping to cheer him.

As she sat on the edge of his bed, he put one aged hand on her forearm and stared up at her with strangely distant eyes.

"You're the image of your grandmother," he said in a voice that cracked slightly and seemed more hoarse than she remembered it. "Caroline was a rare beauty. But I don't know where you get your . . . fiery temperament," he considered, eyeing her affectionately.

"Why from you, Grandpapa," Jewel said, trying to maintain a lightness against his heavy mood.

"Oh, no," he said, smiling sadly. "I tremble to think you've mine. No, I think 'tis your father's fire you have. Yes, indeed, a rakehell in his youth, he was, but the gentle Abigail tamed him." His eyes closed a moment and Jewel squeezed his hand, remembering only too well the day five years ago she was told of her father's death and the horror of it.

"You're full of reminiscences this evening," she said when she'd gathered herself together again.

"'Tis our leaving that does it," he said. "They're buried out there on yon hill." His eyes went to the window.

Then he abruptly let go her hand and closed the Bible with a snap, his face taking on a sudden hardness. "I almost can't bear to leave them in the ground with Angus and his son trampling about. I wish them no peace on it, none ever! You can only guess at my pain. I just thank the Lord that we be getting away from here without that young scoundrel having ruined you as I'm sure he planned." He was looking at her—through her actually—with that look of fierce, even insane bitterness that seemed always aroused in him by thoughts of the McAllisters. Finally, he groaned and sank back against the pillows. "Fetch me another glass of port from the table there, my girl, and then leave me." He waved his hand to have Jewel do his bidding.

Jewel was fearful of his mood and hurried to pour out and take him his drink.

"You worry me, Grandpapa," Jewel said as she straightened the pillows behind him after giving him his glass of port. "You shouldn't have such . . . anger at those people. They—"

"Good night, Jewel," he broke in sharply. "Go to bed. Tomorrow we will be free of them forever."

Jewel, overwhelmed, finally stooped down and gave him a light kiss on the forehead, disturbed to see his eyes staring ahead with that angry faraway look. Quietly she tiptoed out to go to her room, depressed by the uncompromising hatred her grandfather had of the McAllisters. If only he could see Skye as she did!

She paced to her window, open to the night air. With all the curtains gone the room was cell-like in its austerity. The moon was now gliding higher, casting its silvery shadows on the lawns and pastures. The sounds of a bagpipe drifted briefly on the night wind and then faded. Its mournful sound seemed to beckon to her. A Scottish bagpipe. Did Skye play? she wondered, and felt such a desolation as she thought of him. Tomorrow she was to leave this town forever, and in a few weeks' time, leave this country forever.

She would never see again the one man she had ever loved, the man she knew in her heart she was meant to marry. And because of something that had happened forty years ago, her whole life was to be sacrificed.

A panic seized her. She couldn't leave and not see him one last time. It wasn't fair for her to be denied her own good-byes in her own way. He didn't even know that she loved him! She had to see him if for no other reason than to let him know that it wasn't her will that was sending her away, but that of those to whom she felt she owed loyalty. She would never rest if she didn't.

As she stole downstairs to sneak out of the house and head through the fields to Skye's, she suddenly remembered the gown he had sent her. The idea of wearing it on this last night seemed perfect. It would symbolize her acceptance of him, her surrender to him, even as she would leave him forever. She hurried to the dressing room and feverishly took Skye's gift down from the cupboard. Stripping off her old dress, she pulled on the beautiful violet-blue gown. It shimmered in the dim candlelight, molding around her breasts perfectly, just baring their swelling tops. Her shoulders were displayed entirely by the gown's daring design, the cape sleeves draping over the tops of her arms, leaving the rest bare. It fell from below her breasts in a soft line to her ankles and she marveled again that Skye could have guessed her measurements, and then flushed with an excited embarrassment as she realized that he had examined her shape at close range and in some detail.

Slipping into the silk mules, she picked up the lace fan and was ready to go. Excitement bubbled inside her. All thoughts that she should not go were banished as if they'd never been. One dance with Skye, that's all she wanted. And she would not be denied.

The moon provided all the light she needed as she rushed over the pastures to the dance.

Her heart beat faster as she neared the sounds of fiddlers and gay laughter. Carriages, carts and horses were drawn up outside the big barn and the celebration seemed in full swing, although Jewel thought it must already be late in the evening. The big barn glowed from the light of sperm-oil lanterns, the cavernous doors open to the night air. As she neared the entrance, Jewel trembled like a debutante on the brink of her induction into society before a full court and her king. The air seemed charged with energy.

Through the open door she could see long white draped tables lining the two walls, baskets of summer flowers and food in abundance on each, the guests sitting round, heartily enjoying themselves. The musicians were ensconsed in one corner and the center floor was open to the dancers and mingling crowd. Giddily she took a step forward into the barn.

Chapter Sixteen

As she walked slowly forward, Jewel noticed that those guests clustered near the entrance who turned casually to look at her seemed to fall silent, and in the light of the oil lamps the eyes of the men gleamed with admiration. Although the dancing continued, it seemed to Jewel that an unnatural hush began to fall over the entire room. She held her head high and looked around with as much confidence as she could muster. Abruptly the music ended with a burst of laughter and a scattering of applause, and the center of the barn floor began to clear. Jewel was now aware that most of the women's faces looking at her were filled with a disapproval that shocked her. As the silence around her deepened, she searched for a friendly face, feeling frozen at the universal coolness. How differently she now viewed the townspeople that were turning their backs on her. It stirred her rebellious spirit and, lifting her head higher, she continued to walk forward with slow dignity, having no destination other than showing that she would not be cowed.

Suddenly a group of people clustered at the other end of the room broke apart, many turning to look nervously at someone in their midst. And then there was Skye. She saw his dark-clad figure, towering over the others, wheel around at someone's whisper to turn his green eyes on her. Although she was dimly aware that Melissa stood near him, for a long moment it seemed that they were alone in the room. She had stopped now, in the exact center of the floor, her heart pounding in her throat. She had to take a deep breath to steady herself.

Skye's eyes held hers a long time and then he broke their locked gaze to stoop to whisper something to Melissa and then he strode across the floor toward her. As he came closer, his eyes swept over her, and when he halted in front of her she saw that his face was filled not only with joy but with more powerful emotional turmoil than she had ever seen in him.

"You came," he whispered hoarsely, taking her two hands in his, and at last smiling down at her, a passionate gleam in the depths of his eyes. Jewel was trembling but felt an immense rightness at the warmth of his hands enveloping hers.

"Yes," she managed to whisper, almost overwhelmed by the feelings surging and moiling within her.

"You're more beautiful than I'd even imagined," he said, still holding her hands, the silence around them seeming to Jewel to be like a continuous threatening of thunder.

"I—" she began.

"Why, Skye," Melissa suddenly broke in appearing

beside them. "Do bring Miss Lockridge to meet our friends." She was fanning herself and trying to disguise her tight smile.

Skye turned slowly to look at Melissa and then back to Jewel with the emotion drained from his face and replaced with a polite smile.

"Why, yes," he said. "I invite you to our table for a bite before dancing. The musicians are in top form tonight and my cooks have outdone themselves." He took Jewel's arm and then Melissa's and led the two back to the main table.

"Your gown is superb, Miss Lockridge," Melissa said, her eyes flashing with pique. "I must know where you had it made."

"It was a gift," Jewel murmured quietly, not looking at Skye.

"You have competition tonight, Melissa," he said casually. "I thought only you knew French dressmakers, but your secret is out, it seems."

Melissa laughed lightly. "Ah, but you have discovered all my secrets, Skye, and use them to your own advantage."

Jewel flushed with embarrassment at the woman's hint of intimacy with Skye.

They had arrived at the main table and Skye introduced her to his guests, which included Melissa's father and several young men from Albany. One, a Frenchman named Jacques DeMarchaud, bowed over her hand and kissed it in continental fashion. Skye seated Jewel beside him and Melissa took her place on the other side, immediately drawing his attention to herself with a remark about the music which had begun again. Jewel was very much aware of Skye at her elbow, who, while dividing his attentions equally among his guests, brought her senses alive with the light brush of his hand while he filled her glass with wine or offered her tidbits of delicious food. Skye's other guests resumed their conversation, talking around her with a wary acceptance. Jacques was the only one who made her feel at ease among them as he chatted easily of the night's activities. When the musicians struck up a lively tune, Skye turned to her.

"Are you ready to dance?" he asked.

Jewel threw a quick glance at Melissa. "It isn't wise," she whispered, flustered. "I wanted to put an end to the speculation about us, not add fuel to it."

"While I want to let the fires blaze," Skye murmured, his green eyes burning into hers. "We are at cross-purposes, beautiful lady, but as it's my birthday . . ." Smiling he got to his feet and reached down for her hand. "I'm claiming a present of this dance." Flushing and aware of the eyes of all the guests upon them, she arose and put her hand on his arm. As he led her to the dance floor, he whispered down into her ear. "I think I'd go crazy if I couldn't find some excuse to take you in my arms." He laughed teasingly when he saw Jewel blush.

As she positioned herself, she saw Angus glare at her from his place near the musicians. She'd noticed that he occasionally played the bagpipes with them, depending on the tunes they offered.

"Your father disapproves," Jewel said, drawing his attention to where her eyes had strayed.

Skye's face darkened.

"He won't interrupt us," he said tightly. "We've called a truce where you're concerned. You must know by now, I'll let nothing stand in the way of my determination to win you."

Jewel took in her breath, feeling a weakness assault her muddled senses, as Skye led them in a frolicking reel. She unwound as she danced, thoroughly enjoying the romp, her cheeks flushing with pleasure. For the first time she noticed Aaron and was struck by the anguished look he gave her as he passed by her with another partner. When Skye quirked an eyebrow in question, she shrugged, not understanding the look any better than Skye.

"Perhaps he wants to play the role of protective brother tonight," she said.

Immediately after the dance finished, Jacques DeMarchaud claimed her, and Skye switched partners gracefully.

"I've heard much about you from Melissa," Jacques said, his French accent charming, while they traversed the dance floor.

"We hardly know one another," Jewel said in a surprised voice.

"Ah, but Skye has spoken to her of you and I am privy to her confidences," he returned, his dark eyes studying her face. "But I see you didn't know Skye has been, ah, helpful to the Worthingtons since their return from Paris, in a business venture. And, of course, to myself."

Jewel was startled by his revelations. "I didn't

know. Skye and I, we're . . . not well acquainted," Jewel said.

"You English!" he laughed. "Your reticence always amazes me. I will be free with my admission that I was jealous of Skye's attentions to Melissa before I met you. But now, I am no longer sure where his affections lie."

"I'm not sure I understand what you're saying," Jewel put forward uncertainly.

"No?" said Jacques, his eyes narrowing down at her in concentration. "Surely you must know the Worthingtons wish Skye and Melissa, ah, to form an alliance—a permanent one."

"I . . . didn't know," Jewel replied, wondering why he was saying all this to her.

"Seeing how he looked at you when you entered," said Jacques, smiling, "and seeing you two dancing made it obvious where his heart lies. Let us hope that his heart overrules his business sense, no?"

Jewel flushed, disconcerted by his information, but could think of nothing to reply. The dance ended and Jacques made a bow, as Skye presented himself for the next dance.

He drew her into his arms to the lilting strains of a waltz. The light touch of his hands sent spirally waves of warmth to her limbs. Jewel felt his eyes touch her gently heaving bosom and then rise to catch hers, as he whirled her gracefully around the room.

"You take my breath away, Jewel," he said huskily. "There are moments when I'm with you that I feel like a boy caught with a prize I don't deserve. It's all I can do to restrain myself from carrying you off and away from all other competition."

Jewel lowered her gaze to his white shirt, trying to control the soaring of her emotions. "You must stop . . . courting me, Skye," she said, bracing herself to tell him what he should know. "My grandfather has arranged our leaving," she murmured. "Tomorrow we'll be off to New York, and then to Scotland."

Skye's hands tightened their grip on her. "Then I must act quickly," he said, his face darkening.

Jewel raised her eyes to his in question and she flushed with the intimacy of their locked gazes. The dance ended and Skye led her back to the table, excusing himself to talk to the musicians.

Aaron came over to her and asked to dance. Jewel saw he was tense, and felt reluctant, but it was easier to dance than to create an excuse before Skye's guests, who watched her as if she were an exotic creature rather than merely another guest. As they walked to the floor, Jewel asked him if he'd seen Sarah and Ashbury and was told they'd left before she arrived. Jewel felt a tug inside to know she would not see them again.

Aaron danced her around the floor slowly, his steps formal compared to Skye's, and without Skye's soaring flow and power. "Does your family know you're here?" he asked.

Jewel shook her head negatively and saw Aaron's lips tighten.

"You do like to live dangerously. I've learned more about you these past few weeks than in the ten years we've known your family, and the one year of our engagement. Why did you come?"

"Why to dance—with Hudson's finest," Jewel answered lightly. "The same as you, Aaron."

"I don't have your history with our host," he shot back quickly.

"A history that soon closes. I leave in a day's time," Jewel returned.

"Yes, I know," he said.

"And yet you didn't come to say good-bye?" Jewel said, raising her lovely eyes to his.

"I had planned to be at the dock to see you off," he said tersely. "I have been hoping your sojourn abroad will dispel the unpleasantness of this summer and in time reconcile you to a life less remarkable for its adventurous escapades—and more in tune with mine," he added meaningfully.

"Oh?" Jewel said. "And then what?"

"And then we may resume the closeness we once had," Aaron said with sudden urgency, his eyes, she saw now filled with emotion. "McAllister and Melissa Worthington will be married by then," he went on. "I wouldn't be surprised if he moves to Albany with her. I doubt, though, that your grandfather will return as long as Angus is alive."

"Then why would I?" Jewel asked pointedly, amazed at what he seemed to be implying.

"For me!" he whispered urgently. "I will be bereft when you leave, Jewel." Aaron's brown eyes sought hers. "There's no one to compare with you. Don't you know how painful it has been for me to see you chasing that man like a. . . . He's a charlatan, Jewel, and I'm real. I'm the one who will be awaiting your return."

Jewel missed a step and Aaron stopped, his hand clenching hers tightly. The music ended and Skye's deep voice filled the room.

He called to the assembly for attention and announced a new entertainment.

"For the young and old alike," he said, "but only the single—a Mohawk choosing ceremony."

He launched into a story of a time he had been in an Indian encampment on the night of a full moon such as this and had watched with fascination as the unattached formed two circles, the women in the center, the men on the outside dancing counter to the women. The dance progressed to the beat of a drum and chanting until it suddenly stopped and each woman found herself standing in front of her true marriage partner.

"Of course," Skye added with a grin, "you're free to choose whether your particular partner will be for a lifetime or just the next dance. The Mohawks took their dance seriously, knowing Mother Earth had her own wisdom."

There was a murmur of excitement among the assembly and Jewel felt a chill run down her spine.

She felt Aaron's presence, and turning, saw him back away from her, his eyes never leaving hers, to take his place on the outside with the men. Jewel held back, not wanting to participate. Then she felt Skye at her elbow, and he drew her forward to the women's circle and took his place with the men in the outer circle.

"When we're all in our places, we'll begin," Skye said from in front of her. "And douse the lanterns, we'll need darkness for this dance."

The servants went to each of the oil lamps and either put them out or removed them temporarily from the barn. The remaining light got dimmer and dimmer and there was nervous chatter and a few maidenly giggles.

"What are you doing?" Jewel whispered to Skye from behind her fan.

"You needn't worry," Skye whispered back. "I can't find you in the dark unless the Great Spirit so wills," he said, his voice filled with amusement. Jewel's heart skipped expectantly.

The lanterns were finally extinguished and a hush fell on the crowd. Jewel lost contact with Skye and felt disoriented in the dark. The women twittered with excitement and the men jostled each other for position in the outside circle amid laughter. Skye once more gave instructions about which way the two circles were to dance and that all were to stop completely when the music stopped and then turn to the one who would be their intended.

The music began and the men and women circled each other, the women with arms linked dancing clockwise and the men counterclockwise, bumping along clumsily, all enjoying themselves. Jewel could not tell one outline from another and was caught up in the dance with the others.

The dance seemed to go on and on, gasps and laughter all about her, when suddenly the music ceased and the young people came to a standstill. A silence descended on the group while servants began to light the lanterns. As Jewel strained her eyes into the darkness before her, a tall figure began to emerge and when the lights at last sputtered on, her eyes were locked with the brilliant green ones of Skye standing before her.

She held his gaze, seeing in his face the same surprise and joy she knew must be in her own. Around them she could hear cries of surprise and nervous laughter and a single exaggerated "Oh, no!" Finally Skye stepped forward and bowed low before her.

"The Great Spirit has spoken," he whispered roguishly and Jewel's eyes shone with joy. She raised her fan to hide her bursting smile.

The musicians began to strike up a waltz and the crowd buzzed with the results of the choosing ceremony. There was still much laughter and some teasing going on at the partners drawn. Aaron, Jewel saw, had drawn Betsy Turnbull, a plumpish young lady from Claverick Landing, and he looked stiff and uncomfortable.

Skye took Jewel in his arms and she abandoned herself to the pleasure of finding her heart as fulfilled as her arms.

"How did you find me?" she asked, when she could speak again. "I know it must have been some trick of yours."

"How suspicious and unromantic of you," he countered easily, smiling. "And you're right—it was all planned out in advance."

Jewel felt a sinking disappointment at this admission, but smiled back at him as they continued to whirl.

"I had assumed that I could detect you by your perfume—roses, I believe—and planned to signal the musicians to stop when I stomped my boots, but as soon as the dance had really gotten going I was as confused as the next man." He grinned.

"Then how . . . how is it that you . . . you and I—"

"I don't know, Jewel," he said, looking at her intently. "I'm afraid we are victims of the ancient wisdom of the Mohawks."

She searched his face to see if he was still teasing her and saw with total certainty that he wasn't.

"The music stopped then . . . ?" she asked.

"Because the leader had given up hope of hearing my signal and knew the dance must end," Skye answered. "Jewel," he went on with that fierce seriousness that she'd seen so often on his face this night. "The choosing ceremony is only telling us what our own hearts have been telling us from the first moment we met."

"I have heard that you and Melissa—" she began.

"It doesn't matter what you've heard," he said, whirling her toward the barn's back entrance. "You're a foolish woman if you don't know by now that I desire only you."

Jewel flushed with happiness, her feet feeling as though they had wings. Skye's eyes captured hers and held them in a deep mating. Jewel took in a shaky breath.

"I don't care if all the Melissas in the world want

you," Jewel said in a rush. "I only know that this moment I want you and I won't let anyone interfere with our last night together."

"You're reckless," Skye whispered huskily, his hands tightening on her, a faint flush on his own emotion-filled face.

"Yes." Jewel trembled slightly. "Reckless! I love you, Skye."

Skye faltered on a step and waltzed them purposely out the back door of the barn. "This is not the place for this," he whispered as he guided them to the darkened meadow out back, his large hands burning her body.

Skye had her firmly by the arm and led her into the night, his pace swift as he directed them away from the back of the barn where several men were having a smoke. The full moon was now directly overhead and its light poured out upon the gently swaying grasses creating the image of a silver sea. Skye guided them down a path and stopped in the corner of the meadow near an old crooked apple tree, whose branches twisted grotesquely in the moonlight.

"Jewel," Skye said, his voice deepening. Turning her to him, he put his large, heated hands on her waist.

"I know all of your reservations and I understand how difficult it is for you." He paused as his eyes rested on hers, his face darkly serious. "But I'll do all in my power to ease that burden, if you'll have me." He bent his head and fleetingly brushed his lips against her, his touch igniting a flame in her. "I want you to marry me, Jewel," he whispered huskily.

Jewel had her hands on his broad chest and they curled, digging into him, as her breath seemed to leave her.

"Let me announce our betrothal tonight before everyone, let them all know of our love for each other." He paused, not able to fathom her silence. "Jewel, darling," he whispered, bending to press a gentle kiss on her parted lips, "I want you to be my wife."

He would have taken her lips then, so tantalizingly moist and warm, but he wanted her answer.

A small gasp escaped Jewel, and she leaned her forehead against his broad shoulder, her arms circling him, too lost in the moment to speak. When Skye pressed tender kisses on her exposed nape, she shuddered, her body molding itself against him in a state of rapture. She felt his hand reaching to cup her face and lift it to force her eyes to meet his.

"Don't look at me like that," he whispered, joy glowing on his face in the moonlight.

And then, suddenly, the hurricane of Jewel's happiness was dampened by the memory of her grandfather sitting like an avenging angel in his bedroom at Riverwatch. All of the old man's hatred and heartache flooded into her consciousness and she remembered that this love could exist for just this one last night.

"I didn't mean to . . . I just wanted you to know . . . Skye, I can't." Her voice betrayed a suppressed sob, and she tore herself free from his grasp and fled from him into the night.

Skye stood in shocked immobility, but only for a

moment, and then he rushed after her, his feet thundering on the earth. Jewel was tearing across the back field for home, disappearing through a small copse of windbreaking trees.

"Jewel!" Skye said as he caught up to her, stopping her headlong flight by lifting her up into his arms and then coming to a halt. As he cradled her body close to his, the full moonlight revealed the tears on her cheeks.

"I'm sorry," she whispered, looking up at him and trying to catch her breath. "I shouldn't have said . . . that I love you. I'm always saying and doing idiotic things. I didn't want you to feel obligated . . ."

Skye stopped her senseless rush of words by lowering his head and placing his lips on hers, a kiss meant to stop her emotional flow, but turning into a message of his longing and loving passion. It felt so good to be in his arms, totally supported by him and now crushed against him by the strength of his embrace. He lifted his lips to gaze again into her eyes.

"Jewel," he whispered against her ear, his voice hoarse with the intensity of his emotion. "If you return half the measure of my feeling for you, then there isn't anyone that can part us. I'll do everything in my power to make you happy. We don't have to stay here. We can leave, go someplace else, start over." His lips touched tender kisses on her ears, then her neck, her jawline, and then again her mouth, igniting a fire in her veins and making Jewel curl her arms around his neck, wanting the opium of his kiss. All reason fled as they joined together, surrendering themselves to each other.

Skye lifted his mouth from hers slowly and then began to carry her forward. Jewel found she didn't care where he was taking her, so perfect was this night. If only it would never end.

"I love you so," she whispered softly, aware of the pulsing beat of her own desire and the heat of his matching hers.

Skye looked down at her briefly, tenderly brushed his lips against hers and then moved on. Finally he placed her on her feet and she saw that he had brought her to the small guest house used occasionally by Skye as a retreat from the main house. As he led her inside she saw it was clean and sparse. Her nerves tingled with excitement, as Skye drew the shutters tight and lit a candle.

"Do you want this?" he asked softly, his voice full of gentle concern.

Jewel smiled radiantly. Skye's eyes leapt with passion and he came to her, drawing her tightly against him, Jewel burning like a flame in his arms.

"I do want you," she whispered and pressed feverish kisses against his cheek, seeking his lips with her upturned face. "I want you," she cried passionately.

Skye gave a soft groan and his mouth smothered hers, devouring its sweetness with a fierceness that brought a moan from deep inside her. His tongue deepened its caress inside her honeyed mouth, reaching for and mating with hers. Jewel melted against him, her senses whirling. She pressed his neck down in a desperate effort to meet her heightening desire, feeling his body harden against hers in response.

Skye raised his lips, his breath hot against her face

and then turned her gently around to undo the tiny buttons of her gown, his fingers sending shivers of pleasure down her spine. When he reached the last button she stopped his hands and turned to him.

"Let me," she whispered, her soft voice expressing her desire to please him.

Skye's face filled with a loving awe as he watched Jewel slowly remove her gown, her chemise and then slip out of her silken underthings. She trembled slightly when she stood naked before him feeling his eyes on her body. Her nipples hardened as his eyes roamed her perfection, running over her tapering limbs, her rounded hips, to the peaked creamy mounds and up to her eyes, where their naked passion drew from her a gasp. She smiled tremulously and raised her hands to undo her hair, letting it fall in a dark mass down her back. Skye sucked in his breath, unable to wait a moment more before touching her.

Gently, without words, he picked her up and placed her on the single bed, then removed his own clothes, letting them fall in a heap on the floor.

"You are as I dreamed you would be, so many nights, my love," he whispered as he eased his body down beside hers, his eyes never leaving her face. His fingers trailed a line of fire over the soft curves of her body, his manhood hard against her.

Jewel shivered in anticipation, turning to him, her lips seeking the hard heat of his flesh, letting her tongue flick against his shoulder, tiny wet kisses climbing to his neck.

Skye's strong arms pulled her close, his thighs meeting hers, his hand making a tantalizing path down her belly to her thighs and to the seat of her desire, her molten cavern opening to his touch. He brought his mouth down to an aroused nipple, his tongue swirling around it while his fingers gently caressed against the slippery mound of her opening. He lowered his mouth to its moistness, Jewel shuddering with the newness of it, the intensity shattering her. She moaned and writhed against him.

Skye could take no more, his member fired to a burning pitch, and he climbed on top of her parted thighs. Thrusting inward, he began to move fiercely within her, unleashing his power, taking her along with him in his wild passion. When his hands cupped her upward to meet him, she felt as if her entire body were filled with him, as if the intensity of their savage joining would split her, force her to scream in joyful agony. Suppressed gasps escaped from Jewel's kiss-swollen lips, Skye joining her with his own urgent sounds. Just when she thought her whole being couldn't possibly stand anymore of this intense pleasure she felt him lower his mouth onto hers, and with his kiss a shimmering ecstasy broke over them both. Jewel felt herself soaring, released, joined to him so closely she no longer knew where they were separate, her love flowing into him, their hearts beating as one.

Jewel lay spent beside him, their legs intertwined, laughing softly in his ear as she nibbled its rim gently between small teeth.

Skye laughed with her, rolling with her on the bed. "You belong with me," he whispered against her lips.

Jewel stopped her playful nibbling and lay atop him, feeling him rise again beneath her thigh. She traced a finger over his lips, kissing him gently, then let her fingers touch his face lovingly, as if tracing its contours for memory.

"For this one night, I belong to you," she whispered back, her low voice filled with sadness.

Skye ceased his movements, his legs still wrapped around hers and brought his arms up to take her by the shoulders.

"You're mine for the rest of our lives," he said confidently. When Jewel lay her silken head on his hard chest, and he felt tears escaping onto his skin, he lifted her face by the chin. "Why tears?" he asked, his voice showing his bewilderment, his eyes intent on her beautiful face.

"It means," she said, her voice quavering, "that I must leave now."

Skye brought himself up onto his elbows and Jewel rolled off him.

He grabbed her arm as she made to climb off the bed.

"I'm being refused?" he asked, disbelieving.

Jewel caressed the hand that held her and then shakily plucked at it for her release. Skye let her go, watching as she got up and walked to her clothing.

Skye felt stunned. Then he sat up while Jewel dressed.

"What does this mean, Jewel?" he asked and when she didn't answer, he got up and hastily pulled on his breeches, shirt and boots and walked over to her.

"Don't I deserve an answer?" he asked, hurt in his voice.

Jewel continued to dress, slipping into her shoes

and beginning to redo her tumbled hair with trembling fingers.

"What happiness would we have, Skye?" she said despairingly, stopping her fumbling fingers. "Think on it! Your father hates me and my family. And my grandfather would never accept us, he might even become ill again. Can I turn my back on him when he needs me most, he who has nurtured me all of my life?" Her lips trembled and her eyes begged him to understand.

Skye pulled on his coat, shrugging into it, his face contorted with his pain.

"I'm baffled, Jewel," he looked back at the shambles of the bed. "What happened on my bed just now? Was it real? I've just offered to share my life with you, to do whatever I have to make it possible for us. Are you such a coward you'd run away?"

Jewel's hands faltered and she left her hair half tumbled. "I'm afraid to risk it," she said desperately. "What if my grandfather died because of us?"

Skye watched the only woman he'd ever loved disappearing, and a bitterness crept into him he had never felt before.

"Are you still hoping Aaron will marry you?" he asked unreasonably, fighting a threatening rage.

"No!" she answered, strained. "How can you think I'd want him?"

"What do you think will happen to you in Scotland?" he demanded, grasping at straws in his agony. "Do you plan to end your days a spinster at your mother's side?"

Jewel lifted her face to his, wanting to ask him to let

their memory of each other be this last joining, but seeing the irrational fire in his face, she knew he was beyond reason.

"Perhaps some kindly old gentleman will take pity on an ill-used maid and make me his wife!" After she'd spoken she nearly screamed, wishing the terrible words back instantly.

Skye stiffened with anger and then caught the pride in her words and swore softly to himself.

"Then don't forget these, lady, you might need them to barter with," he said bitterly, holding out her grandmother's pearls to her.

Jewel looked at them, dumbstruck, as she realized he must have purchased them for her. A sob tore from her throat and she rushed past him and out the door.

Skye ran after her.

"Oh, no, you don't leave me like that, Jewel," he called after her, catching her outside the door, his hand in a viselike grip on her arm.

They both stopped in their tracks as the moonlight revealed another figure, and they recognized Aaron, his face drawn and white as he stood looking at them.

"Damn it, man, what are you doing here?" Skye ground out, his face showing his fury.

"Keep your hands off of her!" Aaron shouted, his fists clenched.

"Aaron!" Jewel cried. "Oh, Aaron, go home. You can do nothing here."

Aaron leapt for Skye's throat, his strength drawn from his uncontrollable anger. They catapulted backwards on the earth, the two men grunting until Skye's superior strength pinned Aaron down.

"Stop it! Both of you! Stop it!" Jewel screamed.

Skye released Aaron and the two got to their feet, Aaron's breathing labored as he dabbed at his bleeding nose with his handkerchief.

"I challenge you! I challenge you to a duel of honor," Aaron rasped at Skye.

"I don't duel," Skye said, his rage now controlled. "Especially not with lawyers ill-equipped for killing. I'm a crack shot, man, and adept with the knife. I've long years of war and hunting behind me. Come to your senses, Flemming. If it's a fight you want, I'll go another round right now."

The sound of running feet came to their ears and Angus rushed forward, a lantern held high in his hand, stopping when he saw Aaron pressing his handkerchief to his nose and Skye pacing like an aroused lion. Jewel stood stock-still in the background.

"What goes on here, Skye?" Angus asked, his eyes going from one to the other of the men. He lowered the lamp to the ground and put his hands on his hips as he surmised the two were fighting over Jewel. "Jackasses! But that woman is never far from trouble!"

"I've challenged your son to a duel of honor."

"And I've refused," Skye said dismissively.

"Well now, ain't that sweet," Angus said, crossing his arms over his chest. "You're both bigger fools than I thought." He narrowed his eyes at Aaron. "Ain't you forgetting something? Only gentlemen duel with gentlemen, or some such nonsense. You're making my son a man of class," he smirked.

Aaron had not remembered that in the heat of the moment and he cleared his throat. "I hadn't given the matter complete thought," he said with a frown.

"Aye," said Angus, scowling, "nor you either, Skye. You've left a lass at the party worth a hundred times this one, and if ye don't hurry back a bunch of our business will be scuttled proper."

"I don't give a damn," Skye barked back. "Jewel, we're still not finished. And as for you, *Mr.* Flemming, if I wanted a shot at you, you wouldn't escape on that excuse, but I don't."

"I'm leaving," Jewel said suddenly, desperately wanting to end the confrontation before someone was hurt. "Aaron, will you please escort me to Riverwatch?" She took a few tentative steps toward home and was relieved to see Aaron come to her side to accompany her.

"If you think you've escaped, Jewel, you're mistaken," she heard Skye say harshly from behind her. "All the lawyers and crazy old men in the world can't keep us apart."

Jewel, an ache in her heart and throat, stumbled on toward Riverwatch, Aaron trailing behind blindly.

Chapter Seventeen

THE THUNDERSTORM THAT STRUCK IN THE MIDDLE OF THE night echoed the storm inside Jewel that had her tossing and turning and flailing at her pillow throughout her short night of supposed rest. The circles beneath her eyes in the early morning testified to her sleeplessness. Feeling listlessly empty, she roused herself at her mother's call, surprised to see the sun already a quarter the way up from the horizon and a carriage out in front of Riverwatch being loaded with their few trunks and boxes. As she stumbled to get dressed she felt dizzy with fatigue.

"Jewel, I can't find Sarah anyplace," her mother announced, bursting into the room. "Where has she got to? I thought she was with you," Abigail said in a rush, twisting her hands in the skirt of her traveling dress.

Jewel was startled into remembering her sister's leaving and wondered what had happened to the letter Sarah was supposed to have left for her mother.

"Sarah has eloped with Ashbury, Mama," Jewel said automatically. "She said she wrote you a letter explaining all and left it on your dressing table."

Abigail paled. "Is that what that letter was? I was too much in a hurry this morning to read it." She checked the flow of her words. "Eloped?" she repeated. "Oh dear!" Her blue eyes brimmed with tears.

"Ashbury loves Sarah," Jewel said, going to her mother to comfort her. "He's a good man and will take care of her. She would have died if she had to leave him." *As I am dying,* she thought.

Abigail sat down on a chair. "Yes, I suppose so," she whispered, dabbing her face with her lace handkerchief. "But now is such a terrible time for her to leave us. Edmund . . . and she's so young!"

"You were her age when you married, Mama," Jewel reminded her.

"What shall I tell your grandfather?" Abigail asked quietly.

"We'll convince him it's right," Jewel said wearily, not looking forward to another explanation.

Abigail looked up at Jewel, finally seeing her daughter. "And you, Jewel, you went to the McAllisters last night, didn't you?"

"Yes, Mama," Jewel answered with the same weariness. "And now it's over and I'm leaving."

Abigail stared at her daughter's pale and distraught face and decided not to press her further.

"Your grandfather doesn't know and I suppose we had best not . . . upset him," she said tentatively, again almost to herself.

"Yes, Mama," said Jewel, pulling her brush through her hair and securing it in a twist at the back.

"It seems Aaron stayed over last night," Abigail continued, still peering carefully at her daughter. "And spent an hour with Edmund this morning. They . . . I think they were talking about you."

Jewel looked back at her mother but could feel nothing and said nothing.

"It seems he is ready to forgive us our lack of wealth and wants to marry you." Her mother spoke the words almost as if she didn't quite believe his change of heart herself.

Aaron? Resuming their pledge after all that had happened and all he knew? Jewel stared at her mother.

"I don't believe it," she said warily.

"I confess his unsteadiness is puzzling to me," Abigail said. "He was as distracted as I've ever seen him and seemed quite unlike himself."

"And what did Grandpapa say?" Jewel asked.

"He accepted for you, though he seemed quite upset about something himself." Abigail hesitated. "Jewel, is there anything you need to confide to me. I am your mother."

Jewel bit her upper lip a moment. "Aaron and Skye quarreled last night at the celebration. Mama, I was there and heard it all."

"This quarrel between Aaron and Skye, what was it about?" Abigail searched her daughter's face fearfully.

"They both seem to want me, Mother," Jewel

answered dully. "Aaron was angry that I was with Skye."

Abigail paled. "We'd better . . . better go down now," she said. "Everything is in the carriage and I think your grandfather is waiting for us."

Jewel took the last of the linen off her bed and stuffed it into her large traveling bag. The gown she had worn last night was crumpled on a chair off in the corner—a last reminder of her lost love and the only thing to be left in her room besides the bed. Abigail followed Jewel's gaze and flushed at the sight of the gown.

"The gown . . . it was from him?" she asked softly.

"Yes, Mama," Jewel replied and turned to the door. "Let's go."

Edmund was sweating with the exertion of having gotten himself ready and off to Hudson so early in the morning, and he barely seemed to notice as Jewel climbed in beside him. He bellowed at the driver of the open carriage hired to take them to the docks, thumping his walking stick loudly on the floor.

"Let's away, driver," Edmund shouted at the portly, harassed-looking man sitting in front. Then, as the carriage pulled away, he sighed and looked back at the receding house and then forced his eyes away.

"Blast it!" he raged. "We can't be away from here fast enough!"

As Jewel saw her childhood home fading from view she set her teeth to fight back the sinking feeling and the welling of tears. Like her grandfather she forced her eyes away to stare straight ahead at her mother's blue hat.

"And you, girl," Edmund suddenly exploded. "To think you defied me at the end! That chit Sarah running off with that fool Ashbury. And you! Disgracing us by cavorting with that infernal McAllister bastard! At a barn dance! A barn's meant for cows, not people. Gentry use houses!" he added inconsequently, reddening in the face and puffing out his cheeks.

"He's not a bastard and he asked me to marry him!" Jewel said, feeling defiant as she heard her lover abused by her grandfather in his old guise as patriarch.

Abigail sobbed into her handkerchief, already distraught with Sarah's elopement and the leaving of Riverwatch and now having to face the chasm between her father-in-law and Jewel.

Edmund pulled himself upright, his eyes steely as he fought to control himself.

"You'll not mention his name to me again and that's final!" Edmund barked.

Jewel averted her head to the passing meadow—Skye's land—her feelings stony cold. She was exhausted from a night of tears and had nothing left inside her. She could no longer even feel regret as Riverwatch faded from view down the long rough lane toward Hudson.

"You'll be marrying Aaron if anyone at all!" her grandfather dictated to her further, responding to her last statement.

"I won't!" Jewel said mutinously.

"You will," he bellowed back. "In one year's time. I've given my word. A good man wants to marry you in spite of your carryings-on, and you think to refuse him? Did that son of Satan bed with you? Answer me that!"

"Yes!" Jewel said, her eyes blazing and her cheeks flushed. "And not against my will!"

Abigail wailed loudly and the carriage lurched forward faster, as if the driver were frightened at the people warring in his carriage and couldn't get rid of them fast enough.

"By Heaven! You shameless wench! You hear that, Abigail?" Edmund reddened in the face. "He's had his way with her!" He whipped out his handkerchief and coughed loudly, thumping his stick again as if he could barely restrain himself from striking Jewel with it.

"She's not to leave your sight! Not once! The bastard! If ever I see him, I'll have him jailed, hung on the spot. Mark my words, young woman! He'll be dead before I let him set eyes on you again! And stop that blubbering, woman," he yelled at Abigail. "It's indecent! Indecent!"

Abigail subsided into quiet sobbing and Jewel slumped into her seat staring disconsolately, her own rash words beating her like the stick her grandfather wielded. Would she never learn to hold her tongue? She had meant to plead for Skye, to hold a calm discussion with her grandfather, however useless. She wanted them to know him as she had come to know him. Perhaps in time, her grandfather would have relented. Now, she was certain she had condemned him to the reputation her grandfather had given him without evidence. She had made her cause even more hopeless than it had been before.

The streets of Hudson were quiet, it being Sunday, as they rushed through the town. The driver nearly turned over a slow cart crossing his path as he hurried toward the docks. Several citizens were out sweeping their steps and dogs barked at their passing.

Edmund glowered at the driver when they unloaded at the dock, cheating the man of part of his pay for the rough journey. The driver scowled back, giving one of their trunks a kick, but hurrying away without demanding a cent more. No doubt he would spread his tale while in his cups that evening at his favorite tavern.

The small sloop awaiting them was almost ready to cast off when they arrived, and Aaron was standing at the foot of the gangplank to see them off. Edmund hurried forward with Abigail, exchanged a few hurried whispers with Aaron, and then escorted her up onto the ship, casting one last fearsome glance back at Jewel, who, at Aaron's restraining hand, stopped in front of him.

"I would like one last word with you before you sail," he said with quiet dignity.

Without replying, Jewel looked up at him.

"It's still possible for you," Aaron explained evenly, "to erase the scandalous rumors that will undoubtedly be flying around the village in the coming days, and thus spare your family the embarrassment your precipitous actions last night might cause."

Jewel met his distant gaze without feeling or expression. "Yes?" she said.

"Should you agree to become my betrothed, you and your family can leave here with your honor intact," he explained, his voice softening.

"My honor is my affair and you needn't concern yourself," Jewel answered quietly, unconsciously raising her head high as she spoke.

"And your mother's?" Aaron asked gently. "And Edmund's? Do you owe them nothing?"

Jewel looked at the sloop rocking quietly in the river, then back up the quiet main street of the village.

"And you, Aaron," she finally said. "What is there in this for you?"

"You, Jewel," he answered with strong feeling. "You."

Chapter Eighteen

"NAY, SKYE, DON'T GO," ANGUS PLEADED LATE THAT same morning. The two men were walking toward the stables.

"I'm going," Skye snapped back, maintaining his long strides. He hadn't seen the last guest off until the wee hours of the morning and had himself drunk too much. But when he'd awakened at noon, he had decided to go immediately to Riverwatch and ask Edmund to relent and let him marry Jewel.

"I can't let you go and beg from *him,*" Angus insisted. "Great Scots, you're being not only a traitor to me, but a damn fool as well! Ye've got the Worthingtons eating out of your hand, a chance for us to have the inside track on thousands of acres, and your infatuation with this lass will wreck it all."

"Saddle Outlaw," Skye ordered Robbie who had appeared at the men's approach. Then he turned to Angus.

"I may be a fool, but I'm no traitor."

"You are!" Angus snapped back, reddening as the

two men confronted each other. "Ye know what the Lockridges have done to our family and yet ye would ask one to be your wife—to take our name as if your grandfather hadn't been hung and your uncle and aunt ruined by them."

"They weren't hurt by Jewel," Skye countered. "She's as innocent of the damn feud as I am and I won't let it stop me."

"And what about me?" Angus suddenly pleaded. "Do ye think nothing of the dishonor it is to me to bring a Lockridge into my home. I won't have it!"

Skye twisted away in the agony of his conflict and slammed a fist into the side of the stable.

"Then I'll move out," he said, finally turning back to his father. "I mean no disrespect, but I want Jewel—"

"Then take her as your mistress," Angus grated. "Bed her as often as ye like, aye, bring her here if you have to, but don't lower yourself and insult me by begging that vicious old man to let you marry her."

Again Skye grimaced, not wanting to go against his father, but knowing his life would be empty without Jewel.

"I'm sorry," he said. "I'm afraid it's beyond bedding. I want children. I want Jewel as my wife."

"What about Melissa Worthington and all ye spoke about six months ago?"

"Six months ago I hadn't met Jewel," Skye replied, swinging himself up onto Outlaw.

"I won't accept it!" Angus shouted, stamping his feet. "You go off to Edmund Lockridge, then I swear ye'll never be welcome here again!"

Skye looked down at the rigid and angry figure of his father, memories of all they had been through together rising to fill his heart. He hesitated. Could he cross the man who had reared and shared everything with him?

"You don't know what you're saying," he whispered hoarsely.

"I said it!" Angus spat. "I meant it! Ye be no son of mine if a Lockridge girl means more to you than your own father."

Outlaw stirred restlessly beneath him, and Skye could neither leave nor stay.

"And are you the father I've known to deny me the one woman I've ever loved?" he asked quietly. "You, who always said you were glad you had a son who stood up to you."

Angus blinked and turned away.

"Don't try to thwart me with your highfalutin' words," he finally said. "Stand up to me all ye want on anything but this!"

Skye leaned forward to stroke the restless Outlaw's neck.

"I let you take your revenge on Edmund Lockridge," he said quietly. "And let the women fall with him. But now it's over. Jewel had nothing to do with the feud and I'm going after her." He gently heeled Outlaw into a walk and moved away from his father.

"Stay here!" Angus shouted. "I order you to stay!"

Not looking back, Skye heeled Outlaw into a trot and the big horse sped down the path leading off the estate.

"Don't come back, ye bastard! Ye hear me! I'm done with you!"

Hearing words that made his heart sink and his head reel, Skye dug his heels into his big black horse and galloped off toward Riverwatch.

With Skye's urgency communicating to his horse, Outlaw galloped forward as if heading for his stables rather than Riverwatch. When he finally came over the crest of the rise before the house, Skye saw no signs of the family. He leapt off Outlaw by the porch and threw the reins over the railing. In six strides he was across the porch and banging on the front door.

After what seemed like five minutes but was hardly ten seconds, a frightened Tommy opened the door and peered up at him.

"Where's Edmund Lockridge?" Skye said abruptly, brushing past the boy to see the empty hallway and salon.

"They've already gone, sir," Tommy said with widened eyes. "Early this morning, it was."

"Where?" Skye asked, wheeling upon the nervous boy.

"To Hudson . . . in Mr. Phelp's carriage," Tommy answered. "They're taking a boat downriver to New York. I thought you knew, sir."

Skye looked down at the boy. "You're sure?"

"Yes, sir."

Skye was out of the house and had leapt up onto Outlaw before Tommy could get out the door to watch him ride off.

"Oh, fool! Fool! Fool!" Skye lashed himself as he

heeled Outlaw off toward the village three miles away. Jewel had warned him she was leaving the next day but it had never occurred to him that the Lockridges could possibly get away before the afternoon. And under the influence of her grandfather, Jewel would undoubtedly let herself sail off to New York. Hell! If he had to drag her off the ship, he would!

The ride into the village took barely a quarter hour, but Outlaw was lathered as Skye slowed down to a trot in the main street toward the river's wharf. As Skye's eyes searched the river southward for ships sailing to New York, he saw nothing large, but the river bent less than a mile to the south and he knew he might have missed them. He rode straight to his own dock to speak to his shipping agent, Morton Adams, who would know what ships had sailed. He could see two sailing ships he didn't immediately recognize at the Livingston's dock and hoped one might be the ship the Lockridges were planning to sail on.

He found Adams drinking a pint of ale with two other men in the main warehouse.

"I'm looking for the Lockridge family," Skye clipped, stopping in the open doorway. "They're planning to sail to New York. Do you know what ships are leaving today?"

Morton Adams, a sturdy man with a weather-beaten face, lowered his tankard and smiled.

"Good day to you, Mr. McAllister," he said jovially. "To New York? Why I think the *Crescent* sails tomorrow. She's layin' at the Livingston's dock."

"No others?" Skye asked, impatient to leave.

"Frank Culpepper's sloop sailed about an hour ago," said one of the other men, puffing on a clay pipe. "Frank ofttimes takes passengers. Can't say I saw the Lockridges. It being Sunday, I mind my own business this day."

"Thank you," Skye said and rushed away, his whole body tensed at the thought that he might have missed her. Culpepper's sloop was among the fastest on the river and it had caught the falling tide just right. He doubted he had a ship that could overtake it.

Still, they might have boarded the Livingston's *Crescent.* Leaving Outlaw with a stableboy to be brushed down and watered, Skye strode down to the river toward the Livingston's warehouse and dock. As he walked he saw the elegantly dressed Aaron Flemming approaching him. Before they could meet, Aaron halted and Skye marched the last five strides up to him.

"I'm looking for Edmund Lockridge," he said neutrally. "Do you know where I can find him?"

Aaron gazed back at Skye with a mixture of fear and dislike, but he didn't flinch and even let a hint of a smile appear on his clean-cut features.

"Edmund Lockridge?" he asked, raising an eyebrow. "I have the impression he intended to sail for New York."

"Aye, so I've heard," Skye snapped in return. "Is he aboard the *Crescent?*"

"The *Crescent?*" said Aaron, with infuriating slowness. "No, I don't think so."

"Damn it, man, where is he? Where's Jewel?"

Aaron's face clouded over and he placed his walking stick firmly on the ground in front of him.

"You may, I concede, have some business with Mr. Lockridge," Aaron replied coolly, "but you have none with the elder Miss Lockridge."

"That's for me to decide," Skye countered. "If she's aboard the *Crescent,* I'll find her." Skye brushed past Aaron to continue toward the Livingston dock, but as he strode on he heard Aaron's sharp call.

"McAllister!"

Skye turned around.

"Well?" he rasped.

"The Lockridges have already sailed for New York," Aaron said crisply. "They left more than an hour ago."

Skye saw in Aaron's straightforward gaze that what he was saying was true.

"If that's so," he replied, "I'll have to sail to New York on the *Crescent* to transact my business."

Aaron came boldly forward, his eyes filled with anger.

"I repeat: You can have no further business with Jewel Lockridge," he said. "Is that clear?"

"And who are you to speak for Jewel?" Skye returned with an icy stare.

"I am her fiancé," Aaron announced determinedly. "And I say you have nothing whatever to say to her from this day on."

"Her fiancé?" Skye echoed. "That was ended weeks ago."

"Yes," said Aaron. "It was. But this morning I

renewed my pledge and Jewel agreed to become my wife when she returns from Scotland in a year's time."

Skye searched Aaron's smug face for duplicity, but could find no sign of it.

"What sham have you forced on her?" he said, clenching his fists. "Why do the two who plan to marry rush to the opposite ends of the earth when faced with marrying?"

Aaron's face reddened.

"We part, sir," he spit out icily, "because of your indecent behavior, and to give the scandal in which you have involved an innocent girl time to die."

Skye could barely control the urge to fling Aaron bodily into the mired ruts of the road beside them.

"How do I know Jewel agreed to this farce of a betrothal?" he asked. "How do I know this isn't all a pack of lies thrown out to keep me from her?"

"I give you my word on my honor as a gentleman. And gentlemen, sir, do not lie," Aaron answered with dignity.

"Bullshit!" Skye growled. "The fancier the title, the bigger the liar! Jewel doesn't love you! This farce . . ."

"Here!" Aaron interrupted, as he pulled from his vest a piece of parchment and handed it to Skye. "It's her signature on our request to Reverend Barrows to post the bans for our wedding a year from today."

Skye grabbed it, looked at it and then tore it in half.

"Her grandfather made her do this," he muttered. "The two of you have no consideration for *her* feelings!"

"And you, sir," Aaron replied with heat, "have done all in your power to ruin her reputation and damage her chances for happiness!"

"I want to marry her, man!"

"You're too late," Aaron said coldly. "She's gone and she is going to be my wife."

Skye wheeled away from Aaron almost out of control with frustration and anger.

"Damn," he said, turning back to Aaron. "If you loved her, you wouldn't send her away because of anything she did."

"That, sir, is not the way it's done in genteel families," Aaron responded, baring his teeth in a feigned smile, "as I fear you wouldn't know."

Skye took two steps forward and brought his face within inches of Aaron's. "Jewel is mine, *Mr.* Flemming," he hissed hoarsely. "All the legal documents in the world can't change that."

"Your presumption is false," Aaron countered, not flinching. "And all your animal wiles can't change that."

Skye grasped Aaron's shirtfront and lifted him bodily off the ground.

"I'll see you buried first," he said.

"Let me go, you scoundrel!" Aaron said, gasping for breath. "You've made a laughingstock of me and I demand satisfaction. If you're not a coward yourself, then fight me in a fair duel!"

"Aye, I'll fight you this time," Skye said, flinging Aaron away. "Name your weapons."

Aaron, staggering backwards, recovered himself and straightened his shirt.

"Rapiers, Mr. McAllister," said Aaron, shaking with distress now that he'd committed himself. "My seconds will be Donald Browne and John Livingston."

"Rapiers, eh?" Skye said, realizing it was the one weapon he hadn't anticipated and hadn't been trained to use. "I might have known. At dawn tomorrow?"

"Agreed."

"At Riverwatch."

"Most appropriate," said Aaron coldly.

"For the hand of Jewel."

"No! Whether I live or die you're unworthy of her."

"No man may be worthy of her, Flemming," Skye said with a last bitter smile, "but she has given her heart to me."

At daybreak the next morning an early autumn chill created a low mist along the riverbank. As Skye and his two seconds, the first two men he could locate, Morton Adams and Robbie, made their way on foot from the mansion to the appointed site, Skye felt a deep foreboding. He hadn't told his father of the duel, hadn't seen his father since their angry confrontation the afternoon before, and he knew that their estrangement coupled with his longing for Jewel were responsible for his feelings of gloom. At first he had assumed it was a natural fear of the upcoming duel. He knew that he was clumsy and inexperienced with the light rapier, a poor match for the school-trained Aaron. Still he had confidence in his strength and agility and believed he had a good chance of fighting his way through the confrontation. Yet, his sense of foreboding deepened.

As they crept along through the silent mist, Adams in front, Robbie behind, Skye thought of the woman he loved. Had she in truth, freely consented to marry Aaron? Had he meant so little to her that she could spurn him within hours of their coupling? It didn't seem possible, yet Flemming seemed utterly convinced of their betrothal and saw Skye as but a villainous seducer. What hogwash! Yet, in that frail, artificial genteel world that Edmund Lockridge and Aaron inhabited, perhaps that's how people thought.

At last they emerged into the clearing at Pickle's Landing below Riverwatch and he saw at the other side, barely visible through the mist, Aaron and his two seconds. The river was flowing silently by to the right, only thirty feet of it visible in the fog.

"You're going through with this folly?" Morton Adams whispered, stopping in front of Skye.

"Aye," said Skye, realizing that he had let his love for Jewel sidetrack him into a duel that *was* pretty close to folly.

"This fop isn't worth the scuttling, if you ask me," Adams commented, squinting up at Skye.

"I don't intend to kill him," Skye replied quietly.

"But I'll wager he intends to kill you," Adams went on, his round tanned face showing his worry.

"Go make the arrangements," Skye snapped back, and he walked away to the edge of the river.

"Well," he heard Adams say to Robbie, "if Flemming begins to cut Skye up, I guess we can shoot him," and then laugh in a self-mocking way.

Skye stared out through the mist at the grey flow of the river, a few branches floating down from a storm the week before. He thought of Jewel and felt a helpless rage at her disappearance, anger at her caving in to her grandfather and Aaron. So much spirit to be crushed so early in life. Did it make any sense to go after her? A hand on his shoulder brought him back to the riverbank.

"Mr. Flemming wants to know if you apologize," Adams reported.

"For what?" Skye rasped back.

"Messing with Miss Lockridge, I gather," said Adams, shifting uneasily.

"No."

"I figured." Adams turned and walked back to the conference of seconds.

It took ten more minutes before Adams finally led Skye up to Aaron and the dignified John Livingston, his chief second. The two men were to fight in the clearing until one man had yielded or was no longer able to resist—presumably because he was dead or mortally wounded. They might have fought until one man drew blood but Aaron had refused those terms.

Skye was given his choice of the two rapiers offered by Livingston and took one without a glance or comment. Aaron stood pale and silent, his breath visible in the chill dawn.

Finally the seconds, except for John Livingston, walked away to the edge of the river, leaving Skye and Aaron facing each other a few feet apart, their rapiers held loosely at their sides. John Livingston, dressed in a morning coat and hat, stood between them for a few seconds, looked at first one and then the other, then stepped away, making a gesture with his arm for the duel to begin.

In a second Aaron had taken two quick steps forward and thrust his weapon at Skye, who parried it with a blunt blow and made a clumsy retreat. The sense of foreboding that had oppressed Skye since rising, left him with the first sharp clash of the long, slender-bladed swords. He saw that his awkward retreat brought a curl of a smile to Aaron's face. Seeing that smile and the slow confident advance of Aaron's rapier made Skye realize how uncertain of himself he was in such a fight. He backed up, not daring to thrust at Aaron because of his fear of leaving himself exposed. He began to copy Aaron's stance and footwork, depending on his hunter's reflexes to parry Aaron's own attacks.

But in the next few minutes Aaron's skill took telling advantage of Skye's inexperience. Three times the point of Aaron's rapier found Skye's flesh, once in the thigh, once in the soft flesh of his side and once on his forearm. The tip of Aaron's sword glistened with Skye's blood. Skye backed and parried, backed and parried, once finding himself in the shallow water of the river before circling once again into the clearing. He began to feel a dizziness from the tension of his desperate effort to save his life. Always as he backed away he tried to get a feel for the sudden movements Aaron would make and tried to sense where and when he might safely strike back, but the one time he did thrust, Aaron had easily parried the blow and pierced Skye's side. As the sweat poured from him and he grunted with the fierceness of his effort, he suddenly realized that Aaron had stopped moving and was standing in place looking off to his right where John Livingston was motioning for the fighting to halt.

"I say that blood has been drawn," he heard Livingston saying, "and honor upheld. You gentlemen should cease."

Aaron, like Skye, was breathing heavily and with his face as covered with sweat, finally replied.

"The duel is until someone yields," he said coldly. "Mr. McAllister has not yielded. And until he agrees never to see Jewel Lockridge again I insist we continue."

"Mr. McAllister, I beg of you, sir," Livingston pleaded, "end this folly before you are killed."

"I have no desire to be killed," Skye said quietly, "nor any desire to kill Mr. Flemming. However, I intend to marry Miss Lockridge." As the two men stared at him, Skye concluded, "Besides I'm beginning to get the hang of this oversized needle."

"But Mr. McAllister—"

"*En garde,* sir," said Skye, and when Aaron nodded and took his defensive position, Skye began to back away again. But this time when Aaron came forward Skye suddenly rushed at him, parried his rapier when it was thrust at him and then crashed his body into Aaron's, knocking him onto his back with his breath gone. In an instant Skye was over him, the point of his sword at his throat.

"Do you yield?" Skye asked harshly, planting one foot on Aaron's chest.

"Let me up," Aaron hissed, his face in a pained grimace. "That block was no part of dueling."

"No?" said Skye. "I rather fancied it myself. And my second said nothing to me about not striking with the shoulder instead of the sword."

The seconds had all hurried up and stood in a group around the fallen Aaron and the triumphant Skye.

"You must yield," said Livingston to Aaron, "or forfeit your life."

"Nay, I don't even ask him to yield," said Skye. "Only that he not insist on another of these dangerous games if I decide I want to see Miss Lockridge."

"That's reasonable, Aaron," said Livingston. "For God's sake, man, he's letting you off the hook."

Aaron only stared silently upwards until finally Skye took his foot from his chest, flipped his rapier off toward the river, and marched away.

Chapter Nineteen

JEWEL'S JOURNEY DOWNRIVER TO NEW YORK SEEMED endless. On past occasions she had looked forward to the wonderful feeling of being on a boat and experiencing the beauty and grandeur of the river's high bluffs and green banks and of watching the many boats and ships plying up and down the river. But this time rather than looking forward, Jewel only looked back—toward the past she was leaving behind. Her grandfather had been too angry with her to bother with anything except the briefest and most necessary communication. And her mother had spent most of the time moaning and clinging to the ship's side, staring at the land and occasionally leaning over to heave the contents of her stomach into the water. She left the railing only to go to her room and fall into an exhausted sleep below. Jewel stayed by her mother's side to offer what comfort she could. It wasn't until two days later when they were safely inside the nonswaying room of the Blue Bottle Inn that Abigail revived.

While she sipped peppermint tea by a window overlooking the busy street below their shabby but genteel inn, and Jewel began unpacking a few toiletries and their nightdresses, she launched into what was uppermost in her mind.

"Jewel," she began quietly, her expression tight, "was what you told your grandfather on the trip into Hudson . . . true? Have you been . . . intimate with Mr. McAllister?"

Jewel could feel her cheeks staining with telltale red and she nodded, not meeting her mother's eyes.

"My dear child!" Abigail sighed, her worst fears confirmed.

"I love him, Mother," Jewel said simply.

"That is no excuse for such behavior."

"No excuse was necessary," Jewel said, absently playing with her hairbrush. "It was unplanned and . . . natural." Jewel's voice became a soft whisper.

"And so are children, Jewel, or hadn't you thought of that?"

Jewel was startled. She put a hand over her abdomen and looked down a moment. A child! Skye's child! It would be something of him to keep.

"Is it possible?" Abigail asked, her voice wavering.

"You never told me about such things," Jewel said, finally looking at her mother. "I don't know. I didn't think of it. It's possible . . ."

"Dear Heavens!" Abigail said, running a hand over her brow and searching for her handkerchief. "You've lived on the farm all these years, surely you made the connection between animals and . . . Dear Heavens! What are we to do?"

Jewel bent down beside her mother resting her head on her knee and looked up at her. "If I am with child, I will rejoice in it, Mama, and I will care for it, love it with all my heart."

"It's not as simple as that," Abigail said, putting her hand tenderly on top of Jewel's head. "Children need a home and a father. What of Aaron? I can't believe he'll accept . . . such a child. Indeed, I wonder that he's accepted you again after all that has happened. It was most amazing to me."

"Aaron won't marry me, Mama, no matter what he and I and grandfather have said. It's an arrangement made only to quiet Grandpapa's mind. Aaron doesn't like to be bested and I think some of Grandfather's hatred for the McAllisters has made its way into his life. But as for marrying me, I'm certain that when he knows how I feel about Skye, how I will always feel about Skye, he will never do it."

"Oh dear! I wish all this could have ended properly, for all our sakes." Abigail sighed. "If you are . . . with child, then we must devise a plan. We'll tell everyone in Scotland you're a widow. Perhaps you'll have a chance to find a suitable husband." Abigail's eyes had a faraway look as she invented the story.

Jewel got up from the floor. "Oh, Mama, you know I don't want to go to Scotland. And you don't, either. This land is our home."

"I would like to be able to stay in Hudson," Abigail said dreamily, "but you know your grandfather, and, well, it just doesn't seem possible."

"We have to make our own possibilities, Mama,"

Jewel commented, and began to consider what she could do.

Later, Jewel went downstairs to the common room to find her grandfather. He was seated on a bench at a long table enjoying a cup of grog and surrounded by men enjoying drinks of their own. Seeing her approach he beckoned her to sit beside him. Jewel drew her shawl around her as she saw the men at the table casting interested looks in her direction. She was introduced with a few simple words as his granddaughter and then was expected, she saw, to sit and listen respectfully. Jewel felt impatient but decided, since her grandfather had bent this far from his previous cold demeanor toward her, that she would bide her time.

The talk around the long table centered on the new political situation in the country and her grandfather was expounding on each topic introduced with relish, talk always having been his element.

"This country is seething, my friend," Edmund said. "Yes, indeed, the congress can't pay its bills and new taxes are levied every day. Why tariffs are collected here in New York from such far-distance states as Connecticut!" He stopped to chuckle at his own witticism and drank heartily.

"I've heard that properties taken from British subjects are to be returned, so at least some good intentions prevail," said a man with a full black beard.

"Perhaps," said Edmund. "But how many have been so fortunate? The states rattle their own power gourds loudly and refuse to obey. And the new landowners refuse outright to give the loyalists back their confiscated lands." He banged his cup on the table. "They'll soon wish they had King George back governing this unruly mob. Mark me!"

"Speaking of King George, there's a move afoot to crown another George—our own Washington," said the bearded man.

"By thunder, you don't say!" Edmund's eyes gleamed. "Now there's a piece of news. Our own king, you say? And what are the chances of his coronation?" He leaned forward expectantly.

"To my way of thinking," a slender young man interjected, "would be a fool's move. Having got rid of one king, why should we want another?"

Jewel was caught by the talk, her eyes flying from one man to another. She had listened at home only to the grumbles of the patriots and the fears of the loyalists.

"Yessir," a young man said, "with our independence we answer only to ourselves and make our own rules. And I tell you this is the time to start a new business. There's fortunes to be made if you've the energy!" he concluded excitedly, swilling down his ale.

"Fortunes?" Edmund said, rubbing his chin thoughtfully. "In what, do you suppose?"

"Why, most anything you can think of," the young man answered. "This country's growing and wide open. I myself am for pushing toward the frontier. There's land to be had."

"And Indians looking for scalps," another guffawed, and the young man reddened.

The men suddenly looked down to remember a young woman sat with them and the talk turned away from warfare with the Indians.

"Rumor has it Massachusetts farmers rose against taxes," the black-bearded man said to change the subject.

"Yes, indeed," Edmund rallied. "Captain Shays formed a small army of men to protest, but to no avail. Put down by militia, they were. Many's the farmer lost his land. Taxed to death. Like I was. If I had been a young man, I'd have joined myself."

Jewel arched a fine eyebrow. Her grandfather? A rebel farmer? That would be a change. Yet he seemed infected by the enthusiasm around him, and she wondered at his interest in this new government and how it fit with returning to Scotland.

"You, Grandpapa? A rebel?" Jewel remarked incredulously, smiling in spite of herself.

"Hush, girl," he grunted for her ears only, " 'tis talk only."

While she had his attention she asked, "May I speak privately with you?"

"Soon, soon," he replied.

The men were all abuzz with their discussion, pro and con, about taxes, the congress and the new spirit prevailing in the country.

"It's a new generation and a new hope and if you're not mired in the past, you'll move with it," the young man said lifting his tankard. "To us!" he toasted, his speech showing he'd reached the limit of his tolerance for grog.

"Hear! Hear!" several rejoined, and the men all

drank the toast whether they agreed or not, their companionability spreading far and wide as their blood pumped with drink.

Someone called for food to be served and her grandfather seemed now to remember Jewel at his side. He bid his good afternoons to all.

"Join us later, Mr. Lockridge," the young man said to his departing back. "You liven our discussions greatly. And bring your family," he put in for himself, causing a flush to appear on Jewel's cheeks as she saw he was looking at her.

"Now, what was so important you had to see me away from my friends?" Edmund asked as he entered his room. He took a chair by the window where he could snatch a look at the goings-on in the street below, his fascination for people and their activities evident. He pushed the curtain aside and anchored it to watch.

Jewel sat in the opposite chair wondering where to begin, grateful that he was allowing the interview at all.

"Well?" her grandfather said, looking back at her, his expression distant. "I'm waiting. I know you've something on your mind."

"I . . . wanted to know about the quarrel between you and the McAllisters. Who started it and why?" she said, coming straight to the point with great uneasiness.

Edmund stared at her, his mouth tightening. "I'm sick to death of it. What matter, now? 'Tis done and I want only to forget the misery of it."

"Did . . . Richard . . . get the McAllisters' daughter with child?" Jewel persisted, wishing someone had given the girl a name. It seemed so callous for her to be anonymous.

Edmund drummed his fingers on the table. "Why do you want to know? Do you want to be compared with her circumstance? Is that it?" he asked testily.

"No, Grandpapa, I don't." Jewel's eyes beseeched her grandfather's. "I only want to know if . . . our family can be faulted at all." Jewel held her breath a moment and then continued. "And please, don't lie to me—not now. I've a right to know."

"Right?" Edmund repeated. "Perhaps." He paused. "This once, I will tell you and then let me hear no more of it." He paused for a moment, as if recollecting the story. "The McAllisters were nobodies," he began. "They had lost their wealth. All they had left was land to be passed on to the sons, and rocky soil it was, too. The girl had nothing to recommend her, no dowry, nothing. She ran after Richard, enticed him. I remember Megan always hanging around the stables, waiting for him, following the poor lad everywhere like a lovesick puppy. And the father let her, couldn't keep her home. Wild she was."

Jewel had her answer. She pictured the love-struck girl following her prince and hoping madly to be recognized. And then, having been noticed, gave herself willingly.

"She'd have died anyway," Edmund continued. "Couldn't bear a child, marriage or not."

Jewel heard his voice as it reasoned the terrible deed away, lost in her own thoughts as she listened.

"And her father was bereft of his only daughter," Jewel concluded, whispering to herself.

Edmund nodded yes. "A raving lunatic he was. 'Twas his own fault for letting her be so free. Spoiled her, doting on her the way he did. Not till the end did she speak a name. Then she called for Richard, named him as the father. And then her father came like a madman after Richard."

"Did Richard deny . . . his part?" Jewel asked.

Edmund's mouth tightened. "What matter? The McAllisters slew him."

"As you want to slay Skye," she whispered calmly, her eyes unwavering on his. "Don't you see you want to repeat the McAllisters' sin against Richard? Is it to go on forever?"

"I'll speak no more on this," Edmund answered coldly. "Hie you back to your mother now." He dismissed her with a flick of his hand.

"One last thing, Grandpapa, and then I'll leave, I promise," Jewel said, screwing up her courage. "You must know Mama and I don't want to leave. 'Tis our home. Please, I beg you to consider staying. Perhaps here in New York, where we can start anew? Or Boston? Anyplace. But . . . we've no home in Scotland, only cousins whom we've not met. What shall we do there? Can't we make a living here? Mama and I can sew. Perhaps we can—"

"That's quite enough. Women! Never satisfied. A man does all he can to provide and still they want to change the rules. I know what's best for you. I'm not forgetting your perfidy and I'll not stay where he can find you. 'Tis enough I'm beset with the new troubles you've caused without your fears of a new place. I know your mother wants to stay here near her sister and Sarah, but she's agreed to leave for your sake."

Jewel got up slowly. "And we've wanted what's best for you. Surely you know our sacrifices are for you."

"Leave. I've no stomach for this discussion, and I've no alternative." He drummed his fingers on the table again.

"You have. You don't have to give up and run away," Jewel countered carefully, wanting to persuade him. "You've a way with words, Grandpapa, and much to contribute to this new country. You could involve yourself in its new affairs. Run for an office, become mayor . . ."

"Mayor?" Edmund looked startled. "Me, a former loyalist? You've an imagination, girl, that's the short and long of it."

"Why not? You've useful knowledge and experience of the world, and you like people."

"Away with you," he said, his harsh tones of earlier dissolved in the wonder of his granddaughter's faith in his capabilities. And Jewel quietly left.

Chapter Twenty

When Skye finally arrived at the Blue Bottle Inn, his mind set on seeing Jewel, he was informed by the innkeeper that only Mr. Lockridge was in. Knowing that sooner or later he would have to deal with him, Skye asked to be shown up to Edmund's room. When he heard the gruff old man's voice bid him enter, he opened the door and strode in.

When he saw Skye, Edmund's eyes widened and he half rose from the chair. He opened his mouth to speak but no words came.

"Hear me out," Skye said calmly, moving up to where Edmund sat in the corner of the small room, the noon light barely filtering in through the one tiny window.

"There's nothing to hear," Edmund finally said, his voice firm and his face set.

"I love Jewel and want to marry her," Skye said, undeterred. "She and I have had nothing to do with this feud and it's not fair of you to ruin her life because of some hurt a generation ago."

"I'll not see my granddaughter married to a McAllister," Edmund countered, turning his face away.

"I'm afraid you will, sir," Skye went on firmly. "The only question is whether you will break up your own family by being stubborn or accept her decision and let your family return to Hudson where they all want to be." When Edmund simply continued to stare out the tiny window Skye moved even closer.

"I'm not asking you to accept my father," he continued. "He's as stubbornly set against this marriage as you—only to accept me, an innocent in the feud, as Jewel's husband."

Edmund swung around to look up at Skye.

"Angus is set against your marrying my Jewel?" he asked in surprise.

"Yes," Skye replied.

"The fool!" Edmund exclaimed. "Why Jewel is the beauty of the county and her name alone is worth a dowry."

"And there might be some people who would consider one of the wealthiest men in the county not a bad catch for such a beauty," Skye suggested, sensing Edmund's softening opposition. "I can offer Jewel not only wealth but also the home she was born and brought up in. And I want you to know that you would be welcome there, too, sir."

Edmund's eyes glazed for a moment as he sunk into a revery of his beloved Riverwatch. Skye waited, watching him, hoping the lifetime of cold bitterness was beginning to thaw.

Finally, Edmund began to slowly shake his head.

"No," he said quietly. "It cannot be. You have

debauched my granddaughter and have ruined her forever."

"I'm asking to marry her, sir," Skye shot back. "It's your refusal to let her marry me that will ruin both her reputation and her life."

Edmund flushed.

"And don't Jewel's wishes matter?" Skye asked with sudden softness.

"Women are fools!" Edmund said with sudden spirit. "They don't know the first thing about what's right unless they're told. They need firm hands. That's the way it's always been and ought—"

"Mr. Lockridge," Skye interrupted, "it's time you faced the consequences of your refusal—Jewel ruined, your family impoverished and forced to have to begin a new life in Scotland. That's how Angus will get his revenge." When he saw Edmund looking up at him with a frown of concentration, he went on. "If you accept me, you can return to Riverwatch and live in comfort the rest of your life, your granddaughter happy, your daughter-in-law reunited with Sarah. Consider your responsibilities, sir."

Edmund continued to look up at Skye, his face clouding, the hatred ebbing. Slowly he let his head turn back to the window.

"Never a McAllister," he finally whispered hoarsely.

"I ask for your blessing, sir," Skye concluded, straightening and moving away. "But I'm determined to marry Jewel with or without it." In three strides he was out the door and on his way to find out where Jewel and her mother had gone.

He stopped to question the innkeeper and was given the address of Abigail's sister. As he was leaving, however, he ran into a breathless Abigail who was hurrying down the roadway toward the inn. The concern on her face made his heart sink.

"What is it?" he asked, stopping her in her mad-dash and waiting for her to catch her breath.

"It's Jewel," she gasped out. "She's gone!"

"Gone? What do you mean gone?" Skye asked.

"She's left us," Abigail wailed. "She refuses to go to Scotland and has gone back to Hudson to marry."

Skye felt his heart leap, then realized that she might mean Aaron.

"When?" he snapped. "How long has she been gone?"

"She left at midday," Abigail said, beginning to get control of herself and almost surprised to realize who she was talking to. "She didn't take anything with her and I don't know how she could have paid the ship's fare."

"Ship?" said Skye, grasping Abigail's arms. "Did you say she's going by ship?"

"The note said she's sailing back to Hudson to marry," Abigail explained, looking puzzled as if Skye should have known that.

"And marry who?" Skye rasped out with a grimace, still holding Abigail's arms.

Abigail stared up at him with a suddenly blank look.

"Why . . . why I don't know," she said. "I . . . I thought it was Mr. Flemming, but I realize now it . . . it must be you."

"It will be me," said Skye, releasing her, "on that you can count." He started to move away and stopped. "Try to get that cantankerous old man to agree to her marrying me, because before you see us again we'll be married, and I know Jewel would like to have you live near us. Understand?"

Abigail looked back at him perplexed and fought for control of her emotions until suddenly she smiled.

"Yes," she said. "Yes, I do—and I will. And . . . and Mr. McAllister?"

"What is it?"

"Bless you," she said. "And I hope you find our Jewel."

"Have no fear, I'll find her," said Skye, and wheeled to rush off to the docks.

Jewel stood impatiently as the old schooner seemed to crawl up the river toward Hudson. The day was drizzly, a mist and cool wind proclaiming the beginning of a change in seasons. She was wrapped tightly in her shawl, alone on deck, too full of energy to go below for shelter. She had been idly watching a sloop quickly covering the distance separating them in the narrow confines of the river, but now turned away again to consider what she was doing.

That very morning she had with swift determination bartered a ring given her in childhood for a fare upriver to Hudson. The captain had fingered the tiny ring with concern for her lack of coin and knew without her having to say that she was running away from something, but he had let her aboard anyway.

Now she was on her way to Skye. Would he forgive

her lack of faith in him? In them? All her doubts in the rightness of her actions now flew like the geese that hurried south down the river away from the coming cold, unerring in their direction.

It was her future that she flew to, and her own life she was taking into her hands. Her grandfather had lived his life as he chose with the past cluttering it like old crockery. Somewhere inside her she believed that as he had loved her once, so he would sometime decide in favor of her, and the future of this new country, and not for himself, and the past, and a foreign land. It would take time for the change, but she would embrace him again when he came. It was Skye, in his wisdom, who taught her to wrest the sweetness of the moment and make it last. It was he who made her see that tomorrow was theirs and the past need not drag like rusted chains behind them. Their own past was free of guilt. They couldn't live their elders' past, nor did they have to carry it into the future—unless they chose.

And she, Jewel, chose to close that door forever, to look ahead, not behind. She felt like the birds carried on the wind—free, her heart light.

Even as she smiled with the joy of her decision, she saw, fascinated, that the fast sloop was almost upon them, and seemed bent on running right up the old schooner's stern. She saw someone on the sloop hailing her ship, and after a series of barely audible shouts she gathered that the sloop wanted to permit someone to board the schooner.

She felt her ship slowing and watched as the sloop began to draw up alongside. Abruptly a man leapt off the moving ship and boarded the schooner at the stern. She stared, disbelieving her eyes. All this time she had been staring forward to Hudson while he had been coming after her from behind! As Skye recovered his balance, his honey-colored hair wet with mist and spray, she ran to him and threw herself into his arms, wanting to press herself inside him, and closed her eyes in the ecstasy of again being home in his arms.

"I love you, lady," she heard him whisper, and felt his warm lips placing kisses on her cool, mist-moistened face. When the boat heeled and Skye braced himself with her in his arms, she felt warm and safe at last.

The two captains hailed each other again, their mission accomplished, and the two ships parted, the sloop—as if it had achieved its only purpose in life—swinging away and back downriver and disappearing from view.

"How did you know I was on this ship?" she asked him, squeezing his arm. "Where have you come from? Oh, it's so good to be in your arms!" she said, wanting to know everything at once, her eyes on his face, his lips, his glowing green eyes, searching all to see if it was still the same.

Skye laughed joyfully, drawing her to him in delight. "I followed you," he said. "You know I can't stay away from you long."

"Nor I, you," she whispered, thankful that they were alone on deck but knowing she couldn't have kept her arms from around his neck if the ship had been crawling with passengers.

"Does this mean that I'm now acceptable and the answer is finally yes?" Skye asked, the joy in his eyes showing that he knew her answer without her words.

"Yes and yes." Jewel laughed lightly, her eyes shining with happiness.

"Then I won't question the how or why of it," he said. "There'll be time enough for all of it in the future. I'll ask the captain to perform a ship's marriage ceremony tonight. I'll not give you a chance to change your mind."

"Can he marry us?" Jewel asked innocently.

"If he's a true captain, he can, and I think I've seen the man at the docks in Hudson, so I've reason to believe his credentials are good."

A thousand questions formed in Jewel's mind and she asked them all, one at a time, Skye indulging his lady with patience, until finally he called a halt in order to go to speak to the captain to arrange their shipboard wedding.

With several passengers as their witnesses and with their chorus of ohs and blessings on the obviously happy couple, Skye and Jewel became man and wife. A simple parchment paper declared their union, and Skye gave it to Jewel for safekeeping.

The captain brought forth a rare bottle of wine to toast the couple, and Jewel gave him a kiss—to his obvious embarrassment. With the little festivities over, the captain took his leave to see about his ship. Skye and Jewel thanked the three passengers for their willingness to share in their nuptials, and then they took themselves to a small private cabin that Skye had prevailed upon the captain to provide for their wedding night—Jewel having only paid for steerage.

"It will be something to tell our grandchildren," Jewel said, smiling radiantly at Skye after they had arrived in the cabin and as he was taking off his coat.

He laughed with pleasure. "That's a long ways from today, my sweet, as we must make our children first." He winked at her teasingly and sat on the single narrow bunk to take off his boots.

"We've already made a start," she said, her eyes lowering to his.

Skye lifted his head from his boot pulling to look at her, startled.

At first he couldn't speak, but as he saw she was serious, he rose slowly and took her into his arms. He looked at her face and then down at her figure and then up again. "Jewel, don't tease about such a subject."

"You're not angry with me?" she asked, her voice in a hush.

"Angry? No, never. . . . Are you certain?" he asked with wonder in his voice.

"Not absolutely, but I think it so," she answered, still uncertain that he was happy as she was with the possibility.

Skye laughed suddenly, first at her answer, which was nicely ambiguous, and then at the incredible joy of thinking she was carrying their child. He drew her close into his arms and held her tightly to him, letting his body speak of the great pleasure she was giving him. "You make this man as happy as any man on this earth could ever hope to be." He planted gentle kisses on her face, then pulled away to look at her. "Why were you sailing to Hudson?" he asked.

Jewel smiled up at him. "I was going back to Hudson to live my life with you, in marriage or out, till death do us part."

Skye brought his lips slowly down to meet hers in a kiss that told of his longing and love and then he picked her up off the floor and moved the few feet to the narrow bunk. For a moment they both looked down at it.

"But there's only room for one person," she finally said, looking genuinely disconcerted.

Skye only smiled. "Oh, you'd be surprised, my dear," he said.

They spent the night wrapped in each other's arms, coupling with the tender fire that was theirs alone to share. Caresses and touches and whispers told of their oneness and their trust, and of the joy each brought to the other. Near dawn Jewel asked about the scars on his arm and thigh and side and Skye made light of them, telling her he had vanquished her knight, Aaron, but was left with these little nicks of bravery, and that Aaron had been wounded only in his vanity.

By daybreak they had slept little but were alive as never before and eager for the new day and their new life to begin.

"Mrs. McAllister," Skye said huskily, offering his arm for her to descend from the cart he had obtained to bring them out to Skye's manse. "May I help you?"

He smiled at her, knowing she was worried by the coming meeting.

Jewel gave him a sweet smile, warming to being addressed as his wife for the first time. He was gallantly trying to make her feel at ease. He had already told her they would see Angus immediately and then return to Hudson where he was arranging to rent a house. Though Jewel wasn't looking forward to this meeting, she knew it was necessary, as was the writing of a letter to her own family in New York informing them of her new status.

Before she could alight, Mrs. Harris appeared at the door of the manse, clearly glad to see Skye returned. When Skye turned and introduced Jewel as his wife, Mrs. Harris was flustered and began to hastily make apologies for her past insults to Jewel. Jewel stopped her profuse explanations with a smile, but before she could say more, Angus appeared in the doorway.

He stared at Jewel sitting in the cart as if the moon had been transported to his doorstep and then looked at Skye. "So, ye've done it," he said without intonation.

"Aye," Skye returned. "Jewel is now my wife." His voice was clear and steady. "We'll be moving into town. It's already being arranged."

The color drained from Angus's face and his shoulders sagged. He looked as if he had aged ten years in the last week.

"With her grandfather's consent?" he asked finally.

"No," Skye said, "with Jewel's consent. He knows

nothing yet of our marriage, though he's been warned."

Angus made a strangling noise in his throat.

"We came for your blessing," Skye said quietly, "for our marriage and our coming child."

Angus's face changed colors again as he took in this last piece of news.

"Did you say coming child?" He looked from Skye to Jewel.

Jewel nodded and gave him a tremulous smile, sensing that he was interested.

A silence fell over the group a moment and Mrs. Harris fluffed her apron nervously.

"You hear that, Mrs. Harris? I'm to be a grandfather," Angus said, breaking the silence, his eyes studying Jewel's radiant face.

Skye turned to leave, his foot already on the lower step when Angus stopped him.

"Why leave a lonely man for rooms in Hudson when there's space here for my grandson and yourselves," he said loudly for them all to hear.

Skye and Jewel exchanged a stunned stare. Then Skye slowly turned back to his father.

"What about a granddaughter?" Skye quirked an eyebrow at his father.

"Son, daughter, what's the difference? It's my grandchild we're talking about. Now why would I want to hear these walls echo with the rattles of my old bones when they can cheer to the lusty cries of little ones?" he said, his eyes beginning to light with a new energy. "Liven up this place to have young ones here. That's what it's meant for."

Angus stepped down to the cart where Jewel still sat bemused by his sudden change. He held up his hand to help her alight. "You're welcome, lass, if you can forgive an old man his sins."

Jewel looked at Skye to see what he thought about all this.

"Don't let him bully you, Jewel," Skye said, "we've a home in Hudson waiting for us."

Jewel looked back at Angus and then at his hand and then placed hers into it and Angus gave her the very first smile she had ever seen cross his lips, the hard face softening with pleasure.

"Aye, you're welcome lass," he repeated. "I had time to think of it all with Skye gone after you, and this house like a tomb, cold and empty. I'll not sweep the graves of the dead any longer, nor let the dust of the past blind my eyes."

"I had much the same conclusion when I left here," Jewel said and put her arms around Angus and hugged him, beginning to laugh.

Skye smiled to see his father stiffen and turn red with the unaccustomed female attention. Angus freed himself of her arms and smiled crookedly. "I'll not have a petticoat trying to change my style that quick."

Jewel laughed. "Oh, I think a little change might be in order."

Angus turned to Mrs. Harris who was broadly beaming with the outcome of this encounter and beside herself wanting to do something. "Do your best to make a wedding feast for my son and his wife."

"That I will, my best roast and pudding!" Mrs. Harris said, bustling away to the kitchen.

Skye stepped forward to Jewel and swept her up into his arms and carried her into the manse.

"Welcome home, Mrs. McAllister," he said softly and lowered his lips to hers.

Epilogue

IT WASN'T UNTIL JAMES EDMUND ANGUS MCALLISTER was born that Edmund Lockridge returned to Riverwatch and was pleased to find himself welcomed back. Abigail had returned a month after Jewel had written her a letter telling of her marriage, and she had moved into Riverwatch with Sarah and Ashbury, who was made manager of Riverwatch. The estate was to be held in trust for the firstborns of both Jewel and Sarah. And to the wonderment of all, Edmund Lockridge became mayor of Hudson.

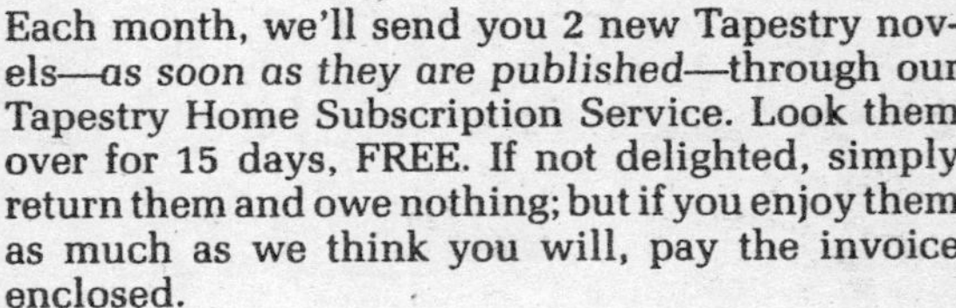